SPELLS OF BREATH & BLADE

BOOK TWO

Spells of Breath and Blade
Tarot Academy, Book Two
Copyright © 2020 by Sarah Piper
SarahPiperBooks.com

Published by Two Gnomes Media

Cover design by Faera Lane

v6

E-book ISBN: 978-1-948455-47-3
Paperback ISBN: 978-1-948455-13-8
Audiobook ISBN: 978-1-494548-91-9

BOOK SERIES BY SARAH PIPER

* * *

<u>Reverse Harem Romance Series</u>

Claimed by Gargoyles

The Witch's Monsters

Tarot Academy

The Witch's Rebels

* * *

<u>M/F Romance Series</u>

Vampire Royals of New York

GET CONNECTED!

I love connecting with readers! There are a few different ways you can keep in touch:

Email: sarah@sarahpiperbooks.com

TikTok: @sarahpiperbooks

Facebook group: Sarah Piper's Sassy Witches

Twitter: @sarahpiperbooks

Newsletter: Never miss a new release or a sale! Sign up for the VIP Readers Club:
sarahpiperbooks.com/readers-club

ONE

STEVIE

It was supposed to be a simple sleeping spell.

Midnight Lullaby, I named it, diligently writing out each ingredient in my new grimoire with a precision that would make my Academy professors proud.

A piping hot brew of valerian root, chamomile, and lemon balm to help me sleep.

A rose quartz crystal on my bedside table for a dose of soothing, loving energy.

Salt poured across my doorways and windowsills to protect me from outside forces.

The Four of Swords card placed beneath a white candle to encourage rest and healing, paired with The Moon card beneath a silver candle for insightful dreams.

Finally, two sprigs of calming lavender tucked under my pillow.

Sounds heavenly, right?

I thought so. Thought the whole magickal, sleepy-time

shebang would send me straight to happy-happy-dream-land without incident.

And after all the incidents of the last few days… The vicious attack by Professor Phaines, losing my mother's grimoire and the Journey Through the Void of Mist and Spirit book to enemy hands, learning that I'm an Arcana witch—an emanation of the Star card—and bound to four mages I'm alternately crushing on and wishing I could just plain crush… Yeah, I *really* needed this to work tonight.

Well. Clearly someone broke into my suite and replaced my chamomile with cayenne pepper, or my restful Four of Swords card with the anxious Nine. It's the only explanation for the way things are going down between the sheets tonight—and no, I don't mean "going down" in the good way.

I'm stuck between asleep and awake, unable to nudge myself fully in either direction. My body senses that I've been in bed for hours, but I'm still vibrating with adrenaline. My heart's going crazy, my muscles keep twitching, and now I can't decide which is worse: being trapped in a nightmare you think is real, or being trapped in a nightmare you *know* is a nightmare and being unable to wake yourself up.

Right now, I'm betting on the latter.

I *know* this shit isn't real. Here on planet reality, my mind is fully present, my eyes wide open. Every few minutes, my darkened bedroom flickers into view, superimposed over the hellscape I seem to be trapped inside in the dream realm. I can *feel* my body lying safe in bed, feel the cool sheets twisted around my legs, smell the spent candle wax scenting the bedroom air, but I can't make myself move an inch. None of my usual nightmare extraction tricks are working—jamming the heels of my hands into my closed eyes, counting backward from ten, pinching myself, shouting at the monsters that they're not real. I even tried to throw myself off the top of a building, hoping to Goddess I'd wake up when I hit the ground.

Nope. Like some immortal video game character who just can't die, I keep spawning back to life, dropped unceremoniously into the center of Arcana Academy. Not the beautiful, colorful campus with its gurgling Tarot fountain and black-and-silver house flags snapping proudly in the breeze, but a post-apocalyptic wasteland identifiable only by the skeletons of once-familiar buildings rising out of the earth in clouds of black smoke. The sparkling red stone pathways crisscrossing the Academy grounds now run red with blood, bent and broken bodies littering the grounds at every turn.

Beyond that, the carnage is still unfolding, the air vibrating with the clash of magick on magick, of metal on metal, of flame on flame. All around me, students and professors alike band together to fight the onslaught of a treacherous magickal enemy with whatever powers they possess.

"Stevie! Run!" Someone shouts from behind, and I spin around to catch Nat dashing toward me on the path, her silver-and-teal hair whipping out behind her. She leaps over a body and lands hard on her heels, slipping in a pool of fresh blood and nearly crashing into me.

"Slow down," I say, grabbing her arms to steady her. "What's happening?"

"They took Isla. We have to run! They're coming!"

"*Who* took Isla? *Who's* coming?"

"Stevie, we can't—" Nat's body jerks, her eyes going wide, then closing. She drops right out of my arms and slumps to the ground. An arrow sticks straight out of her back, still flaming with magick.

I feel her soul pass through me and leave this plane, and it nearly hollows me out inside.

But there's no time for grief. Three dark soldiers barrel down the path from the direction Nat came, one of them pointing at me and shouting while the others nock their arrows. Behind them, a charioteer ushers her beasts into a full gallop across the quad, barreling straight toward a group of students huddled together outside the Breath and Blade dorms. Behind them, their home is engulfed in flames.

"Onward!" the charioteer shouts. The cold determination in her voice chills me to the bone.

She's going to plow straight into them.

"No!" I yell above the din, my feet already carrying me toward the terrified group. That's when I realize I'm not wearing shoes or much in the way of clothing—just a pair of underwear and the hoodie Baz wrapped me up in the night the Claires nearly drowned me in the River of Blood and Sorrow.

Still, I push hard, feet slipping in blood and gore and things I'd rather not contemplate, the entire campus reeking of death and destruction.

Where are the guys? Where is Headmistress Trello? How the hell did this happen?

Sparks fly at my right, and I twist out of the way as two magickal swords clash, the sound reverberating through my head. A male professor I've seen around the library parries with an enemy soldier—a mage dressed in golden armor, his weapons glowing with magick, his eyes as fierce as his blade.

I dart through the melee, narrowly avoiding the jabs of blades, ducking beneath the searing heat of fire spells.

I wish I had a weapon. Something. Anything to help me through this chaos.

As soon as the thought forms, a magick sword appears in my hands, instantly adjusting to a comfortable size and weight. It glows brightly, and I know immediately it's the weapon the Princess of Swords gifted me during our first meeting.

Finally.

Movement at my left, and I spin around fast and jab, catching an enemy soldier in the gut. He clutches the wound as blood pours out from between his fingers, and I yank out my blade and push him away, desperate to reach the students before the charioteer does. She's closing in fast, red dust billowing out in her wake, the horses' hooves like great drumbeats upon the earth.

The students stare with open mouths, paralyzed by shock and fear.

"Move!" I shout in their direction, but it's no use.

Saving my voice, I force all my energy into my limbs and run, charging toward them with a speed I didn't know I possessed. Fires burn all around me, the air black with smoke, my lungs burning, but I can't stop.

Again, my bedroom flickers into view—safe, familiar, serene—but no. I'm not there. I'm here. I'm on campus. There's a battle raging and I have to fight. I can't let her hurt them. I can't let this happen...

Panting hard, I finally reach the group and whirl on my heel in front of them as if my body can stop the inevitable impact. I hold my ground though, soon staring down the largest, most terrifying war horses I've ever seen. Mouths froth as they chomp at their bits, their coats and hooves dripping with blood.

The woman driving them is relentless.

I raise my sword high and call upon some nameless magick, feeling it course into my blade and down into my limbs, but it's no use. The chariot barrels into me, an explosion of white light and golden wheels and the feral screams of the horses...

And then all falls silent. The students are gone. The horses and charioteer have vanished.

I'm unhurt, still standing and gripping my sword, but I'm no longer in front of the dorms. Now, I'm behind the buildings, safe from the battles raging on the other side.

It's calm here. Peaceful.

Something shimmers in the air, and the four Princesses appear before me—my magickal affinities. Cups, in her red dress and wine-dark cloak. Wands, dressed in orange and green, her dress trimmed in Celtic knotwork designs. Swords, her tattered blue cape fluttering in the breeze, a raven perched on her shoulder. And the youngest, Pentacles, wearing her checkerboard gown and velvet cape.

I glance down at my own clothing. Somehow I've lost my hoodie, and now I'm wearing some sort of white gown. On closer inspection, I realize it's a wedding dress—bits of satin hastily pinned together, sequins scattered here, lace and ribbons there, buttons running down one sleeve but not the other. Still in progress, I guess. My hair is woven into a complicated set of braids dotted with white tea roses and sprays of pale blue forget-me-nots, and in my hands, my sword turns into a bouquet of black dahlias.

Immediately, my heart throbs with the bitter ache of betrayal, though I can't explain what's causing it.

Is it a warning? A memory? A vision?

Am I dreaming?

I was in my room, and then I somehow ended up on campus... There was a battle, and... But I thought... I can't...

Where the hell am I?

"Hello?" I call out. My voice echoes back, hollow and terrifying.

The Princesses, ever silent, turn their backs on me and begin walking down a clear path into the yawning landscape behind the Breath and Blade dorms. Tossing the flowers to the ground, I dart after them, winding my way through the towering rock spires. Mist creeps across the ground, clinging to my ankles, slowly climbing its way up until I can't see more than a few feet in front of my own face.

"Kirin?" I call out, rubbing the sudden chill from my arms. Again, the haunting echo calls back.

Kirin... Kirin... irin... rin...

"Ani? Baz?" I try again. "Doctor Devane?"

Vane... vane... vane...

Wearing nothing but this strange, half-made dress, I force my bloodied feet to continue onward, slipping deeper into the mists behind the silent Princesses. Something calls us forward, some force, and so I march, hoping against the odds to find my friends.

I march until I'm sure I've got nothing but raw bones for feet.

I march until my body shivers with cold and hunger.

I march until I no longer feel the stone path beneath me, but the cool, comforting texture of wet earth. Dirt and moss and things that grow. Waxy green leaves dotted with bright red berries brush along the fabric of my dress.

Gingerly, I make my way through the thicket, doing my best not to destroy the bushes, hoping there's a clearing on the other end. Hoping for some clue that will lead me to my brothers.

"Ani!" I call out, but again, I'm met only with the echo of my own voice. "Baz!"

No one responds. Not even the damn breeze.

Where am I?

A trickle of fear slides down my spine, and I whip around in the bushes, scanning for the source of the bad vibes. But there's nothing there. Nothing but swirling silver mist as far as the eye can see.

The mist settles down around me again, blanketing the bushes until only the tallest branches poke through. The visual reminds me of another place, another time… I close my eyes and try to bring it back…

Saguaros, I remember now. Cactus limbs reaching up through the desert mist like the masts of old ships.

Am I home? In Tres Búhos?

But I thought…

I shake my head.

This is my home now. Arcana Academy. I need to find my friends.

No longer concerned about the welfare of the bushes, I open my eyes and pick up the pace, stomping through the thicket until the tangle of leaves finally releases me, spitting me out onto a wide swath of bare dirt. I try to brush the dirt from my dress, but it's no use; the berries have stained it red.

The Princesses have vanished, but movement up ahead captures my attention—a rabbit darting across my path, disappearing in the mist.

"Wait!" I call after him, a clear sign that I'm losing my shit.

Get it together, Stevie. This is insane.

I stop and take a deep breath. Prop my hands on my hips. Look around at my surroundings.

Why am I talking to rabbits? Whose dress is this? Where the hell is everyone?

As if in response, the mist begins to fade away, revealing a massive rock wall before me. It isn't red sandstone. In fact, it doesn't look like any of the rock formations I've seen on campus. It seems older somehow, untouched through the ages. The surface is carved with spirals, and at the base, mistletoe and holly grow wild.

I place my hands against the rough stone and close my eyes, feeling for its energy. Its heartbeat. Deep within, I sense the thrum of ancient magick stirring to life.

A gentle breeze ghosts over my hair, releasing the scent of the roses still tucked into my braids, and I let out a breath.

But the peaceful moment is instantly shattered by the blast of an ancient horn—my only warning before the rock beneath my hands rumbles and cracks, breaking away to reveal a small doorway.

I stumble backward, bracing myself for some new threat.

But there, emerging from the darkness, is only a child— no more than a toddler.

He's naked, his movements slow and sluggish like he's just woken from a long nap.

"Are you okay?" I ask tentatively, reaching out for him. But the child doesn't acknowledge my presence, and the moment my fingertips touch his baby-soft skin, the air around me explodes with warm, golden light.

Magick hums across my skin, and I gasp, understanding dawning in an instant.

Not a lost child.

The Fool reborn. The Source. The Zero.

"Who called you forth?" I ask the tiny being, my voice trembling with reverence. "Why here? Why now?"

Behind him, a druid priest emerges from the cave, the ancient horn dangling from a rope around his waist. He's dressed in a long white tunic and bright green cape, the hood drawn low over his eyes. He pats the child's golden-red curls, then slowly lifts his face toward the light.

His hood slips back, revealing a gaunt face and black, soulless eyes. My knees buckle with fear beneath his cutting gaze, sending me crashing down to the ground. Everything about the man emanates darkness, destruction, chaos.

"Who are you?" I ask, my voice trembling for an entirely different reason now.

The dark druid only smiles. Then, bending toward the baby, he scoops the boy into his arms and presses a kiss to his cheek.

"Let him go!" I shout.

Again, the druid smiles. Then he opens his mouth wide, revealing a giant gaping hole lined with rows of razor-sharp teeth.

"Stop! No!" I scramble to my feet and lunge forward, but I'm not fast enough.

The demonic beast devours him. Through the crunch of

bone and the gurgle of blood, there are no screams. No resistance.

Only death.

Seconds later, the druid gags and chokes, clawing at his own throat, his eyes black as night, his tunic stained red.

But he's not dying.

He's… changing.

Growing larger, broader, his limbs elongating until he's twice the size of a man. Flames erupt over his skin, but they don't burn him. They're part of him now, feeding him, feeding *on* him, a twisted cycle with neither end nor beginning.

He's evil, fueled by pure, unchecked power.

And worse, I realize as a Tarot card appears in my hand, its imagery almost a mirror of the scene before me.

He's one of Dark Arcana.

I'm standing in the presence of Judgment. Trump Twenty.

And there's no reasoning with the beast. Not when he's rocking a suit of flames and I'm standing here in a half-assed wedding dress without a single weapon to my name.

Screw this shit.

I spin on a barefoot heel and take off at a run, darting back into the holly bushes. I get about ten feet away when an invisible force clamps around my midsection, hauling me right back. It slams me against the wall, pinning me flat.

The fire-beast stands before me, pointing a wooden staff at my chest and shouting his vile chant. It echoes inside me, reverberating off the back of my skull.

Called to confess, called to atone
Beg for your flesh, your blood, and your bones
Unwashed and unworthy, you shall be cleansed
For evil Arcana shall meet evil ends

"*I'm* evil? Well… well fuck you!" I shout, the graceless words of a desperate bitch.

Fury burns hot in his eyes, and he aims his staff directly at my face.

"Vile filth!" he hisses, flames popping around him. "You are unfit to carry the magick within you."

"Maybe I am. Or *maybe* you should crawl back into that cave and spend some time reflecting on your life choices instead of berating me. Look at yourself right now! Seriously!"

His flames rage brighter. "You are a disgrace to the Arcana, spirit-blessed."

"And you eat babies for a living, so let's not get ahead of ourselves—"

"Enough!" He wrenches me away from the wall and throws me to the ground, pouncing on top of me. With one hand firmly gripping his staff, his other fiery hand wraps around my neck, burning my flesh. "You *will* stand before the Dark One, Starla Milan. Judged unworthy, sentenced to eternal torment. All who are deemed unworthy shall burn. Your parents will burn. Your friends will burn. *They* will burn."

At his last words, four shadows emerge from the cave. Not children this time, but men.

My men. My brothers.

Thank Goddess!

"Doc!" I shout. "Kirin!" But none of them acknowledge me. "Hey! Ani! Baz!"

Nothing. Not even a flicker of recognition. They stare into the distance, their eyes glazed, their bodies pale and weak, their movements as sluggish as the child's were.

Judgment raises his staff toward them.

One by one, they lift their hands and bow their heads, as if forced into some terrible prayer that no one will ever answer.

"Unworthy!" Judgment shouts.

And with a single swoop of his staff, they're incinerated.

They glow bright for an instant, then darken before my eyes. I watch in shocked horror as their bones turn to ash and blow away like tiny black birds on the current.

There is nothing left to say. Nothing left to fight. Nothing left to live for.

Grief takes hold, and I close my eyes, wishing at once for death. I can't carry this pain. Not again. Not for them.

Starlight, you need to leave now. Starlight… come on, baby. Open your eyes.

That voice… I know that voice…

Starlight…

"Mom!" I gasp. Despite the pain burning through my chest, I open my eyes. I don't see her, but I feel her, my mother's gentle touch on my face, the scent of frankincense and yellow roses tickling my nose…

Leave this place, my love. You've lingered too long. Wake up now. Wake up, Starlight…

Wrenching myself from the nightmare's deadly stranglehold, I bolt upright in bed with a gasp. Sweat beads across my forehead, and my heart feels like a ticking bomb one second away from exploding.

The smell of smoke clings to my hair, the taste of it coating my tongue.

Kicking hard, I free myself from the tangle of sheets and bolt for the bathroom, making it just in time to retch into the sink.

Nightmare, girl. Just a crazy fucking nightmare. You're free. Breathe. Just breathe.

When the heaving stops, I scan the darkness, searching for a glimpse of my mother.

I don't find her. I knew I wouldn't.

What I find instead has me retching all over again.

Dark red footprints lead from the bed to the bathroom, glistening on the white tile floor like rubies in the snow. My feet are practically shredded, throbbing with very real pain that I'm only just now starting to feel. When I hobble back into the bedroom and flick on the lights, I find my white sheets streaked with blood and ash.

My lavender is gone. In its place lies a charred, mangled branch of holly, its once vibrant green leaves curled and darkened, the berries split open like tiny red hearts set aflame.

TWO

BAZ

The sound of high-heels clacking on a stone floor turns my blood to fucking ice.

Not high heels specifically. *Her* heels. The slow, deliberate cadence of the footsteps that always warned of her impending arrival.

Always a minute too late to escape.

"Baz? Is that you, sweetness?"

Her voice echoes across the Iron and Bone common room, as thick and cloying as her perfume.

Even as her vile scent closes around my throat like a fist, even as my vision swims and my head pounds and my heartbeat sets off running like a damn jackrabbit, I refuse to believe it. Refuse to believe that the monster who haunted my adolescence is here, in person, calling my name.

"Baz?"

Memories punch me in the gut, and I'm no longer a grown man sitting by the fire before the crush of another

Monday. I'm no longer an Arcana mage tasked with protecting magick and all who wield it for the greater good. I'm not even a slacker college student nursing himself through a weekend hangover, hiding out here instead of going to class.

Wouldn't be the first time.

But today? Nope. Today I'm nothing but a terrified fucking kid again, fourteen years old and no idea how to fight back against the dark shadows sneaking into my bedroom.

It's all I can do not to piss myself.

And *that* pisses me right off. But that's the power of a true monster, isn't it? They can retract the claws and put on a painted smile, let you think you've escaped, let you think they've forgotten you. But all it takes is a scent, a sound, a single name whispered through dark red lips, and those claws are slicing right through your guts again.

I drop the travel magazine I was reading, rise from the chair, and turn toward the common room entrance with my eyes squeezed shut, still hoping that every last one of my senses is teaming up to trick me.

The cloud of perfume thickens, and I open my eyes.

Please let it be anyone *else…*

But of course it isn't.

The woman beaming at me as she saunters across the room is none other than Janelle Kirkpatrick, Carly's mother, dressed in a tight leopard-print dress, black blazer, and those awful black heels, her lips painted the same blood-red I remember, her dyed black hair skimming her shoulders.

In the handful of years since I've seen her in person, she hasn't aged a day. Now that I think of it, I'm pretty sure she hasn't aged a day since Carly and I were kids.

Wonder what that's *costing her…*

"Baz Redgrave? It *is* you! Oh, honey, it's so *good* to see you."

I brace myself for the unwanted press of her body, holding my breath against the onslaught of her perfume as she wraps her arms tight around my waist. Everything about her makes me twitchy. All I want to do is fucking bolt.

But of course I can't. Our arrangement requires my cooperation.

But it doesn't require my affection. Not anymore.

"What are you doing here, Janelle?" I ask, stepping out of her toxic embrace. My voice comes out a hell of a lot colder than I mean it to, but a lot fucking warmer than I feel toward her.

"Are you joking?" Janelle presses a hand to her chest, glaring at me as if I've just told her she stinks. "The moment I heard about the attack on students—by an esteemed professor, no less—I was on the next flight out from Boston. My daughter's well-being is my top priority. I couldn't rest until I saw with my own eyes that she was safe."

"*Student,*" I correct. "One student was attacked. And it wasn't Carly."

"It may as well have been her. Or you, for that matter." She reaches up to cup my chin, her nails grazing my jaw. To anyone else, the gesture might look motherly. But anyone else wouldn't notice the slight pressure, the sharp nails digging into my skin, the warning in her eyes. "If anything were to happen to either of you... I just couldn't forgive myself, Baz. You know you're like a son to me."

I jerk away from her touch, swallowing down the bitter taste in my mouth.

"Professor Phaines was a friend of yours, no?" I ask, reclaiming my seat by the fire.

Uninvited, she takes the chair across from me, perching on the end like an exotic bird. Preening, as always.

"Apparently not," she says, picking imaginary lint from her stockings.

"I don't suppose you've heard from him?"

At this, the color rises in her cheeks, her polite veneer cracking. "I'm not sure I like what you're insinuating, Baz."

"And I'm not sure I like that you're here, Janelle." I shift in my chair, angling my body toward the flames. Away from her. "If you're truly concerned about Carly and me, just answer my question. The man hurt a friend of mine, and we're all on edge over it. Anything you can tell me about him might help us track him down."

"Headmistress Trello contacted me last night—four days after the attack, mind you, which I was less than thrilled about, as you can imagine. She really should've notified me on—"

"The professor," I press. "What do you know?"

Her lips flatten into a thin line as she shoots me another

warning glare. The kid inside me shudders, old warnings echoing through my skull.

Watch your tone, young man. You know I don't like punishing you, but I will...

"After her myriad apologies, the headmistress enquired about our family's connection to Professor Phaines," Janelle continues. "I'll tell you exactly what I told her—the Professor had fallen out of contact in recent years. I knew he was working closely with Carly and some of the more gifted students at the Academy, but Carly never shared too much about that. You know how she is—very private, very modest about her gifts. She gets that from me."

I choke back a snort. Modest? Sure. She and Carly are the very definition of humble.

"So you're here to what—drag Carly back home?" I ask. "Lock her up in a tower for her own protection?"

"Hardly." She forces out a low chuckle. "You could imagine how well *that* would go over."

When I don't return her smile, she leans closer, her eyes shiny with some trumped-up emotion I have no interest in analyzing.

"The Academy needs me, Baz. My daughter needs me. And I was hoping," she says, reaching across the space between us to rest her hand on my knee, "that you might need me too. Like before. Remember how nice it was? When we were all... a family?"

Her red fingernails trace a pattern on my denim-covered knee, and I close my eyes and bite back a wave of nausea. *Family.* The dreaded f-word. She always did enjoy dangling that out in front of me like a golden carrot. A promise as well as a threat.

The woman was sick back then. Clearly, she's gotten worse.

"There was nothing nice about that and you know it," I mutter, forcing myself to open my eyes and look at her.

Janelle narrows her gaze, the warning behind it intensifying. I force myself not to fidget. As scared as I may feel, that little kid inside me is long gone now, leaving a man in his wake. A broken man, imperfect as hell, but still a man. She can't hurt me anymore. I know that.

Doesn't mean those claws won't take a few swipes at me anyway.

"Oh, now you're just being a poor sport." She purses her lips into an exaggerated pout, then glances around the room, taking it all in for the first time. She didn't come for Carly's orientation this summer and showed no interest when her daughter officially moved onto campus. I would know—I'm the one who got stuck lugging all Carly's shit into the dorm, trying to help her unpack while she cried about her mother's complete lack of interest in her life.

Lack of interest? Yeah. It was all I could do not to grab her by the shoulders and tell her how lucky she was.

But apparently, Carly's lucky streak has run out.

"What did Carly have to say about this unexpected visit?" I ask.

"Carly and I have our… challenges," she says. "I think she was more surprised than anything else. She just… she needs some time to adjust to the idea, that's all."

"The idea of *what*, exactly?" Why is this woman here? Carly's safety? Hardly. Janelle is always working a scheme and this is no different.

"Aren't you going to offer me a drink?" she asks, dodging the question once again.

"It's, what, eight in the morning?"

"I'm still on Boston time."

"Pretty sure it's morning there, too."

When I don't move from my chair, she huffs at me, then stands and slithers over to the kitchen area in search of something strong to drink. A few ransacked cupboards later, she hits the jackpot with a half-empty bottle of vodka undoubtedly leftover from All Hallows' Eve.

The sound of ice cubes clinking into a glass followed by a long, wet pour is just as familiar as her high heels clacking on the floor, and I keep my face turned away, hoping she can't see the sweat beading across my forehead.

My heartbeat is still erratic, my mouth dry and numb. I feel like a hunted animal, which is just how she likes me. All I want to do is bolt for the door, but I can't—and she knows it.

Takes great pleasure in that fact, actually.

Janelle resumes her perch on the chair, locking me in her sights once again. Twirling her glass, she cocks her head and says softly, "You haven't missed me at all, have you?"

When I don't respond, she lowers her eyes and shakes her head as if she's ashamed of me. "Even after everything Charles and I did for you? I thought we raised you better than that, Baz."

Raised me? What a fucking joke. Putting a roof over someone's head and food in his belly when he's got nowhere else to turn may be a kindness or it may be a trap, but either way, it's not the same thing as raising him.

My real parents didn't do such a bang-up job raising me either, too busy treasure-hunting across Europe to pay me much mind. The one who came the closest was my big brother Ford, but that didn't last.

I was ten when I watched the high mages drag him out of the house and throw him into the black sedan—the car that would take him to the worst kind of magickal jail for the worst kind of magickal offenders.

I haven't seen him since.

Guilt burns in my gut.

"I don't remember what it feels like to miss anyone," I tell her. Then, forcing a fake smile, "How is Mr. Kirkpatrick, anyway? Did he travel with you?"

I used to be terrified of the man, but like so many things, that was all part of Janelle's game. *Charles can never find out about us, Baz,* she used to say, her sour vodka-breath hot and damp on my neck. *If he does, it will ruin everything. He'll hurt you. I'm afraid he might even make you leave…*

Hurting me was one thing. But making me leave? I was homeless and broke, terrified down to the fucking bone. It was my weakness, and Janelle made an Olympic sport of exploiting it.

She took the fucking gold, every time.

"Charles? Here?" Janelle waves the idea away, as if it's

the most ridiculous one ever. "He's got much more important business to attend to."

"More important than the—what did you call it? The top priority of your daughter's well-being?"

"You've gotten bolder, Baz Redgrave." Janelle smiles and traces her fingertip around the lip of her glass. Then, glancing up from beneath her lashes with a look that could freeze fire, "I can't decide if I like that or not."

Movement across the room catches my attention, and suddenly everything about this shitty situation fades into the background where it fucking belongs.

"Excuse me," I say, barely sparing Janelle a glance as I rise from the chair and brush past her to get to the one good thing about my entire morning—Stevie in spandex.

THREE

BAZ

Not gonna lie. The sight of that little red Arcana Academy T-shirt hanging off her shoulder, revealing the black strap of her sports bra, is enough to erase half my mind. And don't even get me started on the barely there running shorts or her toned thighs or the rest of those soft curves—curves I've had the distinct pleasure of licking.

But it's her smile that really gets me.

Perfection...

"Oh my Goddess," Stevie says, covering her face as I approach. "Don't look at me. I'm a total hot mess right now. I just came by to get a book I left here last night."

With a smile of my own to match, I slowly peel back her fingers, revealing her face. Her cheeks are red from her run, the morning sun lighting up her bright blue eyes. She looks... alive.

I try not to sigh in relief.

I'm staring. I know it. But I can't help it. Every time I

close my eyes or turn away from her, I see her battered body tied to that tree again, blood leaking down her limbs, her eyes glazed…

"You're beautiful, Little Bird," I say, shoving those memories into a box. "Always."

Stevie rolls her eyes, but she's still smiling, and right now that counts for everything.

I lean against the wall, attempting to block her from Janelle's view. Nosy bitch. I can practically feel her eyes on us. "Out for a run?"

She nods, then taps the phone pocket at her waist. "But don't worry. Doc had my new phone sent over this morning, so I texted Ani to let him know my exact route and timing. I've got the GPS thing on too, so… Yeah. Totally trackable at all times. Yay for surveillance tech!"

"It won't always be like this," I say softly, wishing I could make it better for her. Wishing I could find Phaines and beat the life out of him. Wishing I could do something other than wish.

"It's fine." She blows out a breath, a few curls popping loose from her ponytail. "I'm okay. Honestly, I wasn't even planning to run this morning, but I didn't sleep well last night. Figured some fresh air and a good pounding would help."

"A good… um." I shift on my feet, hoping my dick goes back into hiding before I hurt myself here. "Okay, I'm going to pretend you didn't say that."

Stevie smacks my chest. "*Pavement*, perv. Pounding the pavement."

"So, did it? Help, I mean?"

Her smile fades again. "Not really."

"See? Maybe my way *is* better."

"Maybe." She laughs, but it doesn't last.

Just as quickly as the jokes rise, the awkwardness creeps back in.

I don't know how to do this—not with her. The stilted silences. The uncomfortableness. The blazing desire and all the unsaid shit getting between us.

We're all walking a fine line now, trying to find a new equilibrium, some crazy balance between keeping each other safe and respecting each other's privacy. Trust— what's left of it—is fragile. And though Stevie took the blood oath and willingly joined our Brotherhood, the guys and I have a lot of rebuilding to do. A lot of trust to earn back. And that takes time. Space, too.

Something I keep reminding myself, despite wanting to be close to her. Next to her. Inside her.

After everything that happened with Phaines the other night, and all the Brotherhood stuff, and the long conversations that followed, Stevie finally asked us for some privacy. She needed time to process it, she said. To deal with her own feelings on what happened with Phaines and all the new revelations we'd dropped on her—the secrets we kept from her.

I left her alone all weekend, forcing myself not to message her, not to drop by. Not to stalk her in the common room, hoping to catch sight of her as she curled up by the fireplace with whatever book she'd left behind.

This is the first I've seen Stevie in days, and her presence feels like the fucking sun on my face.

My heart jerks in my chest—a sharp ache like nothing I've ever felt before.

Fuck.

I take back what I told Janelle. Turns out I *do* remember what it feels like to miss someone.

"Hey," I say softly, looking into her worried eyes. "You okay? Really?"

"Yeah. No. I mean…" She smiles, her eyes misting. "I guess I'll always be looking over my shoulder now, right? Waiting for him to show up again. To pop up out of nowhere and finish what he started."

My blood simmers, my fists balling at my sides. "That's not going to happen again, Stevie."

She looks up at me with all the hope in the world, but there's a new emotion behind her eyes now, a hard edge that wasn't there before All Hallows' Eve.

One more reason Phaines is going to suffer when we finally get our hands on him.

"Baz," she says, her eyes fluttering closed. "I need to… I can't… I'm…"

I wait for her to continue, my heart hammering, terrified and hopeful and fucking confused as hell…

But then she just opens her eyes again and laughs, and I know the moment is gone.

"I need a shower," she says instead.

I'm *this* close to asking whether she wants some company, but I hold back. Jokes and innuendos are a lot easier when your heart's not tangled up in it. Now, I have no idea where the fuck we stand. All Hallows' Eve, having her in my arms, in my bed, hearing her breathy moans in my ear… damn. It was everything.

But then Carly showed up, and Stevie and I fought, and she stormed out into the night—straight into the trap Phaines had set for her.

I clench my jaw tight. I want to destroy something. Someone.

Stevie, perceptive as always, reaches out and touches my arm.

And just like that, the rage dissipates.

"You going to the assembly?" she asks, her hand still warm on my bicep. At my obvious confusion, she says, "Trello sent out an email. Mandatory attendance."

I pat my pockets. "Left my phone upstairs. What's up?"

"Apparently, we've got some new security protocols."

"Fuck." I lean in close, keeping my voice low. Janelle is still lurking by the fireplace, pretending to be absorbed in that travel magazine, undoubtedly cocking an ear for some juicy gossip. "She say anything else about Phaines?"

"Nope." Her eyes dart over toward the fireplace, then back to me. In a soft whisper, she says, "Do you know that woman? She keeps glaring daggers at your back."

"That would be Janelle Kirkpatrick," I say. "Carly's mother."

Stevie's eyes widen. "Is she here about Phaines?"

"That's what I'm trying to figure out."

"You said you and Carly grew up together. So I take it you know her mom, too?"

"When I was a kid I... I lived with them for a little while. Kind of a long story."

Stevie narrows her eyes, scrutinizing my face. "But you're not happy about her visit."

"That's putting it mildly."

She watches me closely, trying to get a better read on me. On the situation. Concern flashes in her eyes.

Lesson one in the mysterious school of Stevie Milan—and I should've learned it the first day I met her. Hiding anything from this woman is damn near impossible.

Stevie's still searching my face, waiting for me to fill in the gaps, but all I can do now is shake my head.

It's one thing to stop keeping secrets about one another—we all agreed to that stipulation.

But our own private hells? Far as I'm concerned, that shit is *not* up for discussion—especially where Stevie's concerned. She's seen enough darkness to last a lifetime—I'm not about to pile it on deeper.

"Baz, what's going on? You—" Stevie cuts off abruptly, her eyes darting back over my shoulder again. "Shit. She's coming."

I close my eyes, wishing like hell I could call on my earth magick and bring this whole fucking place down on the woman's head.

"Baz, sweetness, aren't you going to introduce me to your friend?" Janelle inserts herself into our once-cozy space, her fake smile glinting, the pungent scent of booze-breath now competing with her perfume.

"Ah, nope." I draw closer to Stevie, hoping Janelle will take the hint, but of course *that's* not happening.

"You'll have to excuse his rudeness, hon." Janelle edges between us and grabs Stevie's hand, giving it a squeeze. "He's still not over the shock of my visit."

"I can see that," Stevie says, her tone carefully neutral.

"I'm Janelle Kirkpatrick. And you are?"

"Starla Milan."

"Starla Milan?" Janelle's red mouth rounds into a shocked O. "Goddess, you're the poor girl the Professor attacked! Oh, honey, I'm so sorry. Are you… recovering well?" Her gaze trails down Stevie's body, lingering on her bare legs, doubtlessly wondering where the bandages are.

Stevie drops the woman's hand, her face pale. Whatever vibe she's picking up on, she doesn't like it one bit.

"I'm doing much better, thanks," Stevie says coolly. "I heal pretty fast." Then, flashing me a quick smile and a look that says we'll be having a nice long chat about this later, she says, "I need to head upstairs and get ready. See you at the assembly?"

"Do I have a choice?"

"No." Surprising me, she stretches up on her toes and presses a kiss to my cheek, close to the corner of my mouth. The faintest brush of her soft lips sends my whole body into overdrive again. If we were alone, I might just pin her up against the wall, tear off those skimpy running shorts, and—

"Hmm." Next to me, Janelle seethes, her eyes narrowing as Stevie heads toward the stairs. "I'm not sure I like the looks of that one. She seems—"

"Don't." I turn and level her with a dark glare. Janelle might be able to push my buttons—fuck, I might never rid myself of that particular affliction—but no way in hell am I letting her drag Stevie into the mud. "Don't say a word about her. In fact, let's just pretend you never met her."

Janelle tosses back her dark head and laughs, low and throaty, like some kind of cartoon villain. "Oh, Baz. You were always overprotective."

Ignoring her, I head back to the fireplace in search of whatever book Stevie left behind—she forgot it again. Janelle mistakes it for an invitation for another fireside chat.

She settles into the chair again, then digs into her purse for a compact and that horrible red lipstick. "I think that's an admirable quality in a man—protectiveness. It's just… Oh, I don't know. Maybe I shouldn't say anything."

Janelle peers into her compact mirror and cranks up the lipstick, reapplying it like spackling paste, waiting for me to take the bait.

Fucking hell.

"Just say it, Janelle."

She presses her lips together, then runs her pinky finger along the bottom one, rubbing in the color. Still gazing at herself in the mirror, she lifts her eyebrows and says, "Does Carly know about your feelings for this… this woman?"

"Carly and I are—" *Just friends, and that's being generous,* I want to say. But for whatever reason, Carly's got her parents believing we're a thing, and I'm in no position to contradict her. Keeping the Kirkpatrick family happy is a basic survival skill—and it's not just my life on the line.

"—fine," I finish up. "Not that it's any of your business."

"My daughter's heart is every bit my business. Now, I warned her that getting involved with you was a bad idea, but the heart wants what it wants, I suppose." She clicks her compact shut and drops it back into her purse, fixing me with a double-edged grin that makes my skin crawl.

"You've got nothing to worry about, Janelle. And neither does Carly." *Because she and I are never going to happen.*

She stands from the chair and sighs, taking a step to close the distance between us. "Have you heard from Ford lately?"

And there it is. The subtle reminder that she owns me. That for all Charles and Janelle Kirkpatrick did to keep me off the streets and my parents out of the very place my brother ended up, I've got a debt that can never be fully repaid—a debt any one of them can come to collect on, any time they please.

"No, Janelle. I haven't."

"Oh, but *I* have. Well, not *from* him, exactly. But about him. They've got some new guards in place over there. They aren't as… sympathetic to your brother's cause. Rather, I should say, their sympathy is a bit more expensive."

"Point taken."

Leaning in close, she places a hand on my chest, calling up the fearful beat of my heart. It recognizes her touch, her scent, and wants to flee as badly as I do.

"Are you sure?" she asks.

I close my eyes, trying to breathe through my mouth. Hoping that when I open them again, she'll be gone. I'll be in my bed upstairs. This will all be a fucking nightmare.

"Fuck you, Janelle," I mutter.

"Tsk, tsk. Such language." She reaches up and places her palm against my cheek, then removes it.

I feel the change in the air immediately, a soft *whoosh*.

I open my eyes and grab her wrist just before the slap makes contact.

Her eyes blaze with indignation.

"I used to be afraid of you," I say, finding my fuel. My rage. "When I was a kid."

"And now you're all grown up, is that right?" Her tone drips with superiority. It's the same tone she used on me back then. *Baz, sweetie, don't you want your brother to be taken care of? Charles and I are spending a lot of money to keep him safe. But you need to do something for me, too...*

I release my grip, turning my back on her. She's not worth it. Never was. "I have an assembly to attend. Enjoy your visit."

"Baz?" she asks, saccharine-sweet. "There is one more small thing, before you go. Teeny thing, really. The woman? The spirit-blessed?"

I turn on my heel, glaring at her. I'm not sure if Janelle sensed Stevie's abilities or if Carly filled her in at some point, but it's clear she knows Stevie is more than just the student Phaines attacked.

"What about her?"

"It would be a shame, don't you think?" She inspects her fingernails, lifts her shoulders in a casual shrug. "If something were to happen to her? You've already lost *so* much. I would hate to see—"

I've got her against the wall in a heartbeat, my forearm across her throat, my eyes blazing, the very last of my self-control slipping away.

That scared little boy is long gone. All that's left now is a man full of rage, full of hatred, with *very* little left to lose.

Stevie makes that list.

This crazy bitch does not.

"Threaten her again," I say, pressing against her wind-pipe, "and I will *end* you. We clear?"

"Baz? Mom?" Carly's voice cuts through the haze of anger. "What the hell is going on?"

"Ask your mother," I say, backing off. "I'm sure she'd love to explain herself."

Janelle clears her throat, smoothing her hands over her hair. "Just... just a little mother-son misunderstanding is all. We'll work it out."

"You're not my mother."

Ignoring this, she turns her bright smile on Carly. "You look nice, honey. Are you ready for the assembly?"

Carly folds her arms over her chest, immediately suspicious. "How do you know about that?"

"Well... I wanted to surprise you both," she says, her

hands fluttering up around her throat. The throat I should've crushed when I had the chance. "But I suppose you'll find out soon enough."

It's deadly silent in that room, save for the hiss and pop of the fireplace and the low din of students in the hallway, making their way outside.

I cut my gaze to Carly, and we lock eyes. An unspoken understanding passes between us.

Whatever "surprise" Janelle has up her sleeve, Carly and I are the ones who'll have to deal with the fallout. It's always been that way. Probably always will be.

I take a breath. Brace for impact.

Janelle's smile widens, the wolf finally emerging from her sheep's clothing. "Anna Trello has offered me a job."

FOUR

STEVIE

Just over a month into my enrollment at Arcana Academy, the most important lesson I've learned isn't the one about never mixing essence of blackshade with powdered bat wing, or that there's a secret society of Major Arcana mages whose sworn duty is to protect magick, or that the smoked gouda is always the first cheese to run out at Smash's infamous cheese fountain.

No, the key lesson is this: The darker and more dangerous the secret, the faster it travels.

Seriously. It's like Witch Hazel's Third Law of Magick or something. Which is why I'm not all that surprised to find the High Priestess card tucked into my backpack this morning—a reminder of the powerful nature of secrets— followed by Isla and Nat waiting to ambush me outside the assembly hall.

"Stevie!" Nat shouts at my approach, her eyes flashing

with equal parts anger and worry. "Oh, thank Goddess! Everyone's saying you were murdered!"

"Not that I recall." I pat myself down and try for a smile, but my friends are in no mood for it.

"We've been trying to reach you all weekend." Isla crushes me in a hug, her silver teardrop pendant winking in the sunlight. "We've been going crazy!"

"My phone was destroyed," I explain. "I just got my new one this morning. Still catching up on messages." Mostly from the guys, who are still learning how to walk that oh-so-fine line between protective and pestering.

I don't mind, though. I was glad for the space this weekend—totally needed a breather after all their brooding, macho intensity—but by Sunday afternoon, I actually started to miss the fuckers. Seeing Baz this morning set me to rights in a way that copious amounts of tea consumption couldn't—and for me, that's saying something.

"You haven't been answering your door either," Nat adds. "Or your emails or student directory messages. If we had carrier pigeons, we might've tried them, too."

They both stare at me, incredulous.

Shit. I suck.

"I'm sorry, guys. I should've sent a message. I didn't realize the rumors would spread so fast, and I'm not used to having so many people worry about me." Just my best friend Jessa, and she's so busy with her move to Mexico, I didn't want to drop this latest disaster on her. Besides, it's not like I was totally alone. I had the guys waiting on me hand and foot, never letting me out of their sight. Not until

I kicked them out. And even now, I'm not *entirely* out of sight—not with the phone-slash-tracking device.

A necessary evil. For now.

Yeah, I can complain about it all I want, but until Phaines is caught and we figure out the rest of this mess, I like knowing that four powerful mages have always got my back. Besides, trust goes both ways. If I'm insisting they keep me in the loop, I've got to do the same for them.

"We *were* worried," Nat says, her multi-colored hair fluttering in the breeze. The sight of her silver-and-teal tresses takes me back into my nightmare, the battle on campus, the arrow in her back, and I swallow a knot of emotion, feeling even more terrible for leaving them in the dark all weekend.

"The rumors kept getting worse every time we heard them," Isla says. "First you got kidnapped, then beat up, then the whole murder thing… Was it really Professor Phaines?"

I nod and cover my stomach, the memory of his twisting knife still fresh. "Apparently, he wanted my blood for some kind of ritual."

I give them a rundown of the events, leaving out the part about the prophecies and the Dark Arcana—all things the guys and I *must* keep secret, even in a place that thrives on rumors.

It's our only shot at keeping everyone safe.

"Goddess, Stevie," Nat says when I finish the sordid tale. "Are you okay? I swear if you're not, I'm going to kill you right now."

I smile at the familiar threat—one Jessa has uttered many times.

"The first night was a little rough," I admit. "But I'm feeling better now. The cuts have mostly healed, and I'm working on not freaking out at every little shadow."

The nightmares aren't my favorite, either, but Nat and Isla are worried enough as it is. No need to add to it. Besides, the person I really need to speak to about the dream stuff is Doc, and I haven't caught sight of him yet this morning.

"You should've called," Isla says, hurt lingering in her voice. "We would've come right over with soup and wine and movies and fuzzy socks."

"I know. And I love you guys for that. But I think I just needed some time alone to process everything. I was pretty overwhelmed. Still am, in a lot of ways."

The guys stayed with me the first couple of nights after the attack, cooking and taking care of me, much like the girls would've done. It was a kindness I appreciated—one I needed, even.

But by Friday night, I started to feel the walls closing in —and not just because of the attack.

Joining the Brotherhood felt like fate, a hidden purpose that had been waiting to be discovered since the moment I was born. I've never felt as connected to anything—to *anyone*—as I did the moment I signed the Book of Reckoning. It bound me to the mages in ways I can't even describe —a bond we'll carry for eternity.

Yeah, it's kind of a big fucking deal.

But despite the close connection and the sense of belonging I felt, once the newness started to wear off, a different feeling settled in my stomach, heavy as a stone.

And it's not entirely gone, either.

The guys kept secrets from me. Secrets I had a right to know about myself, about the real reasons the prophecies are so important. They misled me, and in some cases, outright lied.

The sting of that betrayal was and is still fresh.

But, unlike our bond, the sting won't last forever. They're doing the best they can with the information they have, just like I am. They wanted to protect me. They thought they'd have more time to bring me into their world.

Obviously, the Universe had other plans.

I can't fault them for that.

And like I said, after too many days apart, I kinda miss the fuckers.

"What's so funny?" Nat asks, narrowing her eyes. Then, looking at Isla, "Are you seeing this?"

"Now she's blushing," Isla says. "Hmm. Something tells me you weren't *totally* alone this weekend."

"No, I was! I swear! I was totally alone..." I laugh, covering my face to hide the blush. "On the weekend, anyway."

"And the other days? Hmm." Nat taps her lips. "Your lover-mage?"

"Which one?" Isla asks.

"Um. All of them? And they're not my lovers! Well, not all of them. It's complicated, okay?"

"I knew those slutty little eyes were going to get you in trouble." Nat links her arm in mine. "Clearly, we have a lot to catch up on."

"And we will," I promise them. "But first... the assembly awaits."

And judging from the dark vibe I'm getting as we file into the crowd, it's not going to be a happy one.

FIVE

The assembly hall is jam-packed with students and faculty, but Isla, Nat, and I manage to find seats together near the front of the room. A minute later, the lights flicker and a hush falls over the crowd as Anna Trello walks onto the stage and takes her place behind the podium.

I turn around and scan the room for the guys, but the only one I see is Baz. He's leaning up against the back wall, sleeves pushed up, sunglasses covering his eyes, the very definition of too cool for school.

"Security protocols, huh?" Nat whispers. "So this is the part where Trello tells us to salt our doorways and always use the buddy system at night?"

"Sounds about right," I say, but I have no idea what Trello's got planned. After the guys told her what happened with Phaines the other night, I thought—naïvely, of course —she might pay me a visit in person, or at least call to see how I was feeling and give me an update on the search.

Instead, I received a brief email expressing generic condolences about the "unfortunate incident," instructing me to keep a lid on all the details. *No need to cause mass panic, Miss Milan.* Her favorite mantra.

"Good morning," Trello begins, and the last remaining fidgeters go still in their seats. "Once again, we are called together not by celebration, but by tragedy—this time, one that struck very close to home. In the late hours of All Hallows' Eve, Professor Phaines—a trusted elder mage and member of the Arcana Academy family—stole precious magickal artifacts from the very library he swore an oath to protect. Even more egregious, he violently assaulted a student in an attempted ritual sacrifice, leaving her for dead in the Forest of Iron and Bone."

A curious murmur ripples across the room as those who hadn't heard the news speculate and turn their heads, searching for the poor victim. For a brief moment, I'm searching too, wondering who could've endured this terrible fate on our own campus.

It takes me a few beats to remember that it was me.

It was one thing talking about it with Isla and Nat. But now, as the pitying eyes of strangers find their way to mine, I'm hit with a rush of dark memories all over again.

Phaines's black boot coming down on my face. The evil gleam in his eyes as he carved my flesh and drained my blood, demanding answers I just couldn't give him. The emptiness I felt, alone in the Forest of Iron and Bone, tied up and bleeding...

"Stevie? Are you okay?" Isla's kind touch on my knee

brings me back to the moment, and I look into her eyes, blinking away the terrible memories.

Concern tightens her brow. "Goddess, you're trembling. Do you want to leave?"

I shake my head, doing my best not to draw more attention to myself. What am I going to do? Run home and cry every time I remember that night? No. Phaines took enough from me already. I need to be here. Present in my own life. With my friends.

Nat puts her arm around my shoulder and gives me an encouraging hug as Trello continues with the news.

"I want to assure each and every one of you that we're doing everything we can to locate Professor Phaines and bring him to justice. We don't believe anyone here is in immediate danger—all indications are that the professor got what he was looking for and is unlikely to return to the scene of the crime. However, your safety is—as always—our top priority, and there are other forces at work beyond our borders that put all of us in a perilous position."

The murmurs intensify, and Trello lifts her hands to quiet them.

"We're receiving numerous reports of larger cities militarizing in the wake of additional clashes between magickal and non-magickal residents," she says. "Protests are growing, along with counter-protests, and many of them are not peaceful. While witches and mages continue to be charged for crimes they likely didn't commit, others are, in fact, using their magick illegally. Sometimes it's in self-defense. Other times, it isn't. In both cases, the authorities have a right to arrest them. That is the law we live by."

"Damn," Nat whispers. "I can't believe how quickly things are going downhill. I kept hoping the military thing would stop with Portland."

"Have you heard anything else about your mom's friend?" I ask, remembering the woman charged last month with torturing her husband and mother-in-law.

Nat shakes her head. "Mom said the family is fearing the worst. No one has heard a word about her—not even from the authorities. They seem to have lost her records. Mom wants to visit them, but she's too scared to go. With the police and military in the city, she doesn't want to make waves."

"Given the circumstances," Trello continues, "and out of an abundance of caution, we thought it best to tighten our security—at least for the time being. We're asking all students and faculty to limit travel through the portals to a minimum, and to be prepared for additional security precautions coming and going. First-year students, this is a reminder that you are not to travel off-campus without an escort. Any attempt to do so will result in disciplinary action and additional restrictions."

"Talk about militarizing," Isla grumbles.

"We've also brought in three additional team members to help with the investigation and to ensure your continued safety." At this, two men and a woman emerge onto the stage, all dressed professionally in dark suits and light-colored shirts, some kind of ID badges clipped to their lapels.

"These fine folks are from the Association for the Preservation of Occult Artifacts. I'll let them tell you a bit more about their role here."

"APOA?" Nat whispers. "Why would she bring those guys in?"

"No idea," I say. "Maybe just to fill in for Phaines at the library?" A sliver of panic edges into my gut. Did Trello tell them about the Arcana artifacts? Can we trust them?

"Good morning," the first man says in a clipped British accent. He looks close to retirement age, with deep lines in his face and eyes that say he's seen some *shit* in his day. "I'm William Eastman. I realize many of you are under the assumption that APOA is nothing more than a bunch of stodgy old librarians obsessed with the past, but I assure you, nothing could be further from the truth. In recent years, APOA has come to encompass a great many divisions, all tasked with protecting magick and serving those who wield it, both inside and outside our revered magickal institutions. My colleagues and I are from the field division tasked with investigating magickal crimes."

The second man steps to the podium, nervously flicking his badge.

"I'm James Quintana," he says. American, judging by the accent. "I... don't do speeches." A few people chuckle at that, and the man loosens up. "But I *do* protect witches and mages. That's my job here. So... right. Thank you."

He steps aside to make way for the last APOA agent, a

woman who introduces herself as Casey Appleton. She sounds American, too, and something about her energy feels familiar, but I don't remember ever seeing her before.

"Thank you for inviting us here," she says. "These are difficult times for everyone, APOA agents included. Some of us have friends and family attending the Academy. Others are graduates. All of us have faced adversity, and all of us have come through it, just as we will again now.

"I realize having security on campus may feel intrusive —that's not our intention. We don't want to limit your freedoms or put you under the microscope, but we *do* need you to be vigilant—now more than ever. Please help us do our jobs. If you see anything out of the ordinary, any new faces on campus other than the people you've seen up here today, any unfamiliar magick, anything that pings your intuition as being even the *slightest* bit off, please tell one of us. In the meantime, we will do our best to keep the disruption to your lives at a minimum and to wrap up our investigation as quickly as possible."

The curious murmurs turn into groans as students begin to speculate just how intrusive and disruptive this "quick" investigation is going to become.

"Students, please," Trello says, reclaiming the mic. "As I've explained, this is for your own safety out of an abundance of caution. Our goal is to return everything to normal as soon as possible. But we cannot do that until Professor Phaines has been captured and we're certain no additional threats remain. Now, are there any questions?"

Someone in the front row a few seats down from us

stands up and says, "Is the stuff with Professor Phaines related to the attacks going on outside?"

Casey Appleton takes this one. "At this point, we have no reason to believe the two are connected, but given the dangers of both situations, we are exercising extreme caution and investigating all possibilities."

"How can they say it's not related?" Isla whispers. "It has to be."

Yeah, no shit. Appleton is definitely hedging. I can feel her evasive energy from here.

There's another question from somewhere behind us. "What happened to the student Phaines attacked? Are they okay?"

Trello finds my eyes across the room, but there's no emotion behind them—not even the tiniest flicker of warmth or compassion. "The student is recovering from the injuries, will still be attending classes, and I'm sure appreciates your thoughts and healing energy."

"Do we still have to go to class?" This from the back wall—a voice I recognize. One that sends shivers up my spine.

Baz.

Most of the students snicker—a little levity to break up the intensity. Unfortunately, Trello doesn't see the humor in Baz's question.

"Not only do you have to attend class, Mr. Redgrave," she says, "but you'll find your classes more intense and rigorous than ever before. This situation is a stark reminder of just how crucial it is for all witches and mages to take their studies seriously and to learn to harness and control their magick. This is not a laughing matter, but one of life and death. Not just because of what happened with Professor Phaines. I don't think any of us will soon forget what we saw on television last month."

My stomach churns at the grim reminder of Danika Lewis's execution, her body left swinging from the gallows for hours as the anti-witchcraft brigade celebrated her murder with selfies and beer.

"So much for the 'abundance of caution' stuff," Nat whispers. "Look at her. She's fucking terrified."

I shift uncomfortably in my seat. Nat's totally right. Trello may be projecting her usual detached authority, but she's practically white-knuckling that podium, and when I tune into her energy, I find subtle waves of fear and uncertainty.

"Professors and other Academy staff will be meeting one-on-one with APOA agents to share anything relevant to the investigation," she continues. "Again, this is more out of an abundance of caution than anything else. We all want to bring the matter of Professor Phaines to a swift conclusion and ensure nothing like this happens again."

Ensure nothing like this happens again? Has she learned nothing from the prophecies, from the last several years of vicious crimes against our kind? Professor Phaines, the setups and attacks going on outside… It's all just beginning.

I press my lips together, biting back my frustration. I understand Trello doesn't want to cause mass panic, but she owes us a reality check here. Instead, she's glossing over the scary parts, hiding under the blankets, and hoping for the best.

As any kid worth his Star Wars sheets knows—hiding under the blankets is not a viable defense strategy when the monster himself lives right under your bed.

There are still a few hands in the air, but Trello is clearly ready to move on. She talks right over the next questioner, still trying to reassure everyone with her "abundance of caution" platitudes.

"You doing okay?" Isla asks me.

Before I can answer, Trello is hushing the room again, prepping us for a final announcement.

"We've got one more introduction to make before sending you off to morning classes," she says, and immediately her energy tenses. The words feel like they're being pulled from her mouth, painfully and reluctantly. "She is a renowned collector and curator," she continues, "and very knowledgeable on magick antiquities and history. She'll be serving as interim librarian and archivist for—"

"Hopefully not just *interim* librarian," comes a woman's voice, deep and throaty. "I'm in it for the long haul, Miss Trello."

Seconds later, the woman herself appears on stage, sauntering toward the microphone with a wave and smile for the crowd as though she's competing in the Miss Magickal Universe pageant.

My whole body goes cold at the sight of her.

"They've already found a replacement?" Nat whispers. "That didn't take long."

"Janelle Kirkpatrick," Trello says, and the woman bows. She actually bows.

No one applauds.

"Oh my Goddess." Nat grimaces. "Kirkpatrick? Is she related to—"

"It's her mother," I confirm. "I had the pleasure of meeting her this morning. Real treat, this one." I shiver, remembering the weird, possessive vibes she gave off around Baz. Obviously they've known each other a long time, but it went way beyond that. She was trying to stake her claim, and didn't like when I encroached on what she perceived as her territory.

I turn my head, searching for Baz along the back wall.

But he's gone.

Janelle takes the podium, vomiting out a prepared speech about what a great honor it is and how amazing her credentials are and isn't it a wonderful time to be a witch? By the time she gets to the part about achieving her life's dream of guiding young witches and mages along the winding path of magickal enlightenment, it's all I can do not to bolt out of there like Baz did.

Bracing myself, I reach out for her energy, half expecting to be smacked in the face with evil and darkness.

But all I get from Janelle Kirkpatrick is a vain, egomaniacal, opportunistic snake, sprinkled with a good dose of horny cougar on the prowl.

As long as you keep your claws away from my mages, have at it, lady.

"Apple doesn't fall far from the tree," Isla says, nodding

toward the end of the row where Carly and two other Claires are seated. Her friends are buried in their phones, but Carly's attention is fixed on her mother, quietly seething.

I can feel her anger from here, simmering beneath her perfectly applied makeup and glossy black hair.

Great.

So Baz can't stand the woman. Trello can't stand the woman. Her own daughter can't stand the woman.

And this is our new Professor Phaines?

I settle back into my chair and close my eyes, pushing away the dark energies surrounding me.

Prophecy research with Kirin just got a *lot* more complicated.

With thirty minutes to spare before my Foundations of Tarot Magick class, the girls and I cruise into Jumpin' Jack's Java for muffins, caffeine, and a little witchy gossip, catching up on all the hookups, breakups, and fuck-ups from All Hallows' Eve.

Pretty sure we all needed the palate cleanser after the doom-and-gloom assembly.

"Out of an abundance of caution," Nat says, rising from our table, "I'm getting another cappuccino for the road. Do you guys want anything else?"

"I'll take a banana nut muffin," Isla says. "Out of an abundance of caution. Stevie?"

I roll my eyes and laugh. "So we're making this a thing now?"

"We are."

"Fine. Out of an abundance of caution, I'm going to decline the offer, as I've had more than my share of sugar and caffeine."

I scoop up our trash and bring it over to the recycler. Just outside the window, I spot Carly.

Alone.

She's hoofing it pretty fast toward our Foundations classroom, bag slung over her shoulder, hair streaming out behind her like the black flags on top of the admin building. Even from this distance, I can tell she's been crying.

"I'll catch you guys later," I tell Isla and Nat, heading for the door. "I need to talk to Carly."

Nat wrinkles her nose. "Why?"

"Time to clear the air on a few things."

Because in addition to how quickly dangerous secrets travel, here's the other thing I've learned:

Burying them doesn't make them disappear. It just gives them more time to sharpen their claws.

SIX

STEVIE

"Carly, wait up!"

Winded from the chase across campus in my gladiator sandals and a miniskirt, I finally catch up to her outside the Foundations classroom.

Thankfully, she stops and looks at me. Not without an epic eye-roll and a highly put-upon sigh, but still. She's actually waiting, giving me a chance to speak. At this rate, we'll be besties in no time.

"So, hey," I say, still a little breathless.

She doesn't say anything at first. Just narrows her red-rimmed eyes and gives me the once-over. Her gaze is cool and assessing, but her energy radiates with pure relief.

"Baz said you were in rough shape when they found you," she finally says. "Guess you bounced back pretty quick. That's good, I guess."

"Aww! Carly, I didn't know you cared so much."

"I don't."

"Lies." I press a hand to my heart and smile. "I can feel the love."

She probably doesn't know I mean that literally. Okay, so maybe it's not *love* I feel from my pseudo-nemesis. But it's not the callous disinterest she's pedaling, either.

She lifts a shoulder, then glances past me as if she's waiting for someone. "What is it you wanted? Class starts soon, and I'd rather not be seen talking with the enemy."

"I'm not your enemy."

Her eyes flick back over me again. "Anyone who thinks she can wear a leather jacket and high-heeled gladiator sandals is the enemy. What do you want?"

Ignoring the jab at my style choices, which are one hundred percent *fire,* I tamp down my annoyance and force out the words I've been holding in ever since Baz told me Carly was the one who alerted them to the danger with Phaines.

"I wanted to thank you, actually. And apologize."

"What the hell for?"

Wow. Apparently saving lives from raving psychopaths is just another day in the life of Carly Kirk-patrick.

But no matter how much she irks me, it *wasn't* just another day for me.

"What you did the other night... Carly, you saved my life. So that's what the thank you is for. As for the apology..." I gaze up at the ceiling and blow out a breath. "I shouldn't have snapped at you on the phone that night. If you hadn't called Baz after that..." I shudder at the thought. "I think we both know how my night would've ended."

"I *told* you I was clairsentient." Carly flicks her hair back, her eyes softening just a bit. "Still think I need to get my aura cleansed?"

"Hmm. Maybe just buffed a little."

"Cute." Carly rolls her eyes again, but I can tell she's holding back a smile. "Anyway, Phaines is a total creeper. Always has been. My parents couldn't stop singing his praises over the years, but he always gave me a bad vibe—even when I was little."

"Really? How so?"

"Just… I don't know. That whole Grandpa Gandalf act. It's a bit much, even for an old mage. I mean, I realize I'm a naturally gifted witch, more advanced than most—"

"Stop with the modesty!" I give her a playful punch in the arm. "Sing your praises loud and proud, girl!"

Again, there's the hint of a smile. "*Anyway*, it always seemed like he was just a little *too* excited about my magick. Then, when he met my friends, it was the same thing all over again. Ooh, so much natural talent! Yes, we must work closely together to ensure your talents are not wasted, blah blah blah."

"What was his end game?" I have my own thoughts on the matter, but it sounds like Carly was working even more closely with him than Kirin and I were, and she's known him a lot longer. Plus, she's not biased by the knowledge that he's one of the Dark Arcana mages—The Hierophant turned bad.

"At first I thought he wanted to just, I don't know, take credit," she says. "My mom is like that too—real big on that 'she gets that from me' kick. Of course, she's the first person to throw you under the magick bus the second anything goes wrong, but as long as you're kicking ass and taking names, it's all because of her amazing parenting skills. Anyway, Phaines—I figured he'd build us up, help us get stronger in our gifts, then parade us around like his own little pets."

"So what changed?"

"It's weird. Like, he was supposed to be this wise old mage teaching us about the ways of the world. But in the end, it was more like he wanted us to teach *him*. He wanted to learn all about our psychic magick, about how we felt or knew or sensed certain things. He'd run all these weird experiments on us, and when they didn't go as planned, he'd get all bent out of shape. He was like an addict. I'm not surprised he went off the rails in the end."

"When you say experiments, what do you mean?"

Carly sighs with annoyance, our momentary truce coming to an end.

Ah, peaceful coexistence. We hardly knew ya!

"So you're working for APOA now?" she snaps.

"Sorry." I lower my eyes. "Just trying to figure out how I could've been so wrong about Phaines."

She opens her mouth like there's another snappy retort locked and loaded, but then she just sighs. "He fooled a lot of people, Stevie. Don't be too hard on yourself."

I glance up at her, surprised at the emotion caught in my throat. "Thanks," I whisper.

"Alternatively, maybe you need *your* aura buffed. I'll see if I can get you the friends-and-family discount."

This has us both laughing, and for a minute I wonder if we've slipped into an alternate dimension. Deciding to push my luck, I say, "So your mom's working here now, huh? That's—"

"Not something I feel like talking about." Carly ices over in an instant, but then her anger melts away the chill, and she's more than ready to chat. "She never even told me she was coming here. Just showed up out of nowhere, announcing to the world that she'd taken this librarian job. She wanted to surprise me, she said." Carly hikes her bag up on her shoulder and lets out a huff. "Well, color me surprised. I wouldn't be more surprised if I woke up tomorrow with a magick wand shoved up my ass and pink sparks shooting out."

"Hey, thanks for the visual. I'll be sure to drink myself into a stupor later in hopes of erasing it."

"I'm serious, Stevie." Carly shakes her head. "We're not close. She didn't even bother to see me off when I left for the Academy. I don't know what the fuck she's doing here, but I can tell you this much. Librarian? Please. She wouldn't know a rare book if it reached up and slapped her on the ass. And don't even get me started on all that 'guiding young witches and mages along the winding path of magickal enlightenment' crap. Go home, mother. You're drunk. Again."

I give her a moment to cool down before I ask my next question. "So if she's not serious about the library stuff, why do you think she's here? Just to watch over you?"

Carly laughs, but this one is as bitter as they come. "I'm pretty sure the last time my doting mother gave two shits about me was when she found out I have three elemental gifts—gifts she thought she could use to her advantage. Well, that didn't work out. So here we are." Carly peeks into the classroom and waves at Blue, her pink-haired partner in crime already seated in the back row. "Anyway, free advice? Steer clear of Janelle Kirkpatrick. I'm not saying she'll carve you up with a knife like her predecessor… But I'm not saying she won't."

On that less-than-encouraging note, Carly turns toward the classroom entrance. But just before she escapes, I grab her arm and give it a squeeze.

Carly sighs and turns back to face me. "Story time is over, little witchling. Time to let Mommy go to class."

"Seriously, Carly. Thank you for making that phone call. I owe you one."

"Great." She leans in close, flashing a wide smile. "I'll be sure to collect."

STEVIE

"Fools!" Professor Maddox shouts, leaping up on her desk at the front of the classroom. "Damn fools!"

Half the students are out of their seats, including me.

Ani's standing next to me, Nat on my other side, all three of us pressing our hands to our hearts. Nervous laughter escapes my lips as I realize this is just more of Professor Maddox's theatrical style. But directly behind us, lazing in his chair like he just woke up from his beauty rest, Baz groans.

"Damn fools is right," he mutters, propping his sunglasses on top of his head. "She pulls this every year."

"Yet for some reason," Ani teases, "you keep coming back for more."

"What can I say? I'm a sucker for good performance art." Then, winking at me, "The louder the better, as far as I'm concerned."

My face flames as I recall our night together, and I sink

into my chair, hoping my friends don't notice.

I'm going to kill that man. Or maybe mount him again. Or maybe both…

At the front of the large, auditorium-style classroom, the professor continues to demonstrate her special brand of crazy. Behind her, William Eastman—the older British guy from APOA—stands like a statue, scanning the place like he's the Secret Service looking for would-be terrorists.

It's unnerving, to say the least, but I guess this is our new normal. Enhanced security. Constant observation. Total discomfort.

"Yes, my magickal mini muffins," Professor Maddox says, apparently unfazed by the man lurking behind her. "Today we'll be exploring an explorer. The most *intrepid* explorer, in fact, of the entire Arcana family. I'm talking about the one, the only, the amazing, The Fool! So." She claps once and hops off the desk, nailing the dismount. "Get out your Tarot decks and your journals. Place the Fool card on the desk in front of you. Yes, Miss Amana, that means you, too. Take your time, we'll wait…" She watches the student in question, then finally turns back to the rest of us. "Now, I want you all to take a deep breath, then let it out slowly. Ground and center, people. Ground and center. Miss Kirkpatrick, playing with your phone is neither grounding nor centering—put it away, please."

I smile to myself, glad I'm not the one on Maddox's radar today. She nailed me pretty good the first few classes, but I think she's starting to come around to my charms.

"For the next ten minutes," she says, "you'll spend time

in quiet contemplation with this magnificent card. Feel its energy, tap into its messages. Then, when you feel called to do so, write a personal essay from the perspective of any of the figures, objects, or emotional impressions in that card."

Baz raises his hand behind us.

"Yes, Mr. Redgrave?"

"What if we don't feel called to do so until next year?"

Ignoring the collective snicker, she says, "I highly suggest you feel called sooner than that, unless you wish to waste your *perfectly* good buns sitting in that chair for the next twelve months."

There's a chorus of groans, but it quickly dies down as we get to work contemplating Baz's perfectly good buns. I mean…

Right.

Moving on!

The Fool card in my deck features a young man dressed in a tunic and wrap, carrying a stick and bundle over his shoulder. He's got his trusty black greyhound for company, and in his free hand, he holds a bouquet of mistletoe. He skips along happily, seemingly oblivious to the fact that he's about to leap off a cliff.

This Fool, Trump Zero, the first card in the Major Arcana… He looks so different here than he did in my nightmare. He was only a baby there, caught in a dark and twisted version of the Judgment card.

Staring at the card now, I take another deep breath and try to get a read on its energy. But instead of picking up on a message like I usually do, this time I feel a gentle tugging sensation in my belly, and then it's like I'm being sucked right into the card itself.

I try not to panic. This is a good thing, right? A sign that my magick is getting stronger?

I steady myself, then look around at my surroundings. I'm sitting in the grass right beside the Fool, right at the cliff's edge.

No, wait. I'm not sitting. I'm standing. On four legs.

I'm the dog.

Just in case this day isn't strange enough.

Well, work with what you've got, right? I yelp to get the young man's attention, pawing at his tunic. After staring out across the abyss for a good few minutes, he finally kneels down beside me, patting my head.

"You're right," he says. "Now *isn't* the time for carelessness. We must be vigilant, friend. Keep our eyes open and see what's right there in front of us. Behind every beauty lies death, behind every death lies beauty. The question is, how do we know which is which? Hmm? We open our eyes and see. Then we *close* our eyes and see. See?"

No. No I don't. But I don't know how to express myself in this strange new landscape, so all I can do is bark.

"I'm sorry to hear that. I really thought you, of all beings, would understand." The Fool stands again and hikes his bundle higher on his shoulder. Turning away from me, he takes a step toward the edge, looking out across the expanse of nothingness once again.

I let out another yelp.

He looks back at me, frowning. "I know. But I told you

to open your eyes, friend. Maybe next time, you'll listen."

And then he leaps.

"No!" I gasp, reaching out for him…

"Stevie?"

I blink rapidly, the cavernous classroom slowly coming back into view. Ani's got his hand on my shoulder, his head bent close to mine, his brow creased with worry.

"Whoa." I take another deep breath, wait for Ani to come fully into focus. "That was… freaky."

"You okay?" he asks. "You were kind of trancing out on us there."

"I had a vision," I say, keeping my voice low. Last thing we need is Agent Seen-Some-Shit nosing around up here, asking questions about my wacky visions. "The Fool told me to open my eyes."

"Among other things." Ani gestures at my notebook, where two pages are filled with my writing, frantic and nearly running off the edges. It reminds me of my mother's prophecies, scribbled in haste, perhaps during a frenetic vision just like mine. "You were writing like mad the whole time."

I glance over the pages, pretty impressed with myself. Somehow, I recorded everything about that vision, right down to the feel of the grass between my doggy paws and the scent of the Fool's wool tunic.

"Maddox is going to love this," I say with a grin. "There's some juicy shit here, if I do say so myself."

"Show off," a deep voice rasps in my ear, and I hold back a shiver at Baz's sudden nearness. Since our night together on All Hallows' Eve, his effect on me has only gotten more intense, despite the issues between us. Earlier this morning, it took every ounce of willpower I possess not to drag him into the nearest supply closet and... *ahem*... forgive him.

Fully.

In fact, if I wasn't so gross and sweaty after my run—and Carly's cougar mom wasn't plotting my swift demise—I might've done just that.

I close my eyes, inhaling his scent. Goddess, I already miss the touch of his hands, the hot press of his mouth, the perfect thrust of his—

"Time's up, team Tarot!" Maddox is on the desk again, rudely breaking into my fantasy. "Please pass your essays forward. Don't worry about perfection—you'll be graded on your interpretations and insights, not on your style or grasp of the English language—yes, I'm looking at you, Mr. Glendale. The dictionary is your friend."

"Stevie?" Ani asks, and I open my eyes to find him watching me with fresh concern. "You okay? You tranced out again."

"Um... no. I'm good."

"Another vision?"

"Fantasy. I mean, yeah. Something like that."

"Fantasy?" His brow furrows. "What do you mean?"

"It's nothing."

No worries! Nothing to see here! Just fantasizing about your best friend's magnificent... wand! Keep calm and carry on!

Turning away from Ani's all-knowing gaze, I pass my

paper forward and pull out my tablet. Maddox wants us to read a few chapters from her book, *Arcana: Magick, Mystery, and Mayhem*, while she grades our papers.

Under normal circumstances, I might actually enjoy the reading time. But William Eastman, who's been in my life all of one hour, is tossing *normal circumstances* right out the window. He's finally left his post behind Professor Maddox's desk, and now paces the aisles of the classroom, stopping at each chair to peer down over our shoulders and inspect our reading material.

No, dude. Not invasive at all.

"Hardcore," Nat mouths to me, and I nod. This guy is even more of a rule-enforcer than Dr. Devane. If the other two APOA agents are like this, bad guys don't stand a chance at this academy.

Maybe that thought should put me at ease, but it doesn't.

After all, Professor Phaines wasn't a bad guy.

Until he was.

And none of us saw it coming—not even his friends and colleagues.

The end of class is a welcome relief, and I hastily put away my things and slip down toward the exit with Nat, Ani, and Baz. But just before I'm home free, I hear the fateful call of my name on Maddox's lips.

"Miss Milan? Just a moment of your time, please."

My friends linger by the doorway, waiting for me, but it's Eastman's glare I feel on my skin.

"Is… is something wrong?" I ask nervously.

"You could say that." Professor Maddox taps the stack of essays impatiently. "Frankly, I'm concerned about your lack of knowledge and awareness around an archetype as foundational as the Fool. His essence is the very source of our magick. The very reason we're even studying this esoteric subject at all."

Behind her, Eastman grunts.

Red-hot shame floods my body. I was so certain she'd appreciate the essay. "I… I'm sorry. I'm still a little rusty on the foundations, I guess."

"A little rusty is an understatement," she says, as though my rustiness is a personal affront.

Damn. After getting off on the wrong foot my first week at the Academy, I've tried really hard to do well in her class, paying strict attention to her lectures and keeping the Baz distraction factor to a minimum—quite an accomplishment on my part.

Or so I thought.

Clearly, I've still got a lot to learn.

"I know I've missed a few classes," I say, "but I'm happy to do some more reading, if you think that will help. I've also been super diligent with my Tarot draws and journaling."

"I appreciate your enthusiasm," she says, "but I don't think reading and practicing draws will be enough. I'm sorry, Miss Milan, but you need tutoring. This level of carelessness is unacceptable. As your professor, I take it as a personal failure on my part to fully engage you in the material."

"It's not, though! You're a great professor. Truly. The performance today was especially riveting. It's just... Is tutoring really necessary?" I can't imagine when I'd fit that in, given all the work Kirin and I have to do on the prophecies, not to mention the search for the Arcana objects, which we haven't even discussed yet. "I'm sure you're very busy with teaching and writing and your own divinatory studies, and—"

"You're struggling, Stevie. That much is clear. What kind of professor would I be if I allowed you to slip through the cracks?" She folds her arms across her chest, unwavering. "I'm hoping I can shine a little more *starlight* on your knowledge gaps."

Starlight?

The subtle emphasis on the word stops me short. The first time I met her, I got the feeling she'd recognized me— at least my name. I thought maybe she knew my mother.

Now, when I glance up into her eyes, I find her watching me intensely, her brows lifted as though she's waiting for me to catch her drift.

Did I hear her right?

"Do you understand, Miss Milan?" she presses, her tone becoming more urgent as Eastman stares at us, making no effort to conceal his eavesdropping. "The importance of this matter?"

"I... think so?"

"Great." Professor Maddox beams. "We start tonight. Are you free at seven?"

"So soon?"

"The sooner the better." She pulls out her phone and taps out a quick text that pings my phone an instant later. "That's the address to my shop at the Promenade—I live in the apartment above. Just text me when you arrive, and I'll buzz you right in."

"Your shop?"

"In addition to teaching and writing, I also own Time Out of Mind. We sell magickal timepieces, antiques, things like that."

"Um. Okay." *Intimidating much?* No wonder she thinks I'm a slacker in need of private lessons. This woman has, like, five different jobs, and I'm still patting myself on the back for learning how to fry an egg without breaking the yolk. "Do I need to bring my tablet or books or anything like that? My Tarot deck?"

"You should always carry your cards, Miss Milan. But you don't need anything special for tonight. Oh, you might want to wear a jacket, though. Who knows where the stars will take us?"

She says this last bit with a breathy, mysterious tone that leaves me wondering what the hell I've just gotten myself into.

Then, with a wink and a quick flick of her wrist, she sends me on my way.

Just before I turn to leave, I catch sight of my essay resting at the top of the stack on her desk.

There, circled on the page in bright red letters, is my grade: A+.

EIGHT

STEVIE

As much as I've griped about Dr. Devane's mega hard-on for rules and regulations, after last night's nightmare-turned-reality-show, all the bad news Trello dropped this morning, and my pending mystery date with Professor Maddox, Doc's authoritative energy is just what I need.

Besides, he's the head of the Brotherhood and the emanation of The Moon card. If anyone's got the 411 on crazy dream scenarios, it's him. And unlike William Eastman, Dr. Devane doesn't make me feel like a criminal just for breathing. Most of the time, anyway.

"Miss Milan? You're uncharacteristically early today." He's behind his desk in the mental magicks classroom, half out of his chair as I approach. His smile is cautious, and for a rare, unguarded moment, I sense a flicker of his energy.

It's surprisingly welcoming. Relieved. Happy to see me.

But there's something darker lurking beneath—something that feels a lot like shame.

"I was hoping we could chat?" I say with a tentative smile. Then, narrowing my eyes, "*You* missed me."

"Nonsense." Doc grins and his flint gray eyes sparkle, the skin crinkling around the edges as he deftly shores up his emotional walls. "But I *am* glad to see you out and about again. How are you feeling?"

"Better. Stronger." I pull up a chair and sit across from him as he settles back into his seat. "I went for a run this morning. Steered clear of the Forest, though."

He shifts in his chair, his smile faltering. I may not be getting a direct hit of his energy at the moment, but even a fool could sense that something's up.

"Doc?"

"I'm..." He lowers his head, ducking my gaze. "You have every right to be mad. Of course you do. I'm sorry. I should've said something. Made my presence known."

I'm about to ask him what the hell he's talking about, but sometimes—when you want the honest, hard-hitting answers—shutting up is the best strategy. Most people would rather spill their deepest secrets than sit too long in the unnerving presence of silence.

"It's just..." He sighs, then finally meets my gaze across the desk again. "Going out alone like that, so soon after the attack..."

Still, I wait, offering no more response than a raised eyebrow.

"Stevie, do you really think it's wise?"

"I think I'm wearing a tracking device," I reply, "and staying on the trails, and sending my itinerary to one of you guys every time I plan an excursion farther away than my own bathroom. How much wiser would you like me to get, Dr. Devane?"

"I..." He closes his mouth, pressing his lips into a thin line like he's trying to hold back the rest. There's a faint rustling of students passing through the hallway outside the door, but here inside the classroom, that ol' silence is a killer, and he finally breaks. "No, you're right. You're absolutely right. I shouldn't have followed you. It was overstepping, and I'm sorry."

"Wait... You *followed* me?" I'm out of my chair, anger racing up my spine like fire. "On my run? The whole time?"

"From the Blazing Pine trailhead all the way to Rock Basin and back again. You didn't know?" Guilt morphs into confusion on his face. "I... I assumed that's what you came here to discuss."

"If I *had* known, I would've maced you. Newsflash, Doc. Women don't like being followed—especially when we're alone, and especially when we spent the better part of two days trying to establish boundaries and rebuild trust." I turn my back on him and pace the room, trying to burn off the frustration.

"I was only trying to protect—"

"Protect?" I spin around and glare at him. "I've got a better word for it. Stalking."

"I've already apologized, Stevie. And I meant it. But tracking device or not, I'd be lying if I said I'm not terrified at the thought of you getting hurt again. You're a target—

we've known that from the start. And frankly, we'd all prefer it if you'd—"

"You'd all *prefer* it?" Wow. Not even four days after they promised to ditch the secrets, the mages are back to making decisions about me behind my back. "Yes, I'm sure you'd all prefer if I stayed locked in my room for the rest of the semester, but I'll tell you right now, that's not happening. So if you insist on following me, I suggest you get yourself a good pair of running shoes, because I'm half your age and I'm going to give you the workout of a lifetime."

I storm across the room to the windows behind the last row of desks, desperate to put some space between us.

"Stevie, I understand why you're upset. But please… Let's talk about this."

Ignoring him, I peer down at the campus below. From my second-floor vantage point, I can just make out the edge of the Tarot fountain, the water glittering in the morning sun. I press my finger to the windowpane, tracing the outline of one of the many red stone paths that wind past it.

Arcana Academy is so beautiful and serene, so magickal, it's hard to believe this is the same place where my parents lost faith in their *own* magick. The same place where dark mages twist that beautiful, life-affirming power into a weapon to torture and maim students, and secrets hang in the air like black clouds waiting to burst.

I sense Doc looming behind me, but I don't turn around. Not even when he places his strong hands on my shoulders, nearly overwhelming me with his sudden nearness.

"We swore an oath, Stevie," he says softly, his warm

breath stirring my hair. "To protect you. To protect each other. That's what Brothers do."

"I'm not upset that you're protecting me. I'm upset you think you have to sneak around to do it. You could've just texted to meet up this morning. We could've gone on the run together—safety in numbers. You're not twenty, Doc. What if you'd had a heart attack out there? Then *you'd* be the one in need of a rescue."

Ignoring the dig about his age, he says, "You wanted space."

"Yes, I wanted space. Actual space. Not the illusion of it." I fold my arms over my chest, still staring out the window even as Doc's warm touch seeps through my jacket. Three witches sit on the edge of the fountain, heads bent together, one of them laughing at something another just said. I wonder if they have any idea how much danger we're in. For all of Trello's dire warnings and abundance-of-caution speeches, she didn't even scratch the surface.

I wonder if Trello herself even knows what we're truly up against.

Judging from the level of secrecy around here, I'm guessing not.

"I thought we all agreed to open communication," I continue. "Now you guys are declaring what's best for me as if I'm not even part of the equation."

"That's not—"

"You say I'm one of you. A member of the Brotherhood, a seer, a powerful Arcana witch. Yet—"

"You are all of those things and more." He releases my

shoulders and steps in front of me, forcing me to meet his gaze. "So much more. But a lot of that 'more' is still locked up inside you—untapped potential. You're still green when it comes to magick, when it comes to comprehending the full scale of what we're facing here. As a more experienced mage and professor—and as the present leader of the Brotherhood—I'm not going to stand by and watch—"

"You're right. I *am* green—probably the greenest witch on campus right now, thanks to my magick-free childhood. I fully admit I need more knowledge and practice—I still can't even make a feather levitate consistently. But there's a big difference between a witch in need of guidance and a child in need of supervision, and right now, you're all treating me like the latter."

"That's not our intent. It's just..." Doc scrubs a hand over his face, his energy leaking around the edges again, so subtle he probably doesn't even realize it. He's trying to hold on to anger, but it's quickly giving way to fear, to his concern for me, to his struggle to do what's right.

And there, flooding into the spaces between all of those emotions, is a deep, dark regret.

The sharp edges of my frustration soften a bit. "It's just *what*, Doc? What aren't you telling me?"

"Stevie," he whispers, reaching up to cup my face in his hands. He peers down at me, his eyes as gray and stormy as the sea.

My nerves jolt at the contact, and for the briefest instant, I catch the scent of the ocean, hear the hush of the waves against the shore.

Then it's gone.

"I want… I *need* to protect you," he says. "Don't ask me to explain it, because I can't. It goes beyond the Brotherhood bond, beyond our age difference, beyond the fact that I'm your professor, beyond anything I've ever felt, even when…" Trailing off, he shakes his head, his thumbs tracing across my cheekbones. "That need… It overwhelms me at times, blinding me to all else, including the fact that I'm probably smothering you. I'm working on it. But it's hard to override that instinct—especially when it comes to you."

"Instinct?"

"Since the very first. Seeing you in the prison, it was…" His gaze burns with new fire. My heart is racing now, my skin tingling at his touch, but I don't dare pull away. "I'd hoped against the odds that we'd gotten you through the worst of it. That bringing you here really *was* the better option. But now I'm not—"

"Stop." I finally step back and take a deep breath, refocusing. "It was my choice to come here."

"Yes, and when you made your choice, I made a promise. I said I'd do everything in my power to keep you safe, to protect you. Since your arrival, you've been attacked multiple times—by fellow students, by an esteemed professor we all trusted, by a rattlesnake, by visions… I've failed you at every turn."

"You also warned me that I'd be in grave danger from the start, that you had no idea who the enemy was, and that it'd be nearly impossible to protect me. You promised me a shit storm, and you delivered in spades. That's not failure, Doc. That's truth in advertising."

Guilt ripples through his energy.

"Not an accusation," I clarify. "Just a reminder that I knew the risks and I signed up anyway. Just like I signed up with the Brotherhood. I'm in this with you guys, and I'm not backing down."

He tries to speak, but I cut him off again.

"And while I fully acknowledge I've got a lot to learn on the magick front, and I shouldn't take stupid risks like ditching my phone and heading off on a three-day solo backpacking trip, I'm not going to stay locked up in my room while you guys fight this battle yourselves. You need me."

"Stevie." Doc offers a small smile, but it's not enough to outweigh the doubt in his tone. "Your loyalty is honorable, but—"

"You think this is about loyalty? To what? Some made-up secret society and a bunch of ancient spellbooks? To the First Fool? To my dead parents? No, Doc. I'm doing this to protect the people *I* care about. You want to try to take that from me? Be my guest. Then you'll have *two* wars on your hands, and you'll definitely lose this one."

Doc stares at me for so long I worry I've given him that heart attack after all. I'm just about to check his pulse when he finally shakes his head, glances down at his watch, and says, "Well, now that we've cleared that up…"

"Have we?"

Doc sighs. "What was it you wanted to chat about,

anyway? Aside from the vaguely stalkerish tendencies of your *elderly* mental magicks professor?"

Laughter rises up inside me, and soon Doc is smiling again, too.

"Does this mean I'm forgiven?" he asks.

"Depends. Does this mean I've finally made my points?"

"All but one." Doc leans in close, his hand finding its way to my shoulder again. In a teasing whisper, he says, "I'm not twice your age, Miss Milan. Not even close."

"I'm twenty-three," I remind him.

"I'm aware."

"So you're—"

"Running out of time before class starts." He heads back to his desk, gesturing for me to follow. "Now tell me what's on your mind. Is it too much to hope for good news?"

"Yes."

"No sugar-coating, I see."

"Truth in advertising. Remember?" I take the chair across from him again and unzip my backpack, fishing out the real reason for my visit.

"What in Goddess's name is that?"

"Oh, just a little barbecued bush, courtesy of our dark-side Arcana counterparts." I hand over the Ziplock bag containing the charred evidence. It looks even worse now, all dried and desiccated, the blood-red berries crusted with ash. "I brought it back last night."

"From where?"

"My nightmares."

NINE

STEVIE

Doc listens attentively, his flint-gray eyes never leaving mine as I tell him about the dream battle, the charioteer, the fires, the injuries, all of it.

"I was healed by the time I got out of the shower," I say, "but there was still blood and dirt all over the floor and bedding. That's how I knew I hadn't imagined it. Well, that and the holly."

"No, Stevie. You didn't imagine it. Dreamed it, yes. But not imagined." Doc removes the branch from the plastic bag, crushing one of the dried leaves between his fingers and bringing it to his nose for a whiff. "Holly has been associated with the Winter Solstice since ancient times."

"The day we honor the Dark Magician." Goosebumps erupt across my skin. "Was this a vision, then? A warning about what's coming? *When* it's coming?"

"That's one possibility—a strong one. What's more concerning to me at the moment is how this branch traveled back with you from the dream realm. Any chance you were sleepwalking?"

"I thought of that, too. But I checked my security settings this morning, and my door hadn't been opened all night. There was nothing weird on the video feed either."

"What about your familiar? Could he have flown you out magickally again?"

"I don't think so." Guilt pokes my heart. "Actually, I haven't seen my owl since the night of the attack."

"He'll come to you again when he's ready, Stevie. He just needs time to heal."

I nod, grateful for the reassurance.

"If we've ruled out sleep-walking," Doc continues, "the next best explanation is the worst one." He sighs, tapping his fingers on the desk. "Someone is trying to get to you from the astral—to break into your subconscious and channel enough power to affect your conscious reality."

"So you think it's more than just a vision? Someone is actually trying to hurt me?"

"Sends a powerful message either way, right?"

"But... How does that even work?"

"No one is totally sure. The realms are extremely complex—just when you think you've figured out how something operates, the rules change. All we know for certain is that realms are fluid, permeable, and they often overlap." He leans forward, elbows on the desk, and makes a sphere with his hands. "Picture a child blowing bubbles through a wand. Sometimes those bubbles chart their own course, drifting on the air currents, always remaining separate. Other times they collide and either pop or absorb into one another. Sometimes they even stick together."

"Then there's that cool trick where you blow a bubble inside of another one."

"Precisely."

I try to picture what he's describing, but we're rapidly approaching mind-blowing territory here. "So if I'm traveling in my dream realm bubble, and someone else is traveling in another bubble, and we bump into each other…"

"A skilled mage or witch can slip between them."

I lift the holly branch, twirling it between my fingers. "And bring things out, back into our material realm?"

"Yes, though I've never seen it happen before."

"Oh, yay! More special snowflake powers for my collection!" I smile, but it doesn't last. "If I can be hurt in my dream realm, does that mean I can be killed?"

It's the age-old question, right? If you die in your dreams, do you ever wake up?

Doc's energy turns icy. "We aren't going to let that happen, Stevie."

"Unless you plan on pumping me full of caffeine and dousing me with ice water every time I nod off, I don't see how you can stop it."

"At the risk of sounding controlling and overbearing…" Doc frowns, deepening the lines around his mouth. "I don't want you sleeping alone."

"Great, me neither!" I laugh. "My bed is officially open for business. Shall we put a message on the student website?"

"This is serious, Stevie. If the Magician and his dark minions are trying to reach you in the dream realm, that means any time you're asleep—literally at your most vulnerable—they will have the advantage. We don't know how many there are, which realms they have access to, how much power they're amassing, how often they can actually get to you. But judging by your visions and dreams, they've got more than enough power to wreak havoc."

"Setting aside the topic of sleeping companions," I say, "what's the connection between my dreams and the actual campus? Everything I saw unfolded right here. The buildings, the pathways… I got turned around in the mist, but it still felt like Arcana Academy, right up through the end."

"There's no doubt in my mind that what you're seeing *is* the academy. We just don't know whether it's a glimpse into the Dark Magician's twisted mind—into the destruction he hopes to cause here—or a premonition of events that have already been set in motion. Events we can't stop, but can only prepare for."

"Neither scenario bodes well for us." Gazing down at the blackened branch, I'm struck with another thought. "Wait. If what I'm seeing is the academy, then the cave—the one with the Fool and the baby-eating druid—exists somewhere on campus."

"I would imagine it does, though I've never seen it."

"Should we try to find it?"

Doc picks up the branch again, gazing at it as if it holds the key to every one of life's mysteries. "No."

"Why not? It could hold clues to the Magician's plans,

or the Arcana objects, or even my mother's prophecies. She was there at the end of my dream, Doc. I know it was her. She—"

"There's only one place where holly thrives on campus, Stevie." He drops the branch and meets my eyes across the desk. "The Void."

The Void.

A shudder wracks my body as Kirin's warning from my first day here echoes in my mind.

It's said that there are places in this world so deep, so dark, so... compelling... when you peer down into them, they literally beckon you to jump...

"*L'Appel du Vide*," I say, just as Kirin did that day. "The call of the void."

"Stevie, this isn't—"

"Dr. Devane?" a woman calls from the doorway, startling us both. "Sorry to interrupt. I'm Casey Appleton from the APOA. I'd like to observe some classes today, and Headmistress Trello suggested I start with yours."

"By all means. Come in." Doc holds my gaze for another beat, then turns to Casey with a welcoming smile. Rising from his chair, he gestures for her to take his place. "I move around when I lecture, so this seat is all yours."

"He paces," I cut in with a smile. "Kind of like a lion stalking its prey."

Doc laughs, his eyes darting to me with a faux-warning glare. "This is Starla Milan, one of my more *vocal* students."

Casey does an excellent job of maintaining her composure, as I'm sure she was trained to do in APOA secret-agent school. But her energy gives her away immediately—a spike of curiosity when Doc said my name, followed by a crushing sense of…

Sympathy?

Immediately, my guard goes up. Does she know me? Know *about* me? Is the sympathy for my dead parents? My dead friend Luke? My recent wrongful imprisonment? My outfit? Maybe she's on Carly's side when it comes to women dressed in leather jackets and gladiator sandals.

"Lovely to meet you, Stevie." She smiles again and reaches for my hand. "I look forward to seeing what you're learning about here."

"Mental manipulation as a form of self-defense," Doc supplies.

"Excellent." Casey laughs, giving my hand a squeeze.

Her touch is warm and confident, and I relax. I'm just being paranoid. All that talk of dark mages infiltrating my dreams and murdering me in my sleep clearly has me on edge.

"Thanks for… um… your service," I say, cringing at my awkwardness. What are you supposed to say to APOA agents?

Fortunately, I'm saved from figuring it out by the wave of students rushing in for class. I nod once more at Casey, then take my seat, immediately scanning the crowd for Baz. Carly and Emory are joined at the hip as usual, but he's nowhere to be found.

A tiny bubble of disappointment floats up inside me, but I pop it post-haste. Baz is my fellow Arcana mage and friend, but that's it. No more sleepovers, no more make-out sessions, no more red-hot, naughty dreams about the devilish man in the meadow…

No. The sooner my body gets the memo on this, the better.

You hear that, slut muffin? When it comes to Baz Redgrave—and any mage for that matter—there will be no more bubbles, flutters, fizzes, fantasies, hot flashes, thigh clenches, throbbing of any parts, or any other symptoms of lust-induced stupidity allowed. Violators will be subject to month-long orgasm deprivation, including those of the self-administered nature…

"By now you've all heard about the attack on campus," Doc begins as the bell rings and the last student rushes in to claim his seat. "You're also aware of the new security protocols, including visiting agents from the APOA." He gestures toward Casey, who offers a quick smile to the group. "Miss Appleton will be observing us today, so let's show her what sharp, efficient minds we all possess. Pair off, and we'll start with the role-playing exercises we talked about last week."

I glance up to find Casey staring at me again, that same strange, sympathetic energy trying to wrap itself around me like a hug—one I don't want or need.

Something about her looks so familiar, too, but I can't figure out where I may have seen her. Was she ever on campus before today, maybe meeting with Trello? Is she an alumnus? Maybe her picture is hanging in one of the dorm museums somewhere. I'll have to do some nosing around later.

With Baz MIA, I partner up with another first-year—a soft-spoken mage named Wyatt I've seen around the Iron and Bone dorms but haven't interacted with much—and we tackle Doc's latest mind games.

Wyatt, it turns out, is obsessed with Dungeons and Dragons, and is therefore an excellent role player. We zoom through the exercises without a hitch, earning a rare compliment from the good doctor that leaves Wyatt beaming and my cheeks warm with pride.

It's only after class ends and Casey wishes us a good day that I realize what else is bothering me about her, aside from the weird sympathy mojo.

Doc introduced me as Starla, but when Casey shook my hand, she called me Stevie.

That means she either heard part of my conversation with Doc before she interrupted us, or she already knew who I was before she got here.

I'm not sure which thought freaks me out more.

"Stevie?" Doc's hand on my shoulder snaps me out of my pondering, and I look around to see I'm the last one here. "Everything okay?"

I rise from my seat, gathering my things. "Do you know that Casey woman? I feel like I've met her before. She looks super familiar, but I can't put my finger on it."

"Allow me to do it for you." He runs a hand through his hair, then smiles, but it's not exactly a happy one. *Resigned* is the word that comes to mind. "That Casey woman is Kirin's sister."

TEN

KIRIN

It's funny the things you remember about a person you spent years trying to forget.

There's a soft knock on my office door, three short taps, and I know immediately it's her. Just like I know she'll barge right in here before I can even—

"Kirin! I've been looking everywhere for you!"

"Casey," I say cautiously.

Her wheat-colored hair is pulled back into a no-nonsense ponytail, and her pale green eyes, so like mine and our father's, shine in the dim light. Ten years later, she still looks exactly the same.

I take off my glasses and rub my eyes, telling myself the sudden sting is from the long hours at the computer screens.

"Can I… Are you busy?" she asks.

"Yes. I mean, I'm… Yeah, come on in." I maneuver

around the front of the desk and clear a stack of books and papers from one of the chairs, gesturing for her to sit.

"You look well," she says stiffly as I retreat back to the relative safety behind my desk. "Academy life suits you, then?"

"It certainly keeps me occupied."

"Never a dull moment, right?" Forcing a smile, she glances around at my disheveled office—hundreds of books lining the shelves and spilling out of cubbies, papers and folders stacked on every flat surface, index cards stuck to a bulletin board I haven't used in years, a collection of unwashed coffee mugs holding court around my monitor.

I can't help but wonder what she sees. An academic scholar? Her less-than-perfect baby brother?

Or just a washed-out mage whose career ended long before it even began?

"Where are you staying?" I pick up the worn stack of Tarot cards I keep on my desk and shuffle—a nervous gesture my inquisitive sister doesn't fail to notice. "Trello didn't tell us she'd called in the calvary. I didn't even know you were coming until you stepped out onto that stage this morning."

Casey's eyebrows lift. Seems I've surprised her, too.

"I would've called ahead," she says, "but I don't have a working number for you."

Ah, passive aggression. There's the old Casey I know and love.

"Anyway, Anna put us up in Red Sands Canyon," she says, and I let out a low whistle. Red Sands Canyon is an exclusive community of well-appointed houses owned by the Academy, used primarily to house visiting dignitaries and wealthy Academy donors. It's not located on campus and is only accessible by a portal, tucked away in a small desert town on the Arizona-Mexico border and hidden from outsiders by magick.

"But," Casey continues, "I asked to be transferred to campus housing. Eastman and Quintana took the Red Sands deal, but I'll be staying in a suite at Breath and Blade. I wanted to be closer to the action, so to speak."

I open my mouth to tell her I live there too, on the graduate floor, but there's no need. She already knows.

With Casey, nothing ever happens by accident.

"For how long?" I ask instead, still shuffling my cards.

"As long as it takes to figure out what the hell is going on here." Her eyes ignite with passion and determination. "To ensure the students are safe."

I set the Tarot cards face-down on the desk between us. "Any leads yet?"

"Just got here, Kirin. Still getting the lay of the land." She reaches out and takes the top card from the deck. Her eyes widen just a fraction when she looks at it, but she doesn't show me her card. "I've never been here before, remember?"

Casey studied at the Paris campus, but that's not what she's talking about. Her subtle dig was about me—about the fact that I've never invited her here. Never even told her I'd taken the research position.

Clearing her throat, she says, "I spent the day with Dr. Devane, observing his mental magicks classes."

I'm about to ask if she learned any new tricks, but instigating her will only make things worse. "He's a great professor," I say instead. "We're lucky to have him on staff."

"Is he your boss?" Casey cocks her head, and with a single look, the family bonding session is officially over.

We're in interrogation mode now.

"No, I report to Trello." I pull a card from the stack—Seven of Wands. At the center, a man stands on top of a stone tower gripping a large wooden staff, preparing himself for battle. Several soldiers march up the hill toward him, spears raised.

I'm being hyper-defensive.

I blow out a breath. Sometimes it's hard to remember Casey isn't the bad guy.

"But we do work together occasionally," I add—a gesture she interprets as an invitation to turn up the heat.

"Work together on what?"

"Research. Translations."

"Could you be more specific?"

"Arcana myths and legends at the moment," I tell her, because she could easily request the library's logs and see exactly which manuscripts I've checked out. Depending on how long this investigation drags on, she could probably get access to my computers too, including the databases of Melissa Milan's prophecies.

"And what is Starla Milan's role in this research?" she asks. "I understand she's working with you as well."

Doing my best to school my features, I nod as if the

mention of Stevie's name isn't a big deal. "Have you met her?"

"In Devane's morning class. Seems like a bright young woman. Eager." She narrows her eyes, undoubtedly searching my face for a reaction, which means she either knows a hell of a lot more than she's letting on—or she's hoping I'll give something away to help her fill in the blanks.

"Fast learner, too," I say. "She's shown an early aptitude for divination as well as interpretation of ancient prophecies. We're working on translating some of her mother's works. Melissa Milan was a—"

"I'm well aware of the tragic Milan backstory," she says dismissively. "Trello tells me the girl is spirit-blessed?"

"She is." I slip my card back into the stack and fold my arms across my chest. My patience with my sister has nearly run its course. "Are we finished here? I've got work to do, and I'm sure there are lots of other people on campus you can grill."

Hurt flickers in her gaze, and my shoulders sag, guilt bubbling up inside me. I'm doing exactly what I said I wouldn't do—letting the ghosts of the past come rushing back in to haunt me.

To haunt us both.

Casey's just trying to do her job—I get that. But when it comes to unsolved mysteries, my sister is like a dog with a bone. The longer she stays here, the more questions she asks, the deeper she digs...

This can't end well. We're all at risk here, especially

Stevie. The last thing I want is for my sister to make the target on Stevie's back any bigger than it already is.

And despite everything, I don't want my sister mixed up in this danger, either.

I used to think I could keep Casey safe. But it turned out the only way to do that was to leave. Now she's here, back in my life and back on campus indefinitely. So what the hell am I supposed to do?

"Casey, I'm sorry." I close my eyes and shake my head, still struggling to keep my emotions in check. "I didn't mean—"

"Janelle Kirkpatrick," she says suddenly, shifting gears so fast I nearly get whiplash. "Did you have any communication with her before the job interview?"

"I haven't had any communication with her, *period*. Did someone tell you there was an interview? Because if that's true, this is the first I'm hearing about it."

"You're the head graduate researcher, and you didn't know Trello was bringing in a replacement for Professor Phaines?"

"I found out about her appointment the same time the rest of the students did—at the assembly this morning."

"You're telling me that for a high-level position like hers, there was no interview, no vetting process, no board review, no input from other professors?"

"As far as I know, Janelle's *on* the board. She's also a donor—probably the most substantial one the Academy has ever had."

"I see." Casey lets out a derisive snort. "Follow the money, and the answers shall appear."

"What do you know about her?"

"Not much. Eastman believes she's interested in a set of magickal antiquities dating back... well, a long time." Casey holds my gaze across the desk, and again I feel her scrutinizing me. Testing me.

Shit. I should've known my sister already had her fingers in this particular pie.

"The legendary Arcana objects, I presume." It's a challenge to keep my tone neutral, but I don't want to assume my sister knows more than she does. Tricking people into oversharing is one of the things that makes her such a good agent—and a lousy sister. "Janelle wouldn't be the first treasure hunter to come sniffing around here."

"You think there's something to it? The legend, I mean?"

"Which one?"

"The one about the objects being buried on the campuses. Some people say the Dark Magician stuff is real—that he's due to rise up again and scour the lands for his precious artifacts, killing and plundering as he goes."

"That is one interpretation, I suppose." I glance over at my monitor, unable to hold her penetrating gaze. "The problem is, there are literally dozens of legends related to the Dark Arcana and the objects—maybe hundreds—most of them long forgotten. We don't have much in the way of primary source material, so it's all just speculation at this point. Like any mythology, I suppose."

Casey rises from her chair and closes the office door,

then sits back down again, her eyes blazing with new intensity.

"Something wrong?" I ask.

"Kirin." She leans in close, tapping her finger on the stack of Tarot cards still sitting between us. "What if they're not legends?"

Then you don't have to worry about it, because chances are... We're all going to be obliterated.

"Really, Case?" I scratch the back of my head and shrug, desperate to get her off this track. "What if a fat man in a red suit flies around the world delivering Christmas presents to all the good little boys and girls?"

"I'm serious."

"So am I. Look, normally I'm the first person to sign up for an expedition down the myths-and-legends rabbit hole, but you're an APOA soldier now. You should know better than anyone about the craziness these legends stir up. Hell, how many Indiana Jones movies and knockoffs have they made? Ancient artifacts, creepy legends, magick... That stuff always brings out the treasure hunters and fanatics. Nine times out of ten, everyone goes home empty-handed."

"Or cursed."

"There is that, yes."

"Magick is real, Kirin. So why not the rest?"

"I'm not saying it's not possible—I wouldn't be in this field if I didn't hold out hope for something like that. But the Arcana artifacts? Come on, Casey. How could something so powerful stay hidden for millennia?"

She levels me with a death-glare. "I don't know, little brother. Let's ask King Tut."

Like I said, dog with a bone.

Tension simmers between us, and I take a deep breath to calm myself. I can't let her upset me. If she does…

"Why are you guys interested in these legends anyway?" I ask. "Don't you have bigger concerns, like finding Phaines and figuring out how to keep the rest of the known world from burning us all at the stake?"

Casey continues to glare at me. "Good to see you're still a stubborn jackass."

"Good to see you're still a—"

"Stop." She holds up her hand, cutting me off. "I didn't come here to fight. And I gave up trying to make you listen to me years ago. But I'm going to give you a piece of advice, anyway." She tosses her Tarot card on my desk—The Tower. It's almost comedic that she thinks the card is about anything other than me—anything other than her own brother, the ticking human time bomb.

"Don't trust Janelle Kirkpatrick," she continues. "We don't know enough about her motives or her background to make any assumptions right now, but she's a known associate of Phaines, and she's been involved in shady antiquities deals in the past. Eastman wants us to keep a close eye on her, so that's what we're going to do."

"Noted. Are we done here?"

"Yeah, Kirin. We're done." Casey jumps out of the chair, jerking her purse strap over her shoulder. "But don't be surprised if you get a visit from Eastman. I'm sure he'd love to catch up."

The anger inside me goes from simmer to boil. Behind me, the bookshelf trembles—so slightly I'm sure Casey doesn't notice. But I do.

Fucking Eastman. I really hoped I'd seen the last of him years ago, but it seems our paths are meant to cross again.

"So you're his little protégé now? How's that working out?" I cringe at my own lack of subtlety. But she can't be surprised. Subtlety was never my strong suit.

"William Eastman is a good man, Kirin. Dedicated. Smart."

"Total prick," I grumble.

Casey goes silent, and when I finally look up to meet her eyes again, I find nothing but a sad girl in front of me, full of shame and regret.

"You didn't have to leave," she says softly. "You would've made an excellent field agent."

The reminder of my long-lost dream feels like a dagger in my chest. "Eastman didn't think so."

"We could've reasoned with him. Given everyone time to—"

"To what, Case? Forget what they saw? Forget the monster in their midst?" I shake my head, shame burning its way up my throat. Yes, Eastman is a world-class asshole. But no matter how much I try to hate the man, Casey's right —he *is* good at his job. He wasn't wrong to ban me from APOA all those years ago.

"Not to forget," Casey says. "To understand. You

could've given everyone more time. Kirin, your gifts are intense and mysterious, but they're also—"

"Not meant for public consumption."

"You didn't even try. Didn't give anyone a chance to fight for you. To help you." Tears glitter in her eyes, and when she speaks again, her voice breaks. "Mom and Dad never blamed you. They just wanted a chance to fix it."

She's right, they didn't blame me—not out loud, anyway. They didn't scold or mistreat me. Didn't threaten me or try to beat it out of me.

But sometimes the weight of disappointment in the eyes of the ones you love hurts as much as a punch in the face, and the only remedy for the pain is to remove yourself from the situation altogether.

I turn my back, focusing on the books on the shelf behind me, organized by subject first, author name second, size third. *This* is the world that makes sense to me. The world on the other side of this desk—my sister, my past, my regrets—that's a world I won't go back to.

I *can't* go back.

"I needed to start over," I say calmly. "I'm sorry that I hurt you, but I had to do this for myself. It was and continues to be my choice. I'm asking you to respect it."

"You didn't even say goodbye. You have no *idea* what that did to Mom and Dad. What it still does to them."

The dagger in my chest lodges in deeper, piercing something vital inside.

My vision blackens at the edges, my insides frothing like a shook-up bottle of champagne.

"It was selfish," she snaps, popping the cork.

And I explode.

I whirl around to face her just as the overhead light sizzles and bursts, raining glass down on my desk. Casey backs up against the wall and covers her head as books leap from the shelves and papers whip around the office in a frenzied storm. One of my monitors tips over, and the stained-glass window at the top of the door cracks.

The whole thing lasts no more than twenty seconds, but by the time I get it under control and the chaos fades, both of us are trembling.

Her with fear.

Me with rage. It's so complete, so all-encompassing, I'm pretty sure my heart is going to implode.

"Still think you can make everyone understand?" In one swift move, I sweep the monitors from my desk, sending them crashing to the floor. "Still think your baby brother isn't a monster?"

For once, my sister is silent. Ignoring my questions, she lowers her eyes and picks her way through the wreckage, opening the door and exiting wordlessly from my life, just like I exited from hers.

The difference is… Casey's not going to stay gone. Nor is Eastman or the APOA or any of the other shit I've spent the last decade trying to outrun.

It's all here, converging on me smack in the middle of Arcana Academy.

And I'm running out of places to hide.

ELEVEN

STEVIE

I'm late for Potions and Charms, stumbling into the class-room just as Professor Broome announces the elixir we'll be working on this week.

"Dream potions," she says, nodding at my apologetic smile as I take a seat next to Isla, "are one of the safest ways to experiment with the power of the subconscious mind. Depending on the herbs and incantations you choose, you can use your potion to aid in lucid dreaming, dream recall, past life regression, travel between realms, and even spirit communications." Her eyes widen, sparkling with the same mystical excitement as always. "So, my little dreamers, grab a mason jar from the counter in back, gather your herbs, and get to work!"

A murmur of excitement ripples through the room—we've all been eager to work on dream stuff. I just wish her timing had been better—dream potions would've come in handy *last* night.

A shiver creeps down my back as images from my nightmares flash through my mind—a horror movie I'm pretty sure is far from over.

"Everything okay?" Isla asks. "You look a little freaked out."

"I'm… No, I'm good." I follow her to the shelves at the back of the room where all the supplies and ingredients are stored. "I actually tried to make my own dream potion last night. Epic disaster."

"Enthusiasm is an admirable quality in a witch," Professor Broome says from behind us, "but overeagerness is the enemy of successful magick."

I turn around to face her, offering another apologetic smile. "Sorry I was late, Professor. And you're right about the overeagerness. I should've waited, but I was having trouble sleeping and wanted to give it a try."

"And?"

"It was a complete failure."

"Hmm." She taps a finger against her lips. "Did you record your spell, your ingredients, and your expected versus actual outcomes?"

"To the letter."

"Then it wasn't a failure, Stevie. It was a learning experience." She beams at me, then ushers us toward the shelves. "Onward!"

"I'm pretty sure she's my favorite professor," Isla says as we line up to collect our ingredients. "Hey, speaking of professors… Nat told me Maddox gave you a hard time after Foundations class today. What happened?"

"Yeah, it was totally weird. She said I was in danger of failing and that I needed one-on-one tutoring. But right before I left, I saw my essay sitting on her desk. She'd already marked it an A+."

"Seriously? So she's lying about the tutoring?"

"I don't know. I didn't get a bad vibe from her or anything. More like… Like she wanted to talk to me about something else, but with that Eastman guy lurking around, she couldn't."

"When are you supposed to get together?"

"I'm meeting her tonight at Time Out of Mind. Apparently, she owns the store and lives in an apartment upstairs."

"Want me to go with you? I'm usually pretty good at sussing out people's motives."

"No, I think I can handle it. Like I said, I didn't get any bad vibes. Actually, I'm pretty sure she knew my Mom."

"Really?"

"They're close in age. Well, the age my mom would've been if…" I blink back tears, wondering if talking about my mother is always going to feel like this—a strange mix of joy at remembering her and despair that she's gone. "Anyway, maybe they were friends."

"Okay. Just text me if she ends up being a crazy cat lady and you need a rescue."

It's finally our turn at the supply area, so Isla and I grab our mason jars and get to it. The shelves are fully stocked with bottles and vials of anything we could possibly need, each ingredient carefully labeled with its name and magickal properties.

Isla goes right for the lucid dream stuff, a mad-scientist grin taking over her face. "I've been wanting to try this all semester."

I pick out a large jar of oat-colored powder and unscrew the lid for a closer look.

"Fairy's Breath," Professor Broome says, coming to stand beside me. "In its powdered form, ingesting it or applying it directly to the skin will help you open up to spirit communications and channeling, but you must exercise extreme caution. Too much could leave you vulnerable to possession." She touches the amulet dangling at her throat. "If you find yourself drawn to this herb, I recommend wearing a grounding stone like black tourmaline or hematite for additional protection. It should help you keep one foot in this realm, even as you're skirting along the astral."

"Can I smell it?" I ask.

Professor Broome nods. "It has a very distinct scent, unlike anything else, though few witches and mages have the ability to detect it."

I swirl the jar beneath my nose, taking a gentle whiff.

I'm almost immediately overcome by the intensity of the scent, and I wrinkle my nose, trying to get used to it. It's not bad, per se. But it's definitely earthy and pungent—a bit like rotting leaves and mushrooms.

"Ah!" Professor Broome smiles, imitating my wrinkled

nose. "I see you're one of the precious few. Perhaps your empathic abilities amplify your sense for this as well."

"Can you smell it?" I ask.

"No. And I'm told that's a blessing."

I've never worked with Fairy's Breath before, so I'm not surprised I didn't recognize it by sight. But the scent triggers something inside me. I've definitely smelled it before, but where? It's not an herb used in teas or baking, and I don't recall ever seeing anything like this in Mom's kitchen.

"Are you going to try it?" Isla asks gently. "To get in touch with your mom?"

It's tempting. And considering my mother has already made contact through my dreams and visions a few times, I wouldn't be surprised if this enhanced our connection even more.

But instinct tells me that spirit communication is not where I need dream practice. Mom will come to me when the time is right—she always has.

"Not this time." I replace the lid and slide the jar back into place. Turning to Professor Broome, I lower my voice and ask, "What would you recommend for communicating with Dark Arcana energies?"

Professor Broome narrows her eyes, but if she thinks my request is odd—or dangerous, for that matter—she doesn't judge.

"Well, what would *you* recommend?" she asks. "What are your goals with that particular communication? Start there."

"I… I think I'd like to learn more about the old legends. Try to understand my roots. Magick's roots."

"Dreamwork is an excellent approach, since so much of our magick is connected to our subconscious. Tell me… Have you dreamed of the Arcana energies before?"

"Yes," I say, then rush to add, "At least, I think so. Dreams are so weird. It's hard to say for sure. But I'm hoping if I can open myself up to their messages, I can figure it out."

She hesitates another beat, then finally nods. "Okay. How would you feel about silversword root and witch's cauldron?"

I find the respective jars and pull them off the shelves, setting them on the counter behind us. "Silversword root for clear communication and seeing through the haze," I muse, inspecting the silvery powder through the glass.

"Very good. And this?" Professor Broome picks up the jar of witch's cauldron. The round, black seed pods are about the size of marbles, but so light and delicate, they're almost sheer.

My cheeks flame, and I lower my voice further. "Honestly, I thought witch's cauldron was for enhancing certain… things. Not dream things. *Other* kinds of bedroom things."

"Potency," she announces, and I crack up.

"Yes," she says. "That's precisely what you want. Crush two or three of them into your mix for added potency. In this case, the pods should help sharpen your dream images and bring additional clarity about their messages."

I grab a pair of tongs and gently remove three pods, grateful that Baz isn't in this class, because I'm pretty sure he'd have a field day with this one.

"Stevie," Professor Broome asks, concern replacing the usual mirth in her eyes. "Working with this sort of energy is very dangerous, and very advanced. Not that you're not capable, but…" She closes her eyes, then opens them again, the concern fading. "No, you're ready. If a witch is called to explore her magick, it's not for me to question her methods. Just to politely inquire."

I give her a reassuring smile. "I appreciate that. I'll be careful, though. It's just… I feel like this is something I need to do now. I can't explain it."

I know there are risks—I was already injured in last night's dream, and Doc confirmed that I could be killed. But instinct says the Dark Magician doesn't want me dead. If he did, it would've happened already.

Call it the twisted ego of a supervillain, but something tells me he wants me to listen. To see him. To know exactly what he's planning for us. And yes, maybe those plans are already set, and there's nothing we can do to stop them, like Doc said. But we *can* prepare. And maybe—if I can show him I'm ready to listen—the Dark Magician will make a mistake and reveal something useful.

"You don't need to explain," Professor Broome says. "Just know that I'm here for any questions, day or night."

"Thanks, Professor."

"Anything else?" she asks, tapping the edge of my mason jar.

"One last thing." I grab a glass eye-dropper from the counter and reach for a bottle of milky white liquid. "I was thinking about adding some moonstone elixir. Since the Moon card rules over the realm of dreams and our subconscious, I thought this might be a good conduit."

"You've got good instincts for this, Stevie," Professor Broome says as I add a few drops to the mix. Her eyes are still sparkling as usual, but this time it's not with pride about my academic prowess or passion for her career choice. It's nostalgia—I feel it in her energy, warm and wholesome, tinged with a hint of sadness and loss.

"Thank you, professor," I say.

"You take after your father." She runs a hand over my hair, a maternal gesture that makes my chest tighten. "Your mother, too. I see both influences in you."

Blinking away the tears before they totally ruin my makeup, I smile and say, "You knew them?"

"Connor was one of my star students. Melissa's gifts were in divination, but she was always a joy to teach, too." Her own eyes mist, then fill with fresh concern. "Stevie, with something like this… the Dark Arcana… I suggest you wear the Eye of Horus hematite during your dreamwork. It will protect you from the more negative forces at play."

"Even if I'm not trying to communicate with spirit?"

"The Dark Arcana *is* spirit energy. Powerful spirit energy at that. Promise me you'll take all necessary precautions?"

"Of course." I touch my throat in search of the Egyptian pendant, but then remember I'm wearing a different necklace today—a rose quartz choker Isla loaned me. "How did you know about the Eye of Horus? It was my mother's."

Professor Broome leaves me with a smile and a mysterious wink, the familiar sparkle back in her eyes. "Who do you think made it for her?"

TWELVE

STEVIE

Why does everything at Arcana Academy have to be so mysterious and confusing?

It's like the administrators all watched too many fantasy movies as kids, and somehow got the impression it's not real magick unless there are plenty of shadows, cryptic messages, and secret meet-ups inside haunted antique stores.

"Yeah, this isn't creepy at *all*," Nat says, rubbing the chill from her arms as we approach the entrance to Time Out of Mind. "Talk about a ghost town."

"Are you sure you're cool to go in there alone?" Isla peers in through the front window, the dim light inside barely enough to see by. "It looks kind of... closed."

"I'm fine," I say. "But I do appreciate the escort service."

After Trello's speech of epic impending doom, I'm not surprised to find the Promenade mall deserted after dark, and I'm glad I decided to ask the girls to walk with me after all. No, I don't want to live my life in fear, or feel like I can't walk out my front door without backup. But I also don't want my gravestone carved with "Starla Milan: Nice Girl, Kinda Cute, Too Stupid To Live."

Tradeoffs!

"Well, wish me good luck and a passing grade." I text Professor Maddox to buzz me in, then send the girls on their way.

The air inside smells like old books, metal, and candle wax, and as I glance around at the many shelves, I'm immediately transported back in time. The one-room shop is tiny, but what it lacks in space it makes up for in really old shit to fill that space. Every shelf is jam-packed with books and knick-knacks, glass jars and bottles in every possible shape and size, statues, ceremonial daggers, sculptures, loose gears and springs, pieces and parts whose origins I can only guess at.

Dominating one end of the room is a glass jewelry case full of watches, pendants, bracelets, rings, and loose gemstones. Nestled beneath a darkened stairwell at the back of the store, a huge grandfather clock keeps watch, its brass hands softly counting the passing moments.

Footsteps creak on the stairs above, and Professor Maddox finally descends into the dim light. I almost don't recognize her—she's dressed in funky ripped jeans and a fitted black sweater, with copper bangles on one arm and a sparkly blue pendant at her throat. Her hair is curled, her makeup so on point even Jessa—queen of the smokey eye—would be jealous.

"Professor Maddox?"

"Nope." She smiles, lighting up her face. I never noticed how pretty she is. "I leave the professor in the classroom. On girls' night, I'm just Kelly."

"But I thought this was a school thing. Tutoring?"

"Change of plans. Tonight, I'm taking you off-campus. Call it a field trip."

Kelly seems genuine, but after my mistakes with Professor Phaines, I'm not taking any chances. I made assumptions that he was exactly who he said he was—who he appeared to be—and those assumptions nearly got me killed. That's not happening again.

I reach out for her energy, looking for any signs of danger or trickery. But Kelly's honesty—along with a good dose of friendly affection—shines through loud and clear.

"Where are we going?" I ask.

"Where the walls don't have ears." Kelly gives me a conspiratorial wink, then grabs the edge of the grandfather clock and gives it a good heave. The whole thing swings open like a door on invisible hinges, revealing a dark closet full of glowing gossamer webs.

Magick webs.

"A portal," I breathe, reaching out to touch them. The strands shimmer between my fingers, making my skin tingle.

"My own personal transportation device," she says. "It's one of the old portals left over from before the Academy upgraded. When they installed the new ones, this little beauty had already been out of service for decades, so they just left it alone. It was here when I moved in, just as dead as can be. But three hours of tinkering, one bottle of cheap red wine, and a dash of hocus-pocus later? Voila!"

"You fixed it yourself?"

Kelly grins. "I'm a witch of many talents."

"Does that mean this portal is off the grid?"

"Maybe," she teases. Then, lowering her voice to a whisper, "You won't give away my secrets, will you?"

I cross an X over my heart and laugh. "Never."

"After you." Kelly gestures for me to step inside, and she follows, shutting the clock behind her. The magick threads envelop us, glowing brighter in our presence and making me feel like we're underwater. It's not scary—just a little disconcerting.

Kelly pulls a Tarot card from her back pocket and shows it to me—a man and woman in a boat, guided to safer shores by a ferryman at the back.

"Six of Swords," I say. "For safe travel?"

"Very good, Stevie." She holds the card in one hand and takes my hand in the other, then speaks an incantation:

> *We travel together through time and space*
> *In my mind's eye, I hold the next place*
> *Steer us safe and guide us true*
> *The Six of Swords will see us through*

The magick flickers, then the underwater feeling intensifies, as if we're sinking into a warm and salty sea. Suddenly, everything starts spinning, the magick strands and Kelly blurring before my eyes. I have just enough time to feel the nausea hit, and then we're stumbling out through another darkened doorway into an alley in an unfamiliar desert town.

The air is warmer here, and after spending the last month inside the climate-controlled confines of the academy, it takes me a minute to get used to the feel of true desert air on my skin—hot and gritty, almost suffocating, as if the red sands are already trying to claim me.

The sun has long since set, but the smell of hot asphalt lingers—a familiar scent that makes my eyes water and my heart beat faster. When I peer down through the short, squat buildings at the end of the alley and see a tumbleweed rolling down the street, I squeeze my eyes shut and let myself believe I'm home.

Tres Búhos... It can't be...

"Welcome to Buena Casita, Arizona," Kelly says with the same dramatic flair I know from class, and I blink the sting of lost memories from my eyes. I glance back through the doorway we just came through—nothing more than a storage room on the backside of a restaurant.

"Whoa," is all I can say.

"Yes, the old portal system is a little hard on the body. You okay?"

"I think so. Just dizzy."

"It will pass once you readjust to being on solid ground again."

"How do we get back?" I ask, checking out the mundane storage room again. There's no magick that I can see—just a few cleaning supplies and some gallon-sized tubs of mayonnaise and pickles. "The only other time I came through a portal was when Dr. Devane first brought me to campus. He had to do a blood spell in the middle of the desert."

"My portal operates a little differently. For one thing, you can only return to campus via another closet or storage space. Any closet will do, as long as it's dark and has a door that closes. You also need your return ticket." She flashes the Six of Swords card again, then tucks it into her purse for safekeeping. "Then you envision my shop, recite the spell, and off you go—the magick will take care of the rest."

"What if you lose the card?"

"Pro tip?" Kelly laughs, linking her arm in mine and leading us away from the storage room. "Don't. No, but seriously. Don't."

"Are you sure this old portal is safe?"

"It is—it's just a bit of a hassle if you're not careful. If you lose the card, you have to call someone from campus to come get you—they'll travel through with their own card and bring you back that way. It's inefficient and not all that secure, which is why they made the upgrades to the rest of the portal system. But I like having my own personal unit. Besides, I mainly use it for popping into town and back— nothing too taxing."

"But that storage room—what if someone had been inside it when we portaled through?"

"Then the magick would've put us in a holding pattern

until it was clear. After five minutes, if it still wasn't clear, the portal would've kicked us back to my store."

"Wow. That's… wow."

"Magick," she says with a wink. "Come on. This way."

She leads us down the alley and onto the sidewalk, then down another block to a little hole-in-the-wall bar called La Naranja Vieja.

"The Old Orange?" I ask.

Saying nothing, Kelly simply offers another mysterious grin, then opens the door, waving me through.

Vieja is right—there are only a handful of other patrons inside, but none of them look under the age of seventy. The space itself is old too, its once-vibrant salmon and orange-painted walls cracked and peeling, the wooden floor planks stripped bare from years of spills and footfalls.

We find a secluded booth in the back corner and slide in, reaching for the menus sticking out from behind the napkin dispenser.

"Order anything you'd like," she says. "It's my treat. And don't let the ambiance fool you. The burgers here are to die for."

My stomach is growling, but I can't seem to focus on the menu. I'm still a little out of sorts from the trip, and no closer to understanding why Kelly was so desperate to meet tonight.

"Professor Maddox," I say, setting the menu back in its place. "I'm—"

"Kelly."

"Okay. Kelly." I smile, hoping it softens my next question. "Don't take this the wrong way, but what exactly are we doing here? You said you wanted to meet about my issues in class, but I saw my essay on your desk today. You gave me an A+. Now we're out here in this random bar in the middle of nowhere, and—"

"What'll it be, girls?" The bartender—a stout woman who looks to be in her eighties—shouts at us from behind the oak bar in the center of the room.

"Strawberry margarita and a bacon cheeseburger for me," Kelly calls back.

"Same," I say, because my brain is too full to think for myself right now.

"You're right, Stevie," Kelly says when we turn to face each other again. "We're not here about school. We're here about your mother."

THIRTEEN

STEVIE

It's nothing less than what I suspected, but still. The word crashes into me like it always does, no matter who's speaking it.

Mother.

"But you already knew that," Kelly says softly. "Didn't you?"

"I... I had a feeling," I admit. "A hope, maybe. The first day of class, there was something about your energy, the way you looked at me... I wondered if you knew her. Then, when you mentioned Starlight earlier... That's what she used to call me."

"She always told me her daughter would be her starlight."

"How well did you know her?"

Kelly reaches into her purse, fishing out a photo and passing it over. There are two girls in the picture, and I recognize Mom immediately—she's wearing that formal silver dress, the same one she's wearing in one of the pictures Trello gave me.

"Is this you?" I ask, pointing at the other girl. Now that I take a closer look, it's obvious that it's Kelly. Same smile, same bright eyes. She and Mom have their arms around each other, their cheeks smooshed together. They both look radiant and happy.

Kelly's eyes shine with emotion. "Melissa—your mother—she was my best friend, Stevie."

I let out a gasp, but the bartender is suddenly here with our drinks. She sets them both on cardboard coasters, but the moment she turns away and I lift my glass, my coaster transforms into a Tarot card.

Four, actually—the Queens.

Kelly's eyes widen as she glances down at the cards. "Has this happened before?"

"Do you mean, have the four Queens crashed the party while I was hanging out in a desert dive bar with the professor whose Tarot class I'm possibly failing? No, this is definitely a first." I laugh, taking a much-needed sip of my frosty margarita. "But Tarot cards have been randomly appearing like this ever since my mom died. Well, the year after—that's when it started. They come and go. I haven't actually seen them in a while."

Kelly smiles and shakes her head. "Very clever, Melissa. Very clever indeed."

"Clever? I don't understand."

"I have a message for you from your mom." She taps the cards between us, then meets my gaze again. "Close your eyes and listen closely. You won't be able to write it down—that was one of her requirements."

My stomach bubbles in anticipation, and as soon as I close my eyes, Kelly begins to whisper—so softly I have to lean forward to hear the words:

Fear not the evasive Queen of Air
Though her manner is coarse, her outcome is fair
By thought or by deed, by word or by blade
Her sacrifice can't be unmade

The Queen of Water extends a gift
Love and compassion to mend the rift
Keep watch by your mind, but open your heart
For that is when her friendship starts

With caution consider the Queen of Fire
Her tongue is sharp and so is her ire
The raven is false, yet darker still
Is the vessel within that yearns to be filled

By the Queen of Earth, you may be vexed
But trust you must her diligence
Sisterhood too, you'll find within
But only when it's welcomed in

She repeats it three times in total, and at each verse, the corresponding elemental Queen appears in my mind—Queen of Swords first, the air element, a wise, no-nonsense woman with long gray hair, dressed in a purple gown and a tattered blue cape, clutching a sword to her chest. Next is Queen of Cups, the water element, standing on a rocky shoreline in a long green cape, holding a chalice beneath a full moon. The fire element, Queen of Wands, sits on a throne wearing a red tunic and cape, a wand held in her right hand while fires burn behind her. And finally, Queen of Pentacles—the earth element—dressed in a red gown and green cape, playing a bodhrán with a bone as she sits on a throne carved with pentacles.

Kelly falls silent, and I sense the message is complete. The queens fade from my mind.

"I still don't understand," I say, opening my eyes. "Is this one of her prophecies?"

"No, not in the larger sense of the word. It's a message just for you."

"But what does it mean?"

"That's for you to discern, Stevie. Melissa didn't offer many more details. She just insisted I memorize it, and pass it along to you verbally after you enrolled at the Academy, whenever I sensed the time was right." She takes a sip of her margarita. "When I heard about Phaines's attack, I knew the time had come."

"But that makes no sense. I thought she broke ties with everyone at the Academy after she and my father left?"

"She did. I never heard from her again, despite my best efforts at trying to reach out. But this message… She shared it with me before she even knew she was pregnant with you, Stevie." Her eyes drift to the Tarot cards still scattered on the table. "She just… knew."

"I've heard she was the best seer the Academy has ever known."

"It's true."

The bartender arrives with our food—two massive plates overloaded with fries and burgers the size of car tires, dripping with cheesy deliciousness. When she leaves again, I pop a fry into my mouth and say, "So do you know why Mom left the Academy? What happened to make my parents completely renounce their magick?"

"I wish I did. Your mother became very secretive in the end. She spent most of her time in the archives, and as much as we cared for each other, our lives were just moving in different directions. Eventually, I stopped seeing her around campus—your father told me she'd even been sleeping in the library, working day and night on her visions and prophecies. Most people thought she'd gone crazy and paranoid—that all the time she spent divining wisdom from behind the veil had finally ruined her mind."

"Is that what you thought?"

Kelly shakes her head emphatically. "Your mother was more lucid than anyone else on campus, including the headmistress."

"Why didn't anyone else seem to see it that way?"

"Understand, Stevie. Sometimes, when we don't speak someone's language, when we don't understand their way of communicating, it's a lot easier to just call them crazy and turn our backs than it is to work toward common ground."

"A lot easier, and a lot deadlier. That's how wars start."

"You're right. And how friendships end and marriages implode and families become estranged. We don't understand each other, we hurt each other, and then we turn our backs. Magick is wonderful, but it can't fix our basic human failings. That's on us." She grabs a knife and cuts her monster burger in half. "You know, there are still so many things about that time that don't add up. I've never been able to figure out why the headmistress forced her out. I'm afraid most of those secrets— just like your mother's visions—died with your parents."

I want to tell her that they *didn't* die—that the very reason I'm here is to decipher Mom's prophecies. That even Trello finally came around to the fact that my mother had something important to say—something that might just save all of our lives.

But like my Arcana nature, my work on the prophecies must remain secret. Not just for my own sake, but for Kelly's as well.

She digs into her food, but my head is spinning with too many questions to allow me to eat anything more than a few bites.

Reciting Mom's message again in my head, I ask, "Do you think she's talking about Queen affinities? People I'm already in contact with here?"

"It's quite likely. There are several students and professors blessed with Queen energies. Queens are very powerful affinities, but not uncommon." She waves her hand over her drink glass, and a thin, pink stream of strawberry margarita rises up, twirling like a streamer between us before diving back into her glass. "Queen of Cups is my affinity."

"Really?"

Kelly nods. "Though I'm not suggesting that verse is about me."

"It could be, though."

"Yes, it could be." She reaches across the table and squeezes my hand, her smile as warm and genuine as her energy, and I can't help but think it *is* about her. The part about keeping watch with my mind but opening my heart makes sense, too. Phaines left me guarded and on edge, and I know I need to be more vigilant than ever. But I also don't want to close myself off to new friends. To love.

"I'm sorry I don't have any answers," Kelly says kindly. "Not the ones you seek, anyway. But I want you to know you have a friend at the Academy, Stevie. Whenever you need one."

"Thank you," I say. Then, with a big grin, "Can my friend hook her girl up when it comes to passing class?"

Kelly laughs. "You have nothing to worry about there. You're a natural with the Tarot, and it's only a matter of time before you master your magick as well. Your essay was actually quite enlightening. I'd love to hear more about your experience with the Fool card meditation sometime, if you're open to sharing? Maybe over some of your infamous tea?" She gives me a wink. "Yes, your mother saw that in your future, too."

"I'd love to." A lump of gratitude lodges in my throat.

Seconds later, the four Queens finally vanish from our table.

Kelly's eyes widen.

"That's normal," I say. "No idea where they come from or where they go, but they always disappear once I figure out their message."

"Now there's an answer I *can* give you." Kelly drains the last of her drink, then lowers her voice. "The cards are from the dream realm."

"The… what?"

"Are you familiar with how the realms work? At least—how we believe they work?"

"Sort of?" I tell her what Doc and I discussed earlier about the realms, leaving out the specifics about my own dreams and the fact that I brought back that extra-crispy holly branch. That is *not* a conversation I feel like getting into right now.

"Well, just as people can travel between realms," Kelly says, "some witches and mages—in rare cases—have learned how to bring things into and out of realms. Your mother was one of those witches. She could bring things out of her dreams."

Yesterday, I might have been more shocked by something like this. But after my own experience with the branch and the injuries, the news that Mom had a similar gift is not surprising.

"I believe she's sending these cards to you," Kelly said. "Once they've served their purpose, they return to her in the dream realm."

"But she's not dreaming," I say. "She's dead."

"Yes, but again, realms overlap."

"She comes to me sometimes," I say, popping another fry into my mouth. "In my dreams."

"That's because it's easier for the dead to speak to us in dreams than it is for them to manifest in our realm. But the Tarot has its own strong magick, and somehow, she's able to send you these cards."

I nod, my brain rapidly approaching overload.

There are so many more things I want to ask her about my mother, magickal and mundane, but before I can formulate my next question, my phone dings in my pocket.

It's Dr. Devane's tone—the one we set up for Brotherhood communications.

"Go ahead and get that," Kelly says, sliding out of the booth. "We should probably head back, and I need to pay the bill and hit the ladies' room first."

I nod and reach for my phone, but really, there's no need to answer. The tone can only mean one thing.

I've been summoned to the Fool's Grave.

The Brotherhood gathers tonight.

FOURTEEN

STEVIE

After Kelly takes us back through the portal and we say our goodbyes with a promise to schedule a tea date soon, I head to Iron and Bone to change for the meeting and await the signal. What signal, I have no freaking idea, but it wouldn't be Arcana Academy without a little cloak-and-dagger confusion.

All Doc said was that I should dress in dark colors and that further instruction would be provided on an as-needed basis.

Well. I've never belonged to a secret society before, much less attended clandestine meetings in the middle of some creepy-ass petrified forest, but I'm pretty sure snacks are a requirement—especially since I didn't eat much at La Naranja Vieja. And if they're not a requirement, they *will* be. Whatever rules and regulations it may violate, a girl can't be expected to embark on this quest-to-destroy-the-one-ring nonsense on an empty stomach.

I quickly change into my nighttime ninja-wear of black spandex and a black long-sleeved T-shirt, then pack a backpack full of peak snackaliciousness: brie and sharp cheddar, rosemary crackers, red grapes, veggies and hummus, and a bag of white cheddar popcorn to eat on the way. I almost grab a bottle of wine, but think better of it, brewing up a quick pot of tea instead. It's my famous Gone Mental brew —a blend of rosemary, peppermint, and sodalite gem essence to encourage alertness, mental clarity, and—word of the hour—honesty.

By the time I'm ready to rock, I'm 99% sure this is all a setup for some televised prank show. But no matter what happens tonight, I've got a thermos full of tea and a cooler full of snacks. What could possibly go wrong?

As if I really needed an answer, my phone buzzes with a text from Baz: *Emergency exit, corridor past common room. 5 min. Tell no one.*

I send him a quick reply: *Is this supposed to be the signal?*

Stevie, he texts. *Why can't you just follow instructions?*

Instructions or orders?

Seriously?

I'm just saying, you guys could stand to be a little clearer in your secret messaging.

!!!

Ok, ok! Be right down!

I grab a black zip-up jacket and my backpack and head downstairs, peeking into the common room as I pass by. Gathered around a long table near the kitchen area, a few students are setting up for what looks to be a pretty serious game of D&D. The only one I recognize is Wyatt, the soft-spoken mage from my Mental Magicks class.

"Stevie!" he calls with a friendly wave. "You want in? We can roll up a player character for you."

"Can't tonight," I say with a frown. It actually sounds kind of fun—normal—but I've got my own real-life D&D quest to deal with right now. "But I'll definitely take a raincheck."

"You got it."

I wish them luck and head down the corridor that leads to the emergency exit. I'm almost to the end when a utility door beside me pops open and a pair of strong hands yank me inside, my kidnapper kicking the door shut behind us.

I tense up for the fight, but the scent of my captor gives him away—that intoxicating mix of woodsmoke, tilled earth, and black pepper that makes my stomach flutter.

The man is a fine wine waiting to be sipped.

But I've still got a *tiny* bit of pride left, so I fold my arms across my chest and say, "Seriously, Baz? A closet? Aren't you taking this whole secret meeting stuff a little too far?"

He leans in close, his scent invading me. There's just enough light for me to make out the shape of his face, the glint in his eyes. "Cozy, right? Kind of romantic, if you ask me."

"Romantic. Sure. So this whole thing was just a setup so you can get me naked again?"

"No way." Baz laughs softly, his breath stirring my hair. "You said you needed space from all that. What kind of a man would I be if I violated your wishes?"

"If this is your idea of space, we've got a problem."

"Agreed. Starting with this." He reaches for the zipper on my jacket, and I lose the rest of my words.

Okay, I really, *really* want to stand firm on this give-me-space thing, but I also really, *really* want him to tear off my clothes, pin me against the wall, and bang the shit out of me.

What can I say? I'm a woman of many contradictions.

Baz gets my jacket unzipped, then says, "Lose it. Now."

Without question, I drop my backpack and slip out of my jacket, letting it hit the floor. My heart's pounding in my chest, my mouth already watering for the taste of his kiss. I can go back to having pride and principles tomorrow. Right now, I'd rather have an orgasm. Or three.

Baz shifts closer, his arms encircling me, his lips hovering so close to mine as he leans in and…

Drapes a blanket over my shoulders?

"What the hell?" I ask.

"Your magickal cloak," he says, stepping back. "In the form of a fleece jacket."

My cheeks burn, and now I'm grateful for the near-darkness. If Baz saw my face right now, he'd know *exactly* where my mind had gone.

Where my hopes had gone.

Shelving my disappointment, I put my arms through the sleeves and zip up. "So how does this thing actually work? The cloaks I saw you guys wearing were long and hooded."

"It'll transform as we get farther from campus. Right now, we just need to look normal."

"Yes, because banging in a utility closet is so normal."

"Um… Did you just—"

"Hiding! *Hiding* in a closet. I'm… wow, it's hot in here. I need air." Ignoring his soft chuckle, I put my backpack on and say, "Just tell me how this thing works so we can get out of here. Are we invisible now?"

"It doesn't make us invisible, just unremarkable. People may see or hear us as we head out, but they'll forget about us the minute we're out of sight."

"How?"

"The material is spelled to affect those who aren't part of the Brotherhood. Non-Arcana."

"Affect them how? By erasing their memories?"

"No, not at all. It just prevents them from imprinting us in the first place. Think of it like a computer file you forgot to save."

"But that makes no sense. If I forgot to save a file, I wouldn't forget the file *existed*. In fact, I'd probably go crazy looking on my hard drive for—"

"Stevie? I think you're confusing me with someone who gives a fuck about accurate technical analogies, and I hate to rain on your nerd parade, but Kirin isn't in this closet with us."

"Hmm." I step closer, letting my breasts brush against his chest, figuring I owe him one after he teased me with the whole zipper thing. "That's a shame, Baz. I can only imagine what sort of trouble the three of us could get into together in here."

"Um." Baz swallows hard, his heart beating a little harder against my chest. "What did you just say?"

"No idea. I guess I forgot to save the file." I break contact and push open the closet door, flooding the space with light. "Now, take me to your cave before the tea gets cold."

FIFTEEN

STEVIE

By the time we reach the cave entrance, our nondescript black fleeces have transformed into the hooded cloaks I remember, only mine is now decorated with white cheddar fingerprints on account of the bag of popcorn I inhaled. Probably should've been more careful with that, but it's too late for wet-wipes now.

We follow the soft glow of torchlight down the path that leads into the cave. Doc and Kirin are already waiting inside, and seconds later, Ani jogs in after us, nearly breathless.

Baz cracks up, pulling Ani in for a side hug and ruffling his hair. "Next time, you're coming with us, Gingersnap."

"What've you got there?" Doc asks, nodding at my backpack.

"Just a few snacks," I say. "I wasn't sure what the protocol was, but in the absence of a sign-up sheet, I brought a little of everything."

"Snacks." He shakes his head as if he's about to scold me, but Doc can't hide the smile quirking his lips.

"And tea." I set the backpack on the ground. "Can't have a meeting without food, Doc. Even if it *is* a secret society meeting in some sketchy-ass desert hideaway."

"No, *especially* not then." Doc winks at me, his dark eyes glittering in the torchlight.

I return his smile, glad we're all reunited again.

But the tension between us lingers, awkward and uncomfortable. I feel like they're all holding their breath, waiting for me to unleash hell.

Especially Kirin.

It's the first time I've seen him since I kicked everyone out of my suite the other night, and now he stands a little off to the side, glancing at me with a small, uncertain smile.

"I'm glad you made it," he says as I approach. "Hopefully, the trek wasn't too—"

I cut him off with a fierce hug, refusing to let go until I feel his arms slide around me, his lips pressing a sweet, protective kiss to the top of my head.

There's so much I want to ask him—about his sister Casey, about how he's feeling—but now is not the time. We've got other business to attend to—serious business, or we'd be chatting about it over beers at Hot Shots instead of in our secret cave.

"Shall we begin, then?" Doc asks.

"Snacks first," I say, kneeling down to unpack the paper plates and goodies from my bag. "No seriousness on empty stomachs."

"Stevie." Doc pinches the bridge of his nose and sighs. "I appreciate your enthusiasm, but we really should get—wait. Is that brie?"

Grinning, I pass him a small plate loaded up with goodies. I make one for each of us, and we spend just a few more minutes eating, sipping tea, and pretending that this is a normal gathering of friends and not a strategy session on how to stop the end of the world.

But pretending only gets us so far, and it's not long before the reality of the situation settles in around us—a heaviness that not even the brie can lighten.

We gather around the altar of petrified wood at the center of the chamber, and Doc takes a moment to show me the carved pentacle on top. It's the first time I've seen it up close like this, and I run my finger over the design, feeling the magick hum beneath my touch.

I nod to show them I'm ready, and then we begin, slicing our palms with the ritual athames and letting our blood drip into the grooves of the pentacle. It glows a bright red, then fades.

"Who gathers here as bonded brothers?" Doc asks, beginning the now-familiar invocation.

The rest of us respond: "We, the Keepers of the Grave."

"Who spills his blood as a symbol of our commitment to one another and in the service and protection of the First?"

"We, the Keepers of the Grave."

"Who vows, by his life or his death, by his silence or his words, in this and all incarnations henceforth, to protect the one true source?"

"We, the Keepers of the Grave."

"We, the Keepers of the Grave," Doc finishes. Then he presses his palm against a rock in the wall, illuminating the alcove that holds the Book of Reckoning.

Using the athames again, we each sign our names in blood. Then Doc places the King of Swords card on top, and we recite the next spell.

> *Let our thoughts be true, our messages clear*
> *Both words and intent are recorded here*
> *Leave nothing unwritten, no secrets to bear*
> *Among brothers in blood, all things are shared.*

The echo of our words fades, and in the dark space behind Doc, four shadows peel away from the cave wall and waver into view.

I gasp. "The Tarot Princesses are here."

"Really?" Doc turns to look, but of course he can't see them. "All four of them? What are they doing?"

"Right now, it looks like they're just observing," I say as they circle us. "Keeping watch."

"No, not keeping watch," Baz says. "They're protecting you, Stevie."

"Thank you," I tell them, and all four nod.

"Your connection to them must be strong as hell," Baz says, not realizing that two of them have come to stand on either side of him.

"One of the many magickal mysteries of Stevie Milan." I smile, but it quickly turns into a laugh.

"What's so funny?" he asks.

"Oh, my girls are *pissed* at you guys." I'm still laughing, taking great pleasure in the fact that the two Princesses are glaring at him like a cheating lover caught red-handed.

"I see." Baz's usual cocky smirk falters, and he swallows hard. "Which ones are here, did you say?"

"Near you? Just swords and wands. But don't worry, I'm sure they won't stab you or set you on fire tonight. Not unless you guys piss me off again."

Both princesses turn to look at me. Their faces are as stern as ever, but I see the laughter in their eyes.

Fucking girl power. Is there anything better?

Well, maybe for my mages, who are currently staring guiltily at their shoes.

I let them suffer a moment longer, then gesture for my Princesses to back off.

"Okay, boys, here's the deal," I say, more than ready to put this whole issue to bed. "What you guys did—keeping things from me—it was super fucked up and totally unacceptable."

"Stevie," Ani says, close to tears, "I'm so sorry."

"I'm sorry too," Kirin says.

"More than you know," Baz says, the emotion in his words surprising me most of all.

"I have no more words to apologize," Doc says. "I can only hope you'll—"

"I said it was fucked up and unacceptable," I say. "But it wasn't unforgivable. I appreciate that you guys backed off this weekend. It gave me time to process, to work through it

—not just your shit, but a good bit of my own. I know you were trying to protect me. I know you thought keeping me in the dark was the best way to do that. And I also know you're never going to pull that shit again. Am I right?"

"Of course we won't," Kirin says, and the others nod.

"But we're past it now. *I'm* past it." I smile at each of them, letting them know just how much I mean this. "I willingly joined this Brotherhood—willingly bonded myself to all of you—and it wasn't just to schlep out here in the middle of the night and watch you brooding like a bunch of emos at a Fall Out Boy show, as fun as that sounds."

"I… don't even know what that means," Doc says.

"It means I know you feel bad about how everything went down, and yeah—we've still got some kinks to work out in this whole… arrangement. But the five of us—the Brotherhood—we really don't have the luxury of time and space apart. The Dark Magician and his allies aren't going to wait around for us to get our shit together. We need a plan, we need to stick together, and we need to keep moving forward. So whatever lingering guilt you feel? Stash it. Or I'll let my Princesses have their way with you."

The tension finally eases, and one by one, my mages smile. We linger in that moment a little longer, and I sense their energies swirl around me—protectiveness, friendship, and the fiercest loyalty I've ever felt.

"Okay," I say. "I think we're ready now."

Doc nods. "Stevie, I'd like you to tell them about your dream."

I do as he asks, leaving no detail out. At the end, I blow

out a breath and say, "And there's more. Apparently, my mother could pull things from her dreams, too."

"Really?" Doc asks. "How did you learn this?"

"I spent some time with Professor Maddox tonight. Turns out she was my mom's best friend." I tell them about Mom's message, along with the information Kelly shared about the dream thing.

"I'm still trying to figure out the message, but the dream thing... I made a dream potion in class today—something I'm hoping will help me connect with the Dark Arcana in my dreams. If I can communicate directly with them, I might be able to—"

"Get yourself killed," Baz says. "Not happening."

"We need to find the Arcana objects, Baz. If the Magician has any idea where they are, maybe I can find out."

"It's way too dangerous. You just finished telling us you got hurt in the dream."

"I got hurt in the library, too. And this forest," I remind him. Rage flashes in his eyes, but I continue on. "There are *no* safe spaces anymore, guys. Not until we find the objects and defeat the Dark Arcana."

Baz opens his mouth to argue, but he knows I'm right.

"Look," I say, "I don't have a death wish. I'd have to take precautions—have someone there with me to pull me out if things are looking crazy. And I'm not saying I have to do this tonight. But I don't think we can rule it out. Right now, it feels like our best option."

"I'm open to the idea, Stevie," Kirin says. "But Baz is right—it's extremely dangerous. I think we should spend a little more time with the prophecies and legends first. Then, if we still don't have any luck, we can try the dream potion."

"That plan would buy us a little more time to figure out the precautions," Ani says. "Just having someone there with you isn't enough."

"I'm not sure what else to do," I admit.

"One of us needs to come with you," he says, and my eyes widen. "Think about it, Stevie. You said Professor Maddox believes your mother is sending you those Tarot cards from the dream realm, right? And she's also bringing them back in."

"Yeah, but I don't understand how that relates to our current dilemma."

"You brought out that holly branch," Ani says. "So maybe, like your mother, you can bring *in* something too."

"Or someone," Kirin says, his eyes lighting up with academic curiosity. "One of us."

"Exactly," Ani says.

"It's a reasonable assumption," Kirin says. "One we can test on safer ground first—a potion to encourage more pleasant, less threatening dreams."

"Puppies and unicorns?" I tease.

Kirin grins. "And rainbows. Don't forget the rainbows."

I consider their suggestions. As eager as I am to jump in and confront the Dark Arcana, the guys are right. We need to do this the smart way. The safe way.

"Okay, I'm with you," I say. "We'll do some experiments. Who wants to volunteer as my first bed mate?"

Everyone raises a hand but Doc, whose eyes are blazing so hot, he's nearly competing with the torches.

I crack up. "Okay, we'll figure that part out later."

Doc clears his throat. "In the meantime, I suggest we come up with a plan to search for the objects on campus. They could literally be anywhere."

"Including," Kirin says, "magickally hidden in or around any of the portals or other heavily warded places. It's not going to be easy."

"Have you guys ever looked for the objects before?" I ask. "Is there anything we can rule out?"

Kirin shakes his head. "Until very recently, we were still mostly convinced they were legends. Our focus has always been on the dark book—well, books. But now…" He trails off, and shame makes my insides burn.

"But now the books are gone," I finish. "Thanks to me."

I close my eyes, picturing the books in Phaines's blood-covered hands—my mother's grimoire and the Journey to the Void of Mist and Spirit. Together, they hold the key to finding the objects—if our hypothesis is correct.

And now they're gone.

"I shouldn't have trusted him," I whisper. "It's my fault—"

"Stevie." Kirin stands before me, his hands on my shoulders. "No. I was going to say—but now we have to accept the fact that we were wrong. *I* was wrong. Not just about the legends, but about… about a lot of things."

His pale green eyes glow in the torchlight, and he holds my gaze for several long moments.

He's not just talking about the objects or the dark legends.

He's talking about me. About *us*.

I close my eyes, remembering him in the library that night, not long after Danika Lewis was executed on live television. Remembering his confession.

I just kept thinking over and over… What if something happened to me or to someone I cared about, and I never even told them how I feel? I'm falling in love with you, Stevie. And I can't let myself do that…

A flicker of hope unfurls in my chest, but I tamp it down. I can't afford to fall into that trap again.

Baz and I? We had a fight on All Hallows' Eve—a bad one, one that we still need to talk about—but in the end, it was just a fight. Kirin? That wasn't a fight. Kirin flat out broke my heart. I'm not saying it can never be mended, but it's not going to happen with a few simple words and longing gazes, no matter how tempting and sincere he is.

No matter how deeply I still care for him.

I give him a soft smile, then step back, turning my attention back to the others.

"Setting aside the problem of the missing books," I say, "what do we do about the Janelle Kirkpatrick factor? She's definitely going to be a problem."

"We stay the fuck away from her," Baz says, his energy turning hot and angry. "And we hope she gets bored of whatever little game she's playing and moves on."

"You think she will?" I ask. "She came here for a reason. And I doubt it's because she's always dreamed of becoming a librarian, or even because she's worried about Carly."

I tell the guys about my chat with Carly before class this morning.

Baz's eyes blaze, and in the mix of his raging energy, I sense a bolt of shame. I try to focus in on it, certain I'm misinterpreting, but it's there, clear as day.

He's ashamed about something.

I glance up and meet his eyes, but he looks away immediately.

"I have to admit," Doc says, "I wasn't expecting Anna to hire a replacement so quickly. Or to call in reinforcements from APOA without looping me in. She's just made our work twice as hard."

"She knows we're looking for the objects?" I ask.

"Not specifically, but your work on the prophecies... She had to know a new librarian would put a crimp in that endeavor. Kirkpatrick is going to want to be involved, just like Phaines was."

"Not if she doesn't know about it," Kirin says.

"So we need a cover," I say. "Shouldn't be hard—I'm a student, you're the researcher helping me with some special project."

"I need to try to limit her access to the archives," Kirin says. "For as long as I can."

"Word of advice?" Baz steps forward again, his arms folded tightly across his chest. "Don't trust that woman. Don't let her get anywhere *near* this thing."

"Maybe we should take a break from the prophecy

work, then," I suggest. "Focus on the search, the Arcana legends, and the dream stuff."

"We need to keep working on the prophecies," Kirin says. "It's all tied together. And we made a lot of progress already."

"But Phaines took the books."

"Yes, but he didn't take the rest of your mother's notes and sketches, or my databases. A lot of the original work is still intact and in our possession. We can try to piece it back together."

"Your mother was quite prolific, Stevie," Doc says. "And you're extremely adept at translating her work. There are still so many prophecies to examine. If your connection to those is as strong as your connection to her book of shadows, then we're still sitting on a treasure trove of information. Information that could help us understand and unravel the Dark Magician's plans."

"You're right." I blow out a breath and nod. "Okay. For now, I think it makes the most sense for Kirin and I to continue working on the prophecies and any other literature we can find about the dark legends and the sacred objects."

"I'd also like Kirin to start working with you on your air magick," Doc says.

"Really?" I ask.

He nods. "You're spirit-blessed, Stevie. Gifted in all four elements. Unfortunately, if we wait for you to complete your official Academy education, we might be too late. We need to use every tool at our disposal to help you learn your magick—the sooner the better."

"Are you cool with that, Kirin?" I ask, keeping my voice neutral. I knew we'd have to spend a lot of time together working on the prophecies, but private magick lessons?

I'm not sure either of us is ready for that much alone time.

"Of course," he says, equally neutral. "I agree with Cass. We need to get you up to speed—and fast. It's too dangerous for you to be without your magick, even here. Even with us watching your back."

"And front," Baz chimes in.

"The point," Kirin says, shooting a nasty glare at Baz, "is that we can't be with you twenty-four seven. I think we'd all feel better if you had at least a few basic magickal skills at your command."

"Fighting skills?" I ask.

"Fighting, maneuvering, out-thinking," Kirin says. "Defensive as well as offensive."

I nod, accepting the challenge.

"In terms of the search," Ani says, "we need to pull out all the maps, grid out the entire campus, and start with the most logical places—places where the energy is more concentrated or the wards are stronger and more complicated. Anything like that would suggest something is being protected."

"Can you take point on that?" Doc asks.

Ani beams. "Happy to."

"I'll do my best to keep Janelle off our trail," Baz says.

"But I have to warn you—she's highly intelligent, relentless, manipulative, and downright ruthless. Whatever her agenda, I promise you—it isn't good."

"I don't get it," I say. "If she has ill intentions, how did she get on campus? Wouldn't the portal magick stop her?"

"Not if she believes she's doing the right thing," Kirin says. "The portal will stop anyone with malicious intentions, but if Kirkpatrick believes that her own cause is noble, the portal may not sense her as a threat. In terms of portal magick, self-serving is not the same as dangerous."

"That means the portal magick is only good for keeping out the most obvious offenders," I say, "and almost everyone else is a potential enemy."

The Princesses, still lingering in the background, nod in unison.

A warning.

It's a few silent moments before anyone speaks again.

"Students and faculty pose another problem," Doc finally says. "Rumors are already flying about Phaines's motives, and the valuable items he may have already stolen —Anna should've at least kept that bit to herself. It won't be long before rumors about the legends and the objects begin to surface. You can bet on that. Secrets have a way of revealing themselves here."

"You're telling me," I say.

"Stevie," Doc says tentatively, "I know how you feel about the use of mental magick, but I don't see a way around this. We can't afford to let any students or other faculty members get too curious about our mission. That curiosity will be as dangerous for them as it is for us."

"What are you suggesting?" I ask.

"I'll do my best to dissuade interest the old-fashioned way, but if it comes down to it, I won't hesitate to use influence magick to get the job done."

My gut clenches. I really don't like the idea of Doc manipulating fellow students like that.

But deep down, I know he's right. If any of them get too close to this, they'll be in danger, and our mission will be compromised before it even gets off the ground.

"For the record," I say, "I don't like it. But I understand."

Goddess, this is all so complicated. Every time I think I've got my own clear lines drawn in the sand, something happens to blur them all over again.

"So what are our next steps?" Ani asks.

"For now, Kirin and Stevie are on prophecy, research, and air magick duty," Doc says. "Baz will deal with Janelle Kirkpatrick. Ani, you've got maps and initial search coordination. And I'll gently nudge our fellow witches and mages off the scent if anyone starts showing interest in the objects or our extracurricular activities."

"It's a plan," I say, and the others nod.

Hope flickers inside me. Our end goal may be a crazy long shot, but even a crazy long shot feels achievable with a plan in place.

"In the meantime," Doc continues, "we must keep up appearances as if none of this is happening. That means I continue to teach my classes, Kirin continues his work in the library, and the rest of you continue to attend your classes as well."

Baz groans, but ultimately agrees.

Clear on our mission, we put the Book and athames away and close out the ceremony.

As Baz does a final sweep to make sure no magickal items were left out, I kneel down to pack up the tea and goodies in my backpack, still processing everything we talked about.

"Guys?" I ask suddenly, my hand gripping the container of brie. "What happens if we actually manage to find one of these things? What do the Arcana objects do, exactly?"

"We have no idea, really," Kirin says. "My guess is they'll amplify our individual powers—whichever elements correspond with the objects."

"Or they might just kill us on contact." Doc grins and points at the container in my hand, and the Princesses vanish behind him. "Are you going to finish that brie?"

SIXTEEN

STEVIE

Baz and I are silent for most of the trek back to Iron and Bone, both lost in our own swirling thoughts. The meeting was intense, and even with all our careful planning, it's no secret we're facing pretty insane odds.

But when Baz's hand brushes against mine in the darkness, concern about the mission isn't what I feel sweeping through his energy.

It's me. Concern about me.

I reach for his hand, lacing our fingers together and giving him a firm squeeze. He relaxes instantly.

I take a breath to speak, but I don't know where to start. Without a wall of jokes between us, I feel totally exposed.

It's been five days since I fell into his arms, into his bed. His wild touch still lingers on my skin, and every time I replay those moments, my whole body ignites.

Yet now, when I try to form even a single question, my words stall out.

Still silent, still holding hands, we walk all the way upstairs to my suite before he finally finds his voice.

"You gonna be okay?" he asks.

Reluctantly, I release his hand and open the door, then turn back around to face him. It's the first I've allowed myself to look at him full on since the meeting, and his eyes are more fiery than ever now, blazing with a million unsaid words, a million burning secrets.

This time, I know they're not about me. Not the kind he owes me, anyway.

"I'm fine, Baz," I say, exhaustion weighing my words. "Just tired."

"Okay. I guess I'll just… Right. See you tomorrow, then?"

This is ridiculous. It's about two hundred degrees Fahrenheit between us, and we're both just standing here like idiots who forgot how to talk.

No, I don't need Baz to lay his soul bare on my doorstep. But I do need him to answer one question.

"Where do you stand with me, Baz?"

A nervous laugh escapes his lips, and he shoves his hands into his pockets, hunching his shoulders. "Is this a trap? It feels like a trap."

"No trap," I assure him, thinking about what Kelly said about communication—how we often give up when we can't figure out what the hell the other person is talking about. I don't want to give up. And waiting around for the other person to figure things out first feels like a form of giving up. "I'm just tired of wasting time trying to figure out the right words to say, so I'm practicing a new strategy."

"Yeah? What's that?"

"Saying whatever the fuck comes to mind, then working out the translations later."

"I see." Baz smiles. "So, where do I stand? That's what you want to know?"

"Are we friends?" I ask.

"That's two questions now, Little Bird. Slow down."

"It's a serious question, though. Are we?"

He cocks his head, his brow furrowing. "Stevie, come on. I've wanted to be your friend since the first day we met and you called me out for acting like a jackass."

"But now I know you weren't acting." I laugh, but it quickly turns into a sigh, and then a whisper. "Baz, I don't... I don't want to be friends with you."

"But I thought—"

"I want to be... something else."

A slow grin slides across his face. "What else, exactly?"

"I don't know. It doesn't even need a label. It just needs to be more than friends. If you're cool with that."

"I'm more than cool with that." He takes a step forward, but I put a hand on his chest and stop him in his tracks.

"But..."

"Ah. The but," he says. "Always the but."

"No labels, no expectations. I'm good with that—seriously. But the stuff with Carly, the constant drama and jealousy and pettiness... I can't deal with that. I know I've contributed to the dynamic, and for that I'm sorry. I wanted to give Carly a chance—still do. I'm trying. But I also want to give my friendship with you a chance, and—"

"You mean our non-friendship."

"Non-friendship. Yes." I shake my head, wishing I *did* have all the right words for this. But I don't, so onward I plow, fumbling my way through it. "I just don't feel like I can do it if she's constantly trying to interfere and pit us against each other."

"I've told you before, Carly and I aren't and never have been an item."

"But now her mother's here and—"

"Janelle won't bother you," he says, anger edging into his voice. "I promise."

"Maybe she won't. But it's not like I can totally avoid her. She's the librarian now. We're bound to cross paths."

His eyes darken, right along with his energy. It's like a storm cloud has just moved in over us.

"What is it?" I ask.

He shakes his head, closing his eyes as if he's trying to forget I even asked.

I wait for him to explain, but he doesn't, and by the time he opens his eyes again, he's totally guarded. Cold.

"I should probably just go," he finally says. "Good night, Stevie."

"That's it? You have nothing else to say?"

"I don't know what you want me to say. I keep trying to tell you there's nothing going on with Carly, but you don't want to hear it. You've got trust issues."

"Hell yeah, I've got trust issues." I glare at him, forcing

myself to keep the hurt out of my voice. "Listen, I've told you about my parents. They were *everything* to me. When I lost them, I didn't think I could survive it. Somehow, I *did* survive, but not fully. It left me guarded and afraid of getting too close to anyone other than my best friend Jessa."

"What are you saying?"

"I'm saying I can meet you partway there, Baz, but I need you to come the rest of the way." I reach up to touch his face, my thumb tracing his lips. "The other night, after we were together? You asked me if I could just trust you. All of you guys have asked me that at one point or another. And I'm trying, Baz. I really am. But the thing is, I need you to trust me, too."

"I know." Baz sighs, warm breath ghosting over my thumb. "Fuck, Stevie. I know. I'm sorry."

"Sometimes when I look at you," I say, my voice no more than a whisper now, "I feel like… like there's all this stuff inside you. Like you have so much to say to me, but you're too afraid to say it. You just keep trying to outrun it instead."

I give him a chance to confirm or deny it, but he does neither. Just looks at me, the emotion in those red-brown eyes threatening to drown me.

"It doesn't work that way," I try again. "Believe me. Run as fast and far as you want—it's *always* going to catch up with you."

Still, he says nothing.

And finally, I run out of words, too. The right ones, the wrong ones—they're all gone now.

I give him a sad smile, then lower my hand from his face, already missing the feel of his skin.

"Goodnight, Stevie," he whispers.

"Goodnight, Baz." I blow out a breath and step inside, closing the door before I even finish saying his name.

* * *

It's been a crazy long day, followed by an impossibly long night. All I want to do is unwind, change into my PJs, and pass out. Tomorrow's a new day, right? Reset button for the win.

One hour, one bubble bath, and one cup of cinnamon cardamom tea after I shut the door in Baz's face, I'm just about to turn in when my doorbell chimes.

The Devil card flickers behind my eyes, and even before I check the video monitor, I know it's the devil himself— Baz. No doubt back for another argument about trust—it's getting to be a sport with him now.

I yank open the door to find him standing in the hall-way, sexy and full of fire, his energy an overwhelming wave of desire mixed with fear mixed with raw, unchecked vulnerability.

He's hurting. Badly.

I press my hand to my heart. "Baz? What's—"

"You're right." He shoves a hand through his hair and meets my gaze, his own blazing with brand new fire. "I *do* have something to say, Little Bird. And it's about fucking time I said it."

SEVENTEEN

CASS

I'm deep into a bottle of whiskey, completely untethered from all sense of time, when my door chime breaks through the buzz.

I drag myself off the couch, set my drink on the fireplace mantle, and check the video monitor, shocked at the late-night visitor.

"I apologize for the hour," Anna says when I open the door. "I tried to call, but you weren't answering."

"Has something happened?" I ask, adrenaline clearing away the last of the alcohol haze. I can count on one hand the number of times the headmistress has portaled out to my house in the middle of the desert—and none of those were social calls.

She looks up at me, her face haunted, and I brace myself for bad news.

"Another student was attacked tonight," she says. "A second-year mage. He's unharmed, for the most part. He was grabbed on his walk home from a water magicks class by the river. He didn't sustain any injuries, but the perpetrator cut a lock of his hair."

"Hell." I stand aside and invite her in, my mind already working through the possibilities—none of them good. Dark witches and mages have been using personal things like hair, fingernail clippings, and blood for millennia—typically in cursework and other forms of attack magick.

What's even more frightening is that someone took the risk of assaulting a student on campus so soon after Phaines's attack, when the entire campus is on high alert and the APOA agents have set up camp.

"So we're dealing with a magick user," I say, leading her to the living room. We each take a chair near the fireplace, the flames popping and hissing. "A student or faculty member?"

"Anything is possible."

"Well, if it's not someone already on campus, then it's someone who was able to trick the portal magick into letting them through."

It's just like we were talking about tonight at the Brotherhood meeting. Someone who's convinced themselves that their mission is pure.

Anna nods, her mouth drawn tight.

"I assume you've looped in the APOA agents?" I ask, unable to keep the annoyance from my tone. Anna should've looped *me* in the moment she decided to bring them on campus, but she didn't. And here we are.

"Casey Appleton interviewed the student, and she and

James Quintana are combing the area for evidence. In the meantime, I've asked William Eastman to review all of our existing security protocols and technology campus-wide, magick as well as mundane. Flaws in the portal magick's design notwithstanding, he's already expressed concerns that the portals themselves and the in-room security systems could be vulnerable to magickal attack."

"Or a good old-fashioned hacking," I say. "Kirin's been worried about that all along."

"The magick itself is highly stable."

"Yes, but it's not all magick. Some of our equipment is based on regular old computer and internet technology, replete with the same issues and vulnerabilities that exist in the mundane world. The difference is we're not talking about credit card scams or identity theft here. We're talking about a magickal threat that could wipe out the entire campus. The entire magickal population."

"I'm well aware of the stakes, Cassius."

"Then you'll agree when I say we need more outside surveillance. In-room and doorway cameras aren't enough. The campus is vast, and a good portion of it lies in complete darkness at night."

"Students need to restrict their outings at night—that's a safer bet," she says. "Perhaps we need to reschedule the night classes. Consider implementing a curfew."

"This isn't a war zone, Anna. Restricting freedoms is not the way to ensure safety. We need better equipment. Most of it's outdated anyway—long overdue for some upgrades."

"I'll need to request funding for something of that nature. The board needs to approve it and find room in the budget."

"How long will that take?"

Anna lowers her eyes. "Minimum, two weeks. And that's if I trade in a few favors and push hard for emergency funding."

I rise from my chair, anger making it impossible for me to sit still. "So you were able to hire a new librarian within days of Phaines's disappearance—a woman whose qualifications are as thin as paper, mind you—yet it's going to take weeks to get the money for equipment that can keep our students safe?"

"The board overrode my decision about Janelle Kirkpatrick. She carries a lot of influence here, Cass. You know that."

"You think she can be trusted?"

"I don't think her motives are necessarily good ones," Anna admits. "But as for whether she can be trusted? That remains to be seen. We simply need to keep her close."

"This is bullshit and you know it."

"The red tape frustrates me as much as it does you, but we can't override protocol every time we need—"

"Fuck your protocols, Anna. People's lives are at stake here." I turn my back on her, leaning against the mantle. "Some of our students are minors."

Anna has no response for that, and it's a long moment before she speaks again.

"Starla Milan?" she asks, feigning nonchalance. "I trust she's safe?"

The mention of Stevie's safety sends a bolt of worry to my gut that burns worse than the alcohol. I close my eyes, willing myself to calm down before I finally turn back to Anna.

"Kirin and I, along with a few other students she's gotten close with, are doing our best to protect her. That's not the issue."

"The prophecy work must continue, Cassius. At all costs."

"Do you hear yourself? For fuck's sake, Anna, if you'd cared half this much about the prophecies twenty-odd years ago, we wouldn't be in this mess right now."

"That doesn't invalidate my present concerns. Not unless you want to have this same conversation again in another twenty years. Assuming we survive that long."

I turn my back on her again, certain that if I don't, I'll say something I'll regret—something that goes beyond a few crass words.

Dispensing entirely with the pretense of sobriety, I grab my unfinished drink from the mantle and down another swig.

"Cassius," she says, her tone shifting to one of condescending concern. "Starla isn't Elizabeth. Tormenting your-self won't—"

"Don't." I grip my glass so tight, my knuckles turn white. "Don't say another word about it."

"But Elizabeth was—"

"I said *don't*."

"I just meant that—"

In a blur, I whip my glass into the fireplace, shattering it. Anna doesn't flinch. Tough old bitch.

"Are you finished?" she asks calmly, and I nod. We've been here before, Anna and I. I'm sure we'll be here again.

"You've got a spine of steel, Anna," I say, reclaiming my chair. "I've always admired that about you. I just wish you'd remember that steel in front of the fucking board."

She straightens her back and clears her throat, but doesn't bother addressing my comment.

"The senior magickal staff and I will continue to do our best with protection spells throughout campus," she says, "but I agree with you—we do need more funding for equipment. As powerful as our senior members are, there simply aren't enough of us to maintain total protection. We need that energy focused on the portals. Safeguarding against outsiders is the most important thing."

"Phaines wasn't an outsider."

"And I'll live with that knowledge for the rest of my life." Anna sighs, finally showing a chink in her armor. "I'm doing what I can, Cassius. I care about the students. I care about the faculty. I care about every single witch and mage on this campus. But like I said, my hands are tied."

I steeple my hands in my lap. "Is this the same speech you gave the Milans when you drove them out?"

Ignoring the mention of Stevie's parents, Anna rises from her chair and heads for the door.

But the conversation isn't the only thing that's over.

Something has broken between us, some irreparable rift destroying any professional respect I once had for her. Anna senses it, too. I see it in the bend of her neck, the invisible weight pressing down on her shoulders.

And this time, I know it's not an act.

Just before she leaves, she turns to me with watery eyes and says, "I want what's best for the students here. That is *always* my priority. You have to believe that."

"No, Anna. I don't." I shake my head, barely keeping my disgust in check.

Believe her? I'm not even sure I can count her among the good guys anymore.

"Cassius, I—"

"Have a good night, Anna. Oh, and be safe out there. You never know what's lurking in the non-protected shadows."

EIGHTEEN

STEVIE

The look in his eyes is feral, the air crackling like lightning between us, and I know—somehow—that if I let him in tonight, if I let him say what he came here to say, everything between us will change.

For the better or for the worse, I have no idea.

"Please, Stevie," he says, pain lancing his voice. "Let me in."

The words hang between us in the air, so much more than a simple request to get into my suite.

I step aside.

Baz crosses the threshold. Shuts the door behind him.

And then he lets loose.

"I'm sorry. I'm so fucking sorry for All Hallows' Eve. It was the middle of the fucking night, and like a total asshole, I let you walk." He paces my kitchen, pulling his hands through his hair. "It's my fault you left and went to the library. You were supposed to spend the night, but then we fought over fucking *Carly*, of all things. I should've just told her to fuck off, but I didn't, and you were hurt and pissed and you just... You left."

The reminder of Carly's interruption of an otherwise blissful night stings, but I douse it. "It was my choice to leave."

"I should've followed you, though," he says, still pacing like a caged animal.

"Baz—"

"Or just... just made you stay with me so we could talk things out. I didn't—"

"Baz!" I step in front of him and put my hands on his chest, stopping his frantic pacing. His heart is slamming against his rib cage, his skin hot to the touch. "Look at me. Please."

He finally glances down, his eyes wild, rimmed in red.

"You should know by now that you can't make me do anything I don't want to do," I say. "That plan would've blown up in your face."

"But I didn't even try." He places a hand over mine, his shameful, guilty energy rushing through me. "I let you down, Stevie. I swore to protect you, even before we knew you were one of us, and I let you down."

I open my mouth to deny it, but I don't want to lie.

He *did* let me down.

"Yeah, you're right," I say, and Baz lowers his hand, taking a step back and folding his arms across his chest. I move forward, closing the space between us again. "But it's not because we argued that night, or because you couldn't stop that psychopath from attacking me."

He shakes his head.

"No?" I ask. "Oh, really? Now you're going to tell me how I feel? I don't think so." I wrap my hands around his forearms, waiting for him to meet my eyes again. "Look, jerkface. If you're going to sacrifice yourself on an altar of guilt, it should at least be for the right reasons."

He finally looks at me again, and I soften beneath his pained gaze.

"Baz," I say gently, "you let me down because you didn't trust me enough to tell me the truth. Maybe you had your reasons, but it still hurt."

"I'm sorry," he whispers, his eyes glazing with emotion. "I *hate* that I hurt you. That hurt is what drove you out of my arms that night. Out of my bed. And straight to—"

"Stop. You can't blame yourself for this. Our personal issues aside, the only person at fault for my attack is Phaines. Don't you get that?"

He turns his back on me and leans against the kitchen counter, his back and shoulder muscles bunching beneath his shirt. It's all I can do not to go to him, to run my hand down his back, to press a kiss to the back of his neck and whisper in his ear that everything will be okay.

"Baz?"

"This was a mistake. I shouldn't have—"

"Oh, no. Don't shut me out now. You're here, you started this, and you'd damned well better finish, or I swear I'll come up with a spell to turn you into a jellyfish."

"A jellyfish?"

"Call it poetic justice."

There's a faint laugh, but then it's gone.

"You don't get it, Stevie. Finding you out there that night… All that blood…" His energy spikes, a tsunami of red-hot anger washing away the sadness. "I can't stop thinking about it. I should've been there, and I wasn't, and seeing you tied up and bleeding… Fuck. I thought he… I thought you were dead. I can't get that image out of my mind. And if *I* can't scrub it… Shit. I can't even imagine what you're feeling right now."

"I won't lie to you," I say. "It sucks. I'm still looking over my shoulder, half-expecting that psycho to jump out and grab me again. But Baz…" I finally give in to my instincts and run a hand down his back.

He leans into my touch, letting out a soft sigh.

"I *will* be okay," I say. "And that's only because you guys found me in time. All we can do now is move forward with our plan and try to keep each other safe."

He finally turns to face me again, grabbing my hands and pressing them against his chest. His heart is still jack-hammering inside, his skin still hot. "Everything you said about running, about being afraid… I *am* afraid. Terrified. Constantly. And I've been running from it a lot longer than I've known you."

"I'm sorry." I slide my arms around him, resting my cheek against his chest, listening to the frenzied beat of his heart.

"You asked me where I stand with you," he says. "With us."

I pull back to look into his eyes, and he cups my face, his thumbs brushing softly against my ears.

"I want to be with you, Little Bird," he says. "I don't care what you call it or don't call it. I don't care who knows or doesn't know. No boundaries, a million boundaries, whatever you want. All I know is that for me, there's only you. I—"

I press my finger to his lips, then stretch up on my tiptoes and steal the kiss I've been dreaming about since I saw him in the common room this morning. In my mind's eye, I see a flash of the meadow—our meadow, our crowns of flowers and thorns, our heat.

Baz moans softly, cupping the back of my head and drawing me closer as he deepens the kiss.

Goddess, I missed the taste of him, the feel of his hands in my hair, the fire his every touch ignites inside me.

Warm, strong hands trail down my back, and I melt into his embrace, only breaking the kiss to listen to his heart again.

"I can't lose you," he whispers into my hair.

"You won't. I'm here. Right here." I stretch up on my toes for another kiss, but Baz pulls back, shaking his head.

"We can't, Stevie," he says softly. "Not until… Not until I say what I came here to say." Regret and sadness invade his energy, the last of his fiery passion fading into nothingness. "You need to know the truth about me and Carly."

NINETEEN

BAZ

I watch the heat fade from her blue eyes, and for a second I think I've just made the biggest fucking mistake of my life.

But then she nods and says, "I'll make tea," and the soft smile that follows is enough to chase away most of my fears.

"Make it strong," I say. "I need it."

This gets another cute little smirk, and the spark finally returns to her eyes. "I know. I can tell."

Of course she can.

"You go relax," she tells me, shooing me into the living room. "I'll handle this."

While Stevie mixes up one of her magickal brews, I pace the living room, trying to figure out the best way to tell this fucked-up tale. I'm nowhere near ready by the time she appears, two steaming mugs in hand, but there's never going to be a good time for this.

I take one of the mugs and join her on the couch, me on

one end, Stevie curling up at the other. There are only a few feet separating us, but it might as well be miles. It's all I can do not to pull her into my arms, to kiss her until she's breathless again.

But as Stevie looks at me in the dim light, her eyes full of kindness and compassion, I know I can't back out now.

I take a sip of the tea, a sweet and spicy mix that perks me up and gives me just a little more strength to see this through.

"The situation with Carly... it's super complicated and fucked up. Completely dysfunctional. Fairly codependent. Borderline toxic. There are reasons for all that, but before I go there, I need you to know one thing—to believe it, even if it's the only part of this whole story you *do* believe."

Stevie nods. Then, clearly sensing my nervousness, she smiles her sweet smile and says, "I'm here, Baz. I'm not going anywhere."

"Carly and I... This thing between us... It's not sexual or romantic in *any* way. Not even close. I have never lied to you about that, Stevie."

Stevie brings her mug to her lips, blowing a breath across her tea. Steam dances before her eyes, obscuring them for just a moment.

"Okay," she finally says.

"Okay?"

"If you say it's not like that with her, I believe you."

"But?"

"It's just... For whatever reason, Carly *doesn't* believe that. I don't know if it's because you haven't made that clear enough to her, or if she's just super hung up on you, or what the deal is there, but as long as she thinks she has a chance with you—real or imagined—she's going to see me as the enemy. She's going to make my life hell."

"I can't even tell you how many times she and I have talked about this. She knows there's no chance with us. I've never led her to believe otherwise. I couldn't possibly be any more clear about it."

"Yet she's super possessive of you."

"Like I said, it's complicated." I take another sip of tea, then set the mug on the table, knowing that this is it. Once the words are out, I'll never be able to take them back. Stevie will know the most significant part of my history, and in the retelling of it, she'll become a part of that history.

Even if she kicks me out of here and never speaks to me again, we'll always be connected to this moment.

That's the thing about sharing secrets; it bonds us in ways that can never be broken. Not by time, not by distance, not even by hatred.

But Stevie has a right to know. She's earned that much.

"When I was ten," I say, forcing myself not to break our gaze, "I witnessed a murder."

Stevie gasps, and I watch the horror cross her face. "Baz, my Goddess. I'm so sorry."

An unexpected wave of emotion rises inside me, and I clear my throat, trying to stave it off. I can't go a day without thinking about this shit, but it's the first time I've said the words out loud to anyone, and seeing her reaction shakes something loose inside me—a rockslide that could very easily become an avalanche.

But I have to keep going.

"They were both mages. The killer… he was stronger than the other mage, and after a brief fight, he knocked the guy unconscious. He tied him to a post, carved up his body, bled him…" I close my eyes, fighting off the movie flickering behind my eyelids, a thousand frames of torture from the past superimposed onto torture from the present, the body switching between the dead mage and Stevie, tied to a tree in the Forest of Iron and Bone. "In the end, he doused the mage with gasoline and burned him alive."

I open my eyes as a tear tracks down my cheek, but I don't bother wiping it away.

"It happened in a field behind my house. I had a little tree fort out there, some crappy thing my dad built years earlier. I was just inside the tree line, maybe fifteen feet off the ground. Bird's-eye view of the slaughter. I watched the whole thing, too fucking scared to move. I kept hoping he would tire out and leave, that it would end, but the torture just went on and on. The screams… I've never heard a sound like that, not before or since. I don't know how long it took him to die, but by the time the noise stopped, the sun was rising. The killer just sat down in front of the charred body and looked up into the trees. I swear he saw me."

"Holy shit," she breathes. "Did he come after you?"

"Nope. Just smiled. Something about him… he was so unhinged. It kind of snapped me out of my trance, and I remembered I had my phone on me—this cheap little thing I had for emergencies. I called 911. They showed up in minutes—cops, FBI magickal enforcers, you name it. The guy didn't even move. They cuffed him, dragged him away. Someone got me out of the treehouse—brought me inside the house to answer a million questions. The killer—still cuffed—was sitting on the steps out front with one of the cops. I could see him out the window, still smiling that deranged smile. His eyes were black. Everything human about him was just… just gone."

Stevie inches forward on the couch, her knees brushing against my thigh. The contact steadies me, and I grab my mug, downing the rest of my tea.

"They sent him straight to Bone Hollow," I continue. "It's a maximum-security magickal prison. *The* magickal prison. Worst place any mage or witch can imagine. He's on Death Row, too—worst place of the worst place. Sometimes I wonder if the torture he suffers there is worse than the torture he inflicted on the mage."

"You feel guilty," Stevie says gently, her hand on my knee, and I don't bother denying it. "But it sounds like he got what he deserved. And that's a good thing, because my *Goddess*, Baz. What if he were walking around free? Free to kill again? Free to track you down and get revenge?"

"If he were, he'd know right where to look, and I'd probably be dead by sunrise."

Her eyes go wide. "You said he's on Death Row, though. When is he being executed?"

"That's not happening."

"What? Why not?"

"See, back then, when the world wasn't trying to wipe us off the map, they used to let magickal authorities deal with their own. This mage… His crime was horrendous. He was supposed to be executed immediately. But the bribes to keep him alive and kicking? They kept coming in, so the officials kept postponing the date. It's gone on like that for fifteen years, and will go on for fifteen more, I'm sure."

"But… bribes? What kind of person would pay to keep a killer like that alive?"

"Janelle Kirkpatrick," I blurt out.

Stevie gasps, and I shift to face her full on.

The next part is the hardest, but I need to get it out.

"The mage killer? His name is Ford Redgrave," I say. "He's my brother, Stevie."

Her eyes fill with tears. "Fuck, Baz," she whispers. "Holy fucking *fuck*."

"My parents were in Europe, off on one of their magickal treasure hunting excursions. Mr. and Mrs. Indiana Fucking Jones had already been gone a year at that point. By the time they heard about what'd happened, it was too late for them to do anything about it. They blamed me, I think. Ford, for all his fuckups, was always the favorite."

"Not favorite enough for them to stick around and take care of, though. You said they'd already been gone a year by then!"

I shrug. "Treasures *always* came first. Ford came second. I'm not even sure I made the cut."

"So did they finally come back to the states for you after that?"

"Didn't need to. I was already living with another family."

"But who… Oh. *Oh.*" She lowers her eyes and exhales, the pieces clicking into place. "The Kirkpatricks."

"Carly's a few years younger than me, but we knew each other from school and family stuff—our parents ran in the same circles. I stuck up for her a few times over the years—playground bullies, guys trying to cop a feel, that sort of middle school bullshit everyone deals with. We were friends. When she found out what happened with Ford, she insisted I come home with her. That her parents would know what to do. I went along with it, figuring they'd fix me some mac and cheese and send me on my way."

"But they adopted you instead."

"Carly's family has always been wealthy—more than mine. They had plenty to share, and I was more than happy to accept. Janelle loved telling her friends and associates the story about how she'd taken me in—how my parents were too irresponsible, how it was the compassionate thing to do. I was her little trophy boy—something she flashed around as a badge, ensuring everyone knew what a good, selfless person she was. What a bad person my own mother was." I shake my head, the old hurts rushing in again. "Our parents were all collectors. They'd always been in competition. Sometimes I think that's why my parents spent so much time overseas—they could reign supreme over there, flaunting their magickal discoveries without the constant threat of Kirkpatrick one-upmanship."

"And your parents were okay with that? Just letting someone else—a rival, at that—take care of their youngest son?"

"Turns out they didn't have a choice. I found out later it wasn't just their disdain for me that kept them out of the states. They were eyeballs deep in their own legal troubles after spending half their lives robbing everyone, from world-renowned museums to local tribes, smuggling priceless antiquities in and out of every country they'd ever set foot in. There were rumors they'd even killed people."

"They never got caught?"

"Thanks to my kindly benefactors, no." I lower my eyes, shame heating my face. I hate feeling so beholden, but the alternative isn't much better—I'd simply be trading in a lifetime of shame for a lifetime of guilt.

"No wonder you and Carly got close," Stevie says. Sadness echoes in her voice, but there's no jealousy or judgment there. No anger.

"We grew up more like siblings than anything else," I say. "For all their wealth and willingness to share, her parents were pretty fucked up, too. Carly and I stuck together out of necessity. Her house felt like a war zone half the time—Janelle's fault, mostly. Charles could be decent— he's the one that bought me my first camera, actually."

"I remember you said your dad had given you the camera for Christmas," she says softly. "You were talking about Charles."

"He was more of a father to me than my own."

"But Janelle wasn't like a mother?"

"More like a monster."

"What do you mean?"

"Let's just say she was definitely the disciplinarian of the family—a role she thrived in. There were so many times I wanted to help Carly, but defending Carly meant provoking Janelle, and I just…" I close my eyes and shake my head, feeling like I'm trapped in a horror movie, creeping down the basement stairs without a flashlight. One more step, and all the old ghosts will slither out of the darkness and destroy me.

And as much as I want to share my history with Stevie, some of those ghosts need to stay locked up for good.

"Eventually, things between me and Carly changed," I say, opening my eyes. "Suddenly she wanted more than just big-brother protection from me. She wanted things I couldn't give her. Things I *still* can't give her. She knows it, but for whatever reason, she leads her parents to believe otherwise. And if I deny it, I risk pissing off the whole family, and then—"

"They stop paying the bribes." She leans back against the couch and closes her eyes. "Wow. This is… a lot."

"Fucked up, right? I don't know how or why she does it, Stevie. All I know is if it wasn't for Janelle Kirkpatrick's dirty money, my entire family would be dead. Whether they deserve it or not, whether I ever speak to them again or not, I can't handle the idea of that happening—especially knowing I can prevent it. As long as I keep the Kirkpatricks happy, my family gets to live. It's hard and it sucks and I fucking *hate* it, but I can't seem to let it go. To let *them* go."

Stevie says nothing. There's nothing she *can* say. But just the fact that she hasn't sent me packing… It means the fucking world to me.

"So there it is, Little Bird. The shit-show you're signing up for with me." I scrub a hand over my face and groan. "I realize this makes me a complete dickhead. And I have no right to ask you to get anywhere *near* this shit. Anywhere near *me*. But I can't lie to you about this, Stevie. I *want* you near me. More than anything." I look into her eyes, trying to memorize the shape of her face, the curve of her mouth. Even the sound of her voice makes me feel things I didn't think were possible—even when she's yelling at me. Hell, especially then. "No matter what happens tonight, I'm glad I told you."

"Me too," she says, a sad smile touching her lips. "What you went through with your brother… with your family… It sucks. It's a rotten deal, and you never should've gotten stuck with it. But…"

I nod and wait for her to continue, but she's gone silent again, rising from the couch and heading over to the windows that look out across the Forest of Iron and Bone. I watch her standing there, my eyes composing the shot, my memory photographing every detail—the way the moonlight plays off her skin, the shape of her shoulders, the squiggles of that crazy curly hair spilling down her back.

Goddess, what has this woman done to me?

I don't get off on hopping from bed to bed—it's just not

my style. But I haven't been a saint, either. I've had my share of fun between the sheets. Still, the women who came before... It wasn't like this. Stevie's gotten under my skin, right straight through to my heart. I don't know what it means or what to call it, but it's like she said earlier.

I don't want to be friends—that's not enough. Not anymore.

Unfortunately, I'm not sure the non-friendship thing is still an option for her.

"But you can't deal with the Kirkpatrick crazy," I finish up, mostly so she doesn't have to.

I don't expect her to answer, but she turns around anyway, fresh tears shining in her eyes. It's a gut-punch, but nothing less than I expected. She'd have to be insane to stick around for this shit.

"Honestly?" she says. "I don't know, Baz. Carly is pretty... intense. And whatever her true motives in helping your family, Janelle is *way* off-balance, and something tells me she's not going to just let you live your life here. I sensed those tiger claws embedded in your chest the moment I walked into the common room yesterday."

"She's controlling and possessive," I say. "Always has been."

"That's an understatement. And you and I? We're just getting to know each other. All this shit makes it a *lot* harder—and that's not even accounting for all the Arcana insanity we're dealing with."

"I get it. I really do."

"Complications scare the shit out of me."

"I know."

"The answer is *so* obvious, Baz. So clear. Logic says we should shut this whole thing down before we get in any deeper. We should keep our relationship purely Arcana-based, maybe a little friendship on the side, nothing more."

Forcing a smile I don't feel, I cock my head and say, "Yup. That would be the smart choice."

"Best decision of the year."

"You're right."

"But," she says, and I swear in this moment, I've never loved a word more. It's a maybe, that but. A loophole. Hope.

Stevie crosses back to stand in front of me and leans forward, sliding her hands over my shoulders, the tiniest smile curving her lips. "Maybe we need to hit the pause button on what's smart and just do what's right instead."

She pushes me back and climbs into my lap, crashing into my mouth with a kiss that sets my world on fire and makes me fucking believe in miracles again.

And for just a little while, the ghosts haunting my head slink back into the basement, shut the door, and turn off all the lights, disappearing into the darkness.

TWENTY

STEVIE

The first time I slept with Baz was wild and unbidden, all the built-up tension and anger and frustration and lust between us finally exploding in an epic All Hallows' Eve fireworks show.

But tonight, after everything he shared with me, spoken and unspoken, his touch turns slow and tender, both of us wandering into a strange new territory that leaves me unhinged and exposed. Terrified. But also exhilarated.

Rising from the couch, he carries me into the bedroom and gently lays me on the bed, his body hovering over mine, his gaze never leaving my eyes.

We stare at each other for an eternity.

"*Goddess*, you're beautiful," Baz says, his voice breaking into a whisper that tickles my lips.

He watches me a heartbeat longer, then lowers his mouth to mine, kissing me slow and sweet as his fingers work the buttons on my top. One by one, he releases them, unwrapping me like a gift, kissing his way down my throat as I slide my arms out of the sleeves.

His lips are warm and soft, a stark contrast to the cool air on my newly exposed skin, leaving a trail of sparks that sink into my skin and light my insides on fire.

My core is throbbing, my desire winding tighter as his fingers and mouth ghost over the raised pink lines criss-crossing my stomach, still healing from Phaines's brutal dark magick. Even without reaching for his energy, I feel the fire growing inside him too—the rage at what Phaines did to me, the heat between us, a burning desire, all of it colliding into a red-hot inferno on the edge of total combustion. Every touch, every tender kiss seems to cost him a little more, but Baz remains in control, his gentleness as surprising as it is maddening.

Dragging his mouth down my stomach, Baz tugs at my pajama bottoms and underwear, slowly peeling them off until I'm lying nude before him, my skin hot and needy, my heart pounding, everything in me desperate for more.

With the same slow, crazy-making touch, he guides my thighs apart, kissing his way from my hipbone to the inside curve of my knee, then back up again, the heat of his breath misting over my clit as he moves to the other thigh, down and back again, teasing and kissing, touching me everywhere except the place I want it most.

"You're torturing me," I breathe, arching my hips, trying to get closer, desperate to take control.

"Shh." He traces his tongue over my hip bone again,

then moves closer, closer still, his lips grazing my clit and making me gasp. "Don't fight, Little Bird."

"Non-friendship," I pant, torn between savoring the intense pleasure of his delayed gratification game and demanding release right this instant, "does not mean non-touching. I want—oh, *fuck*…"

Suddenly he grips my thighs and licks my clit, then blows a cool breath across my superheated flesh before sucking me hard between his lips. After all the teasing, the raw pleasure of his commanding mouth is almost too intense, his tongue stroking me hard and fast, then slow, bringing me closer and closer…

I slide my hands into his hair, arching my hips against his devouring mouth, and he unleashes a throaty moan that vibrates straight into my core.

Tightening his grip on my thighs, Baz plunges his tongue deep inside me.

The last of my control breaks like a dam, unleashing the full force of pleasure I'd been denied. It crashes through my body in a fierce wave that starts in my core and spreads through my belly, sweeping me over the edge until I'm tumbling and my thighs are trembling and I'm screaming his name, my own long since forgotten.

Baz kisses my thighs, my belly, retracing the path he took on the way down with more soft, slow kisses. When he reaches my jawline, I turn and capture his mouth in another kiss, desperate to breathe him in, to feel his lips moving against mine, to feel the heat of his breath in my mouth.

"Naked," I pant. "You. Now."

He does as I ask, quickly stripping off his clothes and resuming his delicious position on top of me.

His cock is hard and hot, pressing urgently against my thigh, and despite the fact that my body is still trembling with the aftershocks of my last orgasm, I want him inside me. Need him inside me.

"Condoms," I breathe, grateful Isla insisted I stock up that day we went shopping. "Nightstand drawer."

He reaches for the drawer, grabs one from the stash.

He's back on top of me again, his mouth finding mine in the darkness as he shifts between my thighs. He slides inside me, his body shuddering as I wrap my legs around him and bring him in deeper. Again I see our meadow from the Cernunnos card, sunlight glittering through moss-covered trees, grass tickling my bare skin, the faint scents of smoke and fire floating on the warm air.

Without breaking our kiss, Baz flips us so I'm on top. I straddle his hips, his rock-hard cock thickening inside me as his hands roam across my backside.

I pull back and gaze into his eyes, and he stops for just a moment, reaching up to sweep the hair from my face. The look in his eyes is so raw and real, I almost feel like a spy, a lost girl stumbling in the darkness, discovering something rare and fragile, something that was never meant for me. The familiar fears scrape at the edges of my heart, warnings about dangerous mages and loss and broken hearts...

As if he can read my thoughts, Baz traces his thumb across my lower lip and cups my face, drawing me down for another soft kiss.

"Come back, my beautiful Star," he whispers.

"Cernunnos," I whisper back. "Don't leave."

"Never. I promise."

He shifts beneath me, heat cresting between us once again, and I sit up on top of him, rolling my hips to take him in deeper, faster, desperately chasing the blissful orgasm building inside all over again.

But Baz's firm grip on my thighs stops my frenzied pace.

"Slow," he whispers, holding me tight. "Slow."

I look into his red-brown eyes again, losing myself in their liquid heat, in the depths of his intensity. Obeying his command, I slow down until I'm barely moving.

"Just feel," he whispers.

"Feel what?"

He reaches for my hand and presses it against his chest. "Everything."

I close my eyes, bringing myself back from the edge and focusing on all the things I can't see.

Here, in this moment, what I feel isn't the heat and friction of frenzied passion, but the stillness. The silent spaces between the powerful beats of his heart. The gentle mist of our breath mingling in the air. My bedroom smells like him now, like fire and earth, and when he takes my hand in his again, the connection sparks between us, the magick rooting us to each other and to the earth, and it fills me with a sense of belonging that's so right, so perfect, it's as if I've finally found something I've been seeking my entire life.

Arching my back, I rise up slowly, then slide back down

over his cock again, taking him in one delicious moment, one delicious inch at a time. Baz traces his fingers down my throat, my chest, drawing tantalizing circles around my nipples.

I melt beneath his touch, a wave of pleasure building behind the dam once again.

Palming my breast, Baz rocks his hips, so slowly I'm not sure he's moving at all. But the pressure between my thighs is building to a red-hot crescendo, my blood simmering, my nerves singing as a shock of heat races to my core.

Without warning, Baz bolts upright and fists the back of my hair, capturing my mouth in a fierce kiss, his body shuddering beneath me as he finally lets go, setting off a chain reaction that explodes between us.

I'm right there, holding tight to the edge of the cliff, torn between terror and bliss. Maybe I *should* be terrified—terrified of this moment. Of everything Baz told me tonight. Of his past and his present and all the monsters he's still trying to outrun, even if he didn't name them all out loud.

Or maybe it's okay to lose myself to this, to trust that I will always find my way back again. To trust my feelings. To trust *him*.

"Starla," he breathes against my lips, and my choice is made.

I let go, tumbling over the edge of that cliff, hurtling toward the unknown, trusting that he's going to catch me before I hit the ground.

BAZ

Stevie's thrashing around in bed again, but this time it's not because of me.

"Wake up, Little Bird." I wrap my arms around her and pull her against my chest, stroking her back. "It's okay. You're safe."

Finally jolting awake, she pulls back, her wild eyes searching my face in the moonlight. "Baz? What... what happened?"

"Another nightmare, from the looks of it. Do you remember anything?"

"I... yes." She turns over onto her back, then pulls her hand out from beneath the sheet.

She's clutching a bouquet of black dahlias.

"For me? You shouldn't have." I take the flowers from her hand, inspecting them closely. They're dried and desiccated, their edges burned. "You *really* shouldn't have."

"I guess it's a new thing with me now." Stevie sighs, staring up at the ceiling. "It was just like last night. The battle on campus, the Princesses. I followed them through the Breath and Blade lands, but then they vanished before I could figure out where I was. I wandered into the holly bushes again and I… I saw him."

"The Dark Magician?"

"No." Stevie closes her eyes and shakes her head, dropping her voice as if she's afraid of saying the name out loud. "Dark Judgment. At the cave with the Fool."

I set the flowers on the nightstand. "Are you hurt?"

"I don't think so. Not this time." She turns toward me again and rests her head on my chest, her warm, ragged breath swirling against my skin. "I'm at the cave, feeling like there's something I'm supposed to see there, to find… But then I'm just standing there watching him devour the Fool and incinerate you. All of you. You're there, and then you're just… just gone. Ashes. The worst part was I *knew* I could fight him—defeat him, even—if I had my sword. But all I had was that useless bouquet, and there was so much mist and I couldn't find anyone to help… I felt so powerless. I still feel it—that emptiness. Helplessness."

"Okay, first of all, you're not powerless or helpless. Far from it."

"Then he's got a hold over me in some other way, because I couldn't access any magick. I couldn't even move." She shudders against me, and I tighten my hold on her, kissing her forehead. "There's more—different from last time. The ashes—your ashes… He brought you guys back, Baz."

"Brought us back? How?"

"With the staff. There was a chant… ashes… something…" Stevie sighs, then repeats the words from her nightmare:

> *Ashes to ashes, dust to dust*
> *With flame and with fury, the ends are just*
> *Cleansed by fire, Arcana must die*
> *From Death we return, in Darkness we rise*

"He said the spell three times, then pointed his staff at the ashes, turning them into a massive white fire. When the flames finally died down, the four of you were standing there as if you'd never been burned in the first place. You were back."

"Alive?"

"No. Just… back." Her voice drops to a whisper. "Others emerged from the cave then. I recognized some of our professors, students, so many witches and mages. They just kept pouring out… Black eyes, bloodied mouths, their hunger overwhelming… I could feel it." She pulls out of my embrace and looks up at me, her eyes still holding the terror of the dream. "Undead, Baz. They're making an army of undead. That's what I saw the day I got bitten by the snake, too. An army that can't be killed."

She rolls onto her back again and closes her eyes. "And he wanted Ani to kill me."

"What did Ani say?"

"Nothing. He turned toward me, and his eyes—they were as black and dead as the others. There was nothing left of Ani at all—just this shell. He opened his mouth, and black smoke started pouring out… Judgment called him the Black Sun. Said he'd rule over the Dark armies that would usher in the new magickal order. That's when I woke up."

Black Sun?

I've never heard the term, but something about it makes my gut sour. Ani's the emanation of The Sun—goodness and light. Joy. Just picturing him like that…

"Wait. The staff…" I sit up in bed, leaning against the headboard as a terrifying thought hits my brain. "What did it look like? How big?"

"Kind of like a tree branch? The end held a bright red jewel. Do you know of any magickal staffs like that?"

"Staffs, no. But a wand? Yeah, I could think of one wand in particular with that kind of juice."

"*The* wand? Flame and Fury?" Stevie bolts upright beside me, clutching the sheets against her chest. "Can it do that? Bring the dead back to life?"

"That's probably a better question for Kirin. Did you guys come across anything like that in the books?"

"Not yet, but there are so many different legends floating around…" She looks over at me, the terror in her eyes replaced with undaunted determination. "We need to find it, Baz. We can't let any of the Dark Arcana find those objects. This dream… Whatever it's trying to tell me, it's only the beginning."

"I know." I pull her close again and stroke her hair, wishing like hell I could tell her it *was* just a dream. That she's worrying over nothing. But I can't do that, and we both know it.

The sun hasn't risen yet, and after a few minutes of dead silence, we sink back into the cool comfort of the sheets. Stevie turns on her side, her back to me, and I draw close, seeking the contact of her silky-smooth skin, pressing my lips to the base of her neck.

She lets out a soft moan of pleasure that makes me instantly hard.

"For someone who insists he's not the cuddling type," she teases, "you're awful clingy."

"Cass seems to think you shouldn't sleep alone. I volunteered to keep watch. A *close* watch."

"I thought we were supposed to put up fliers or website ads."

"For murder victims? Because any guy that offers to keep you company in bed—that's what he's signing up for."

"Possessive much?"

"Of you?" I growl and bury my face in a mass of curls, my cock already straining against her backside. "No question."

Stevie arches back against me, making the whole situation infinitely worse.

"You're playing with fire again, Little Bird," I warn.

"You're right. You should probably teach me a lesson or something. Maybe I need—"

"I know *exactly* what you need." In one fluid motion, I've got her on her back again, and I climb on top, pinning her wrists above her head as I settle in between her thighs.

I run my tongue along her inner arm, across her shoulder, down to her breast. My mouth closes around her nipple, and I inhale the sweet honeysuckle scent of her skin, tasting and teasing her, damn near losing my mind as she writhes beneath me. The bedroom flickers in my peripheral vision, and suddenly we're at the lake by the standing stones—Stevie's lake—the vision of her Star Arcana energy.

She arches her hips, her wet heat calling to me, begging me, and with no more invitation than that, I roll on a condom and plunge inside her.

After a night of slow, delirious pleasure, we're fast and frenzied now, hot skin sliding against hot skin, kisses devouring kisses, and it's not long before we're both at the edge, teetering on the precipice.

"Baz," she whispers, and I thrust in deep, her body clenching hard around me.

She slides her hands into my hair, pulling me in for a kiss that makes my head spin, and both of us shatter, consumed by a rush of pure, white-hot ecstasy. When I finally pull back for air, I cup her face, and she looks up at me through long lashes, her dark hair spilled across the white pillowcases, her mouth still parted in pleasure.

And when she smiles, radiant and beautiful and all for me, I realize she's not the one playing with fire at all.

I make a silent vow right here and now, a promise that

runs deeper than any blood bond, deeper than any Arcana oath.

No matter what dangers await, no matter what horrors the Dark Arcana conjure, no matter how many armies break upon the walls of this academy, I will *die* before I let this woman come to harm.

TWENTY-TWO

STEVIE

All too soon, sunlight chases away the last of the shadows in my suite, and I drag my happily exhausted body to the shower, fighting the urge to crawl back into my warm bed with the man who—true to his promises—spent the entire night making me forget how to form words.

There's still so much more I want to ask him—about his past, about his story. But despite the horror of his childhood trauma and the loss of his family, I can't help but sense that somewhere in that 'so much more' is where the *real* darkness festers. I felt it last night, leaking out between his words and closing around him like black ink spilled in water.

Whatever Baz went through, whatever games Janelle is still playing with him, it goes far beyond a mage murder and the cutthroat competition between his parents and the Kirkpatricks.

But it's also beyond my business. I'm grateful he told me about his history with Carly, but I'm not going to force him to face any of those other demons, no matter how strongly I can sense them, no matter how badly I want to fix him. Some paths we just have to walk on our own.

After last night's epic sleepover, I thought I'd be nice and let him sleep in while I got ready. But just as I'm about to turn off the shower, he's stepping in there with me, dark hair sticking up in every direction, sheet marks criss-crossing his face.

"What are you staring at?" he asks with a lopsided grin.

"You're kind of adorable when you're half-asleep."

"And you're kind of sexy when you're wet. And naked." He pulls me close, sliding his hands down to cup my backside. "Did I say kind of? I meant *very*."

He kisses me, hot and deep, and for a minute I allow myself to get lost in the feel of his tongue sliding into my mouth, his hands caressing me. But as much as I'd love to dive into another sex-a-thon...

No. Bad idea. We have... classes... and... library stuff and...

Oh, Goddess, this man seriously knows what he's doing...

"Baz, I'm... going to be late and you—"

"One minute."

"What?"

"I can make you come in one minute."

"I seriously doubt—"

He spins me around and pins me against the shower wall, tracing a hot path down the back of my neck with his tongue as he slides two fingers inside me from behind. With his free hand, he reaches around front, teasing my clit with slow, delicious circles.

My body clenches around his fingers, and he plunges in deeper, stroking me until I'm breathless, the dueling pleasure of his thrusts and teasing circles making me lightheaded. He nips my earlobe, his breath hot on my skin.

"Let go," he whispers, thrusting in deeper, faster. "Come undone."

That's all it takes. I can't hold back. I shatter hard and fast, pushing back against his fingers, riding the wave of pleasure until I'm so dizzy I'm seeing stars.

He pulls out slowly, embracing me from behind and resting his forehead on my shoulder as I will my breathing to go back to normal. When it does, I turn in his arms, pressing a kiss to his smirking mouth.

"That might be a new record," he says.

"No idea. I wasn't counting."

"Normally I'm not one for quickies, but it's like I always say. Never pass up an opportunity to start the day off with a proper orgasm."

"Is that what you always say?"

"Okay, no. But now that you're in my life, I'm gonna start." He kisses me again, his cock hard, his mouth doing things to erase my last working brain cell, and soon he's dashing out into the bedroom for the condoms, dripping water everywhere as he races back into the shower, and we're right back where we left off.

We've just finished ensuring *both* of us start the day off properly when my door chimes, followed by a hard rap.

"What time is it?" I ask Baz.

"No idea. Maybe ten?"

"Shit, that must be Kirin!" I step out of the shower and grab a towel from the hook, hastily wrapping it around my body. "I was supposed to meet him at the library at nine!"

Baz shrugs. "He'll get over it."

"*Baz.*"

"If you're trying to make me jealous, Little Bird, it's totally working."

As if to confirm, his energy washes over me—jealousy in the lead, followed closely by disappointment and a tinge of fear.

"Jealous. Really. I'm standing here naked with *you,* while the man I was *supposed* to meet is locked outside."

"You're not naked anymore, though, that's the thing." He reaches for my towel, but I dart away, smacking his grabby hands.

"Naughty mage. I have to get to work. And it's Tuesday. Don't you have a class to go fail? A professor to annoy?"

"Advanced Gem and Mineral Composition. I could *teach* that class. I'm only in it for the easy grade."

He's smirking at me, but the jealousy and hurt still linger. I look up into his eyes, and just like last night, the rawness there is impossible to unsee.

"Baz." I close my eyes, blowing out a breath. "You don't need to be jealous. But the situation with Kirin is... complicated."

I don't want to keep secrets about that. Secrets are what got me into so much trouble to begin with.

"You have feelings for him," he says, doing his best to keep the irritation out of his voice. "I get it. I see it any time the two of you are together."

"I *do* have feelings for him," I say, opening my eyes. "I mean... I did. I don't know. It got kind of fucked up between us a couple of weeks back, and now..."

"Now what?"

"I'm not sure."

"Those kinds of feelings... they don't just go away."

"No," I admit. "But you know something?" I step partway into the shower again and take his face between my hands, pressing a soft kiss to his lips. When I pull back, his eyes are closed, his mouth curved in a smile, and some of the hurt recedes.

"Those kinds of feelings don't have limits, either," I say. "Not for me."

The door chimes again. I leave Baz with a final kiss, then wrap my hair in a towel, dash into my bedroom, and grab my robe.

"Be right there!" I make it to the door and haul it open just as I get the robe tied shut. "I'm so sorry, Kirin. I totally should've—"

I totally should've checked the security monitor, that's what. Because the man standing in my doorway isn't Kirin Weber.

It's Agent William Eastman from APOA, his face turning red with awkward embarrassment as he takes in the sight of me, the top of my robe gaping open, the sound of the shower hissing in the background, my swollen lips and stubble-burned chin a pretty solid indicator of how I've spent my morning.

"Agent Eastman?"

"My apologies for the intrusion, Miss Milan," he says in his clipped British accent. His judgy, by-the-book cop energy hits me so hard and fast, I'm just about ready to drop to my knees and beg for forgiveness for all the carnal sins I've committed in the last several hours.

"I'm here to check the security system," he says, his judgment turning into annoyance.

"I didn't report any issues," I say.

"We're doing a full sweep of all the systems in student and faculty campus housing. You should've received an email."

"I... right. I haven't looked at my phone yet this morning." I offer a chagrined smile, then grab my phone from the kitchen counter. Sure enough, there's an email from Trello about the security checks.

"Got it." I invite him in and show him the setup. "Do what you need to do, sir."

"Thank you, Miss Milan. I'll be but a moment."

"Would you like some tea?" I ask. Brits love their tea, don't they?

"Thank you, no."

I peek over his shoulder, watching as he plugs some kind of device into my security monitor. "What's that for?"

"Just testing the video backup frequency. We need to ensure the system is running automatic backups every hour, should we need to review video footage later."

"I see."

Satisfied with the backup thing, he taps rapid-fire onto the screen, checking out some other settings I decide not to ask about because I won't understand what the hell he's talking about anyway.

"So, you're from England?" I ask instead.

"Yes. And quite busy, as you can imagine."

"Of course. Sorry."

Not one for small talk, then. Okay, fine by me.

While Eastman deals with the rest of the security issues, I put on the kettle for tea, trying to decide what I want for breakfast. Truth be told, I could really go for a muffin and a latte right now, but I'm late enough as it is. I'll have to try to fit in a café run after the library, before my Tarot Divination class.

Before I even make up my mind on the tea options, Eastman is packing up his magick-tech gear and wishing me a good day.

"Do I need to learn any new procedures?" I ask.

"No, not at all. I've simply reinforced the magickal identification system with a few upgrades. All of your presets have been saved, and the entry and lockup procedures are the same. We are, however, advising everyone to periodically review that video footage, even if you don't suspect any tampering. We can't be too careful."

"Of course. Thank you, Mr. Eastman."

I show him out, glad to be free from his overbearing energy. I appreciate his dedication to his job and to keeping us safe, but from now on, I'd prefer he do it from a nice, long distance.

I'm just about to return to the tea-and-breakfast dilemma when my door chimes again—Kirin, my actual date. Well, not date. We're not using that word. Appointment. My appointment. Nice and non-sexy, like a gyno visit.

"Good morning," I say as I open the door, and Kirin beams, his eyes lighting up behind his glasses, and my stomach goes a little fizzy and a single, stupid thought strikes my mind.

If my gyno actually smiled at me like that, I'd never miss an appointment. In fact, I'd schedule one every month, and get on the waitlist for cancellations...

"Stevie?"

"Yes, Doctor? I mean... Kirin! Hi! Come on in." I stand aside as he enters, waiting for my common sense to return from its obvious vacation. It reminds me of our Kettle Black days, back when his mere presence turned me into an Olympic-level competitor in the events of Babbling Like an Idiot and Blinking Rapidly Like a Deer in Headlights. Who Also Has Allergies.

"Sorry I'm running so late," I say, a little breathless. "I overslept... I was just trying to figure out breakfast. Hungry?"

Still smiling, Kirin holds up a to-go tray of coffee cups and a brown paper bag. "I brought muffins and—"

"Is that coffee?" Baz asks, stepping out of the bedroom wearing nothing but a towel and a still-wet six-pack of very sexy, very lickable abs.

And thus concludes the Kirin-Weber-Smiling portion of the day. Thanks for stopping by!

TWENTY-THREE

KIRIN

Stevie's megawatt smile has the power to brighten the darkest days, but the effect is somewhat dimmed by the half-naked man strutting around behind her.

I catch his eye, glaring a few daggers for good measure, but the bastard only shrugs, his smirk as obvious as his hard-on.

"Is your shower out of order?" I ask him, not bothering to keep the bite from my tone.

"No idea." Baz's stupid smirk gets even bigger. "I haven't been home all night. But you're welcome to go downstairs and check it out if you're concerned."

"I'm good. Thanks." I close my eyes, trying to regroup. I know they've got something going—the chemistry between them has always been combustible. I sensed it the first time I introduced them outside Iron and Bone on Stevie's first day on campus.

Can't say I didn't see this coming.

I just wish I didn't have to see it at all.

Yet now I've got an eyeful, my imagination shading in every last detail of what must've happened between the time they left the Brotherhood meeting last night and this *supremely* annoying moment right here.

Fuck.

I force down the bitterness and open my eyes, plastering my smile back in place. No matter how much it burns, I can't be pissed at Baz. For all his ridiculous peacocking, I know he truly cares about her. We all do. And even if it's not love right now—even if it *never* gets that far between them—I've got no right to complain. I'm the asshole who walked away from her. The one who kissed her in every possible way, then ran, ignoring her when she needed me most, hoping the time and the distance would cool my feelings and keep her safe.

Both of those hopes died the night we found her tied to a tree, tortured at the hands of a madman. I could no more keep her safe than I could turn off my feelings for her. But now, if she doesn't want anything to do with me beyond the prophecy and air magick work we're tasked with, I've got no one to blame but myself.

"Sorry, Stevie," I say, doing my best to keep my feelings on lockdown, even as the coffee cups in my hand begin to tremble. "I didn't know you were busy today."

"I'm not," she says with another smile, right at the same time Baz says, "She's *extremely* busy."

Stevie rolls her pretty blue eyes and laughs, a sound that

almost makes up for the irritating presence of half-naked Baz.

Almost.

"Put on some clothes, heathen," she tells him, but the sparkle in her eyes tells me she doesn't find his half-naked presence irritating in the slightest. Then, turning back to me as if this whole crazy moment is no big deal, she nods at the to-go cups in my hands and says, "*Please* tell me those are vanilla cinnamon lattes, and please tell me one of them is for me."

"Keep smiling at me like that, and you can have both of them."

"Okay, I'll keep smiling, but lucky for you, I'm in a sharing mood."

The air in the room is lighter with Baz out of sight, and I can't help but return Stevie's smile. We sit at the kitchen counter and enjoy our lattes and banana chocolate chip muffins, a few moments of bliss before Baz is back to kill the buzz.

"Are you actually going to class?" she asks him.

"Figured I'd give it a shot," he says. "I heard you like smart guys." He grabs his wallet and phone from the countertop, from the spot right next to *her* phone. The one she *didn't* use to call or text me that she'd be late today, because she was too busy with—

I grab my latte and take another sip, willing the anger to recede.

Stevie rises from the counter and walks Baz to the door,

even though it's just a few feet away and he could certainly find the way himself.

I try to focus on the pattern in the granite countertop, looking for all the variations in the rock, but it's impossible not to feel their ebullient, post-sex giddiness emanating across the room.

"What, no kiss goodbye?" The cretin asks her, still lingering in the doorway.

"How about an ass-kicking goodbye?" I grumble.

"Depends on who's doing the kicking," he shoots back, "and whether she's naked or not."

"*Goodbye*, Baz," Stevie says, laughing at us both. She shoves him out the door, but not without the promised kiss, and before I know what I'm doing, I'm standing behind her, watching her watching *him* until she finally—thank Goddess—shuts the door.

"I'm sorry," I whisper, and she whirls around, shocked to find me so close. "I didn't mean to barge in."

Her surprised gasp turns into a soft smile, and she reaches toward my face, gently pushing my glasses back up my nose.

"My fault," she says. "I should've texted to say I was running late."

"It's okay. You were… busy." Jealousy heats me from the inside, and I wonder if this is how a lobster feels, slowly boiling, death encroaching one tiny degree at a time.

Stevie frowns, and I see it in her eyes—sadness, regret, and then, at the very end, a flicker of something more. "Kirin, I—"

A fist pounds on the door, startling us both. She opens it to reveal one very confused, very ragey Baz standing in the doorway, brandishing a tube of lipstick like a switchblade.

"Where did this come from?" he demands.

Stevie grabs it from his hand and opens it up, twisting up the glossy red stick. "No offense, Baz, but this is *so* not your color."

"That's because it's fucking Janelle's. How the fuck it ended up outside your door, I have no idea."

"Wait… what? Are you sure?"

"I told you, the woman practically raised me." He snatches the lipstick from Stevie's hand, his nose wrinkling with disgust. "Maurice Clayton's Daredevil Red. Only brand and color she's ever fucking worn."

Dread sinks in my gut. "What the hell would Janelle be doing outside Stevie's door?"

"Maybe Carly had it," Stevie says.

"What the hell would *Carly* be doing outside your door?" Baz asks.

Stevie shrugs. "Could she have stopped by looking for you?"

"She doesn't have the balls for a confrontation on your turf." Baz chucks the lipstick against the wall in the hallway so hard it leaves a bright red smudge. "We need to see the security footage."

"On it." I grab Stevie's tablet from the counter and pull up the home security feed, checking the video logs from last night. Sure enough, there's our red-lipped perp. "Looks like she stopped by while we were at the meeting last night. But it doesn't look like she rang the bell or knocked."

"No wonder Eastman wants us to review the video footage," Stevie says. "He was here this morning, checking everything out."

I nod. Trello sent an email about the checks this morning.

"What else did he say?" I ask.

"Just that we should make a habit of checking the videos every once in a while to confirm there's nothing shady going on."

"Well, this looks like just the shady shit he had in mind." I angle the tablet so everyone can see the video. Janelle shows up on the floor, looking over her shoulder, snooping around the other doorways and listening to make sure she wasn't followed. Once she confirms the coast is clear, she approaches Stevie's door and pulls something out of her purse, gripping it in her hand. A second object hits the floor.

"Pause," Baz says. "Zoom in."

I do as he says.

"That's the lipstick on the floor," he says, pointing. "Looks like it fell out when she grabbed that other thing."

"What's the other thing?" Stevie asks.

Baz leans in for a closer look. "Hard to tell, but it looks like some kind of crystal point. Keep rolling."

I un-pause the video, and we watch as Janelle sweeps the crystal point over the door, first making a large circle, then moving her hand in a series of lines and squiggles.

"You recognize that gesture?" Baz asks.

"It's some kind of rune," I say, rewinding and watching again at a slower speed. "But from this vantage point, I can't tell whether it's a rune of protection or…" I rewind and watch again. "Or something else."

Baz blows out a breath. "Something else. With her, it's *always* something else."

I watch a few more times, that dread in my stomach growing until it plunges like a hot rock.

"What's wrong?" Stevie asks. "Did you figure it out?"

"Baz is right." I set down the tablet and take off my glasses, polishing the lenses on my shirt. "It's not a protective rune. It's not a benevolent rune at all. As far as I can tell, Janelle Kirkpatrick was trying to spy on you."

"Trying?" Stevie asks.

"She didn't do the rune correctly. She rushed through it, left out the last three lines. This rune is completely ineffective—it didn't even take. If it had, we would've seen a faint blue glow. I'd be able to sense it now, too."

"A spying rune?" Baz asks. "What the fuck even is that?"

"Just like it sounds," I say. "Spying runes can be visual or auditory, or both, depending on her intentions. If it *had* worked, she'd be able to tap into the power of it anytime she wanted to check up on you. It would basically work as if she were standing in the doorway, without the barrier of the door. She'd be able to see anything in the line of sight from the doorway, or hear any sounds that would normally travel that far."

"But it didn't work," Stevie says.

"No. I'm sure of it."

Next to us, Baz seethes. I'm no empath, but I'm intimately familiar with the lead-up to a complete meltdown, and this man is about two seconds from exploding.

"Fuck this." He turns around and charges for the door.

"Where are you going?" I ask.

"I need to find Janelle."

"Don't be stupid, Baz." I dart in front of him and put a hand on his chest, stopping him in his tracks. His heart is going crazy, his breathing rapid. "Calm down."

"Fuck calm. She's trying to hurt Stevie. I warned that bitch, if she even *thought* about it…" He pinches the bridge of his nose, sucking in ragged breaths of air. "I need to eliminate her from the equation. Now. Before she tries something else."

"Far be it for me to advocate non-violence at a time like this," I say, "but personally, I find it best to plot murders on days when the campus *isn't* crawling with APOA agents."

"Baz, Kirin's right," Stevie says, reaching up and stroking his face. The tenderness of her touch on his skin makes me ache, but it has the desired effect, immediately taking Baz down from a 10 to a 4 on the murderous rage scale. "Besides, she didn't hurt me or cast any attack magick. She's just nosing around for something."

"But what?" he asks. "What the fuck could she possibly want with you, unless it's about me?"

The two of them share a glance loaded with some

hidden meaning I couldn't even begin to guess at, but Stevie shakes her head.

"She knows I'm spirit-blessed," Stevie says. "Carly told me her mother was always trying to find a way to manipulate her powers. Maybe she just wants a piece of mine."

"I'm not buying it," Baz says. "She's scheming. She's always scheming. And by now she knows her spell failed, so we can bet she's going to try something else again soon."

"Let her," I say. "This time we'll be ready. Catch her in the act."

Baz considers it, then shakes his head. "Too risky."

"Baz," Stevie says, crossing her arms over her chest. "I'm with Kirin on this one. We have the upper hand here. Let's lie low and let her walk into her own trap."

He opens his mouth to argue, but with a single raised eyebrow, Stevie shuts him down once again.

Finally, he blows out a breath and nods, pulling her close and pressing a kiss to the top of her head.

"So how do you want to play this?" I ask.

"You guys head to the library as planned," he says. "I'll get Cass over here to do a full sweep and an obfuscation spell to take care of any lingering spy energy. I'm also going to set up a crystal grid for additional protection."

"Sounds like a plan," I say.

"Yay, another plan," Stevie says, heading to her bedroom to get dressed. "Any more plans and I'm going to have to start writing them down."

The moment she's out of earshot, Baz is already at the door, ready to bolt.

I grab his arm, digging in hard. "Whatever you're think-ing, brother, don't."

"I can't let it lie, Kirin." He turns to face me. "If Janelle hurts Stevie—"

"Listen. I can't believe I'm about to save your ass on this one, but seriously. Listen to me, Baz. If you go behind Stevie's back on this, *you'll* be the one hurting her. And trust me—that's not a path you want to start on. Not after every-thing we promised her."

His eyes blaze with anger, but my words get through to him.

"No more secrets," he finally says, the last of his anger fading. "Fuck."

"No more secrets."

"You're right."

"I know."

"But Kirin?" He hooks a hand around the back of my neck and leans in close, his voice low and menacing. "Hurt her again, pull that broody disappearing act shit one more time, and no amount of promises will keep me from beating *your* ass."

"Noted."

He releases me and grabs his phone to call Cass, but before he hits the contact button, he offers a genuine smile. "Hey. Thanks for that."

"For letting you threaten me?" I roll my eyes. "Sure thing. Anytime. Always a pleasure."

"For stopping me from screwing up. You really did save my ass."

"Don't mention it."

"You always were the brains of the operation."

"Don't pout, brother. You got the abs." I smack him in the gut and then turn away, listening to the sounds of Stevie singing in her bedroom as she gets dressed, wondering if there will ever be a time when I stop thinking with my head and just follow my fucking heart.

TWENTY-FOUR

STEVIE

With precious little time to lose to bullshit spy games, Kirin and I leave Baz to deal with my suite and head to the library, ready to hit the books—now with the added fun of dodging our new librarian, a woman who's not only trying to spy on me, but possibly looking for the Arcana treasures too.

And let's not forget her territorial issues with Baz.

Or the fact that I'm probably her daughter's *least* favorite witch on campus.

I let out a sigh as we exit the Iron and Bone dorm, wishing I *could've* stayed in the shower with Baz today. That we could've forgotten about everything outside that's trying to kill us—even just for one more day.

But the Arcanapocalypse waits for no one.

A new thought strikes, making my stomach clench.

"Kirin, what if Janelle's working with Phaines?" I ask. "What if that's why she tried to set up that rune?"

"The thought crossed my mind, too. But honestly, Stevie, her runework was quite amateur—way beneath Phaines's league, especially now that he's operating with the Dark Arcana. He wouldn't risk his position by employing someone as careless as Janelle. Besides, he already got what he wanted from the library itself—the books."

"But unless he's figured out a way around the spells, he still needs my magick to read them. What if he sent her here to get to me?"

"We're not going to let that happen."

"Kirin, no offense, but you're being a little naïve. I know you guys don't *want* to let it happen, but she already got to my room. *That* shouldn't have happened either, but it did."

Kirin lowers his eyes, watching his footfalls as a few students pass us on the red stone path. All around us, the campus bustles with life—witches and mages scurrying to class, a group of students practicing levitation on a patch of grass behind us, two mages making out in the shade of a giant saguaro. If anyone is worried about the events going on outside our magickally-protected borders, no one shows any signs of it.

Life, as always, moves on.

But not for us. Not for the Arcana, the Keepers of the Grave.

"I know that, Stevie," he finally says when the students are out of earshot. "We all know that. Whatever Janelle's designs, we didn't think she'd make a move so quickly. Our assumption, our mistake. It won't happen again."

"I made too many assumptions with Phaines," I say, remembering how taken I was by his grandfatherly demeanor.

"Hey." He stops in his tracks, putting a hand on my shoulder. "Stevie, I won't let you out of my sight in there. Not for a minute. I promise."

"I know." I smile, hoping it's enough to reassure us both. "Did you meet her yet? Officially, I mean?"

"No. She spent yesterday getting settled into her new office, and I managed to avoid direct contact. But it's only a matter of time before she wants access to the archives, and I'm the one who has to sign off on that."

"Is she in the security system?"

Kirin shakes his head, leading us down the path again. "I'm trying to hold off as long as possible. There's plenty for her to do that doesn't involve rare manuscripts, but like I said, she's going to want access sooner or later. Probably sooner."

"If she wants to spy on me, the archives lab is probably the best place after my apartment."

"The lab is already warded against spy spells—a precaution the Academy took from the beginning, given the sensitive nature of the documents. I've added some enhancements to the screening process, too. But none of that can stop her from spying the old-fashioned way— snooping and eavesdropping."

"What the hell does she want?"

It's a rhetorical question, but Kirin answers anyway.

"That's what we're hoping to find out. So for now, we play it cool, just like we told Baz. Right?"

"The waiting game… It's so frustrating. I just don't want to get caught with my pants down again."

"I… right. Of course." Kirin looks away, his ears turning red, and I realize the stupidity in what I just said.

Kirin *literally* left me with my pants down in the middle of the library, right after making my whole world explode in technicolor glory. I came, he left. Pun intended.

It's kind of a raw nerve for both of us, and I feel the guilt leaking into his energy, hot and prickly.

I grab his arm, stopping us on the path. "Kirin, I didn't mean—"

"I know you didn't," he says softly. "It's just a… just a saying."

"A stupid one that I didn't mean to say."

"It's okay. I'm the one who screwed up." He looks my way again and tries to smile, but it doesn't reach his eyes, and it's not long before it falls away completely. "Stevie, there's something else I need to tell you."

I feel the shift in his energy, his guilt and concern and protectiveness whisked away by a dark, swirling hole of sadness and loss. The change is so abrupt it makes my own heart feel hollow and cold.

"Kirin…" I look into his eyes and find the same sadness lingering. "I know we need to talk about what happened between us, but I can't. Not yet. Not here. We need to focus on work, and I—"

"It's not…" He closes his eyes and shakes his head. "I

just wanted to tell you about my sister, Casey Appleton. I know you met her in Cass's class yesterday."

My cheeks heat—a mix of embarrassment and, if I'm being honest, disappointment. "Right. Yes, she was observing us. I was going to ask you about her earlier, but the whole Janelle thing took over."

We continue our walk.

"Casey and I aren't close. Before yesterday, I hadn't spoken with her in ten years. Same with my brother and parents. It's just… one of those things."

Pain. Loneliness. It rushes at me hard and fast.

"But… why?" I blurt out. My parents were my whole world, and they were taken from me—something none of us had any choice in. I can't imagine the pain of knowing they still exist somewhere, but for whatever reason, don't exist in *my* life.

It's the same thing I felt last night when Baz told me his story, and I wonder now if Kirin and Baz realize they're not alone in this pain.

"I'll… I'll tell you about it sometime," Kirin says, his energy shuttering a bit. Defensive. Scared. "But my family drama has to wait. We've got bigger priorities right now. I just wanted you to know that despite our personal estrangement, Casey *is* a good agent—it was always her dream to work for APOA, and she's always been honest, hardworking, and smart. She's done well for herself there. I trust her to do her job, and I trust that her heart is in the right place when it comes to keeping students safe."

"What does she think about what's going on here?"

"Well, Phaines is obviously their main concern. She warned me to keep an eye on Janelle, too—said that Eastman is already suspicious of her on account of her past relationship with Phaines and her history with treasure hunting."

"Baz mentioned something about that, too," I say. "Does Casey know about my mother's prophecies?"

"That they exist? Yes. I also confirmed that you and I are working on the translations—she would've figured it out eventually anyway. But I haven't told her about the Dark Arcana or what we suspect Phaines was really after."

"So your trust of her only goes so far."

"For now."

The path curves, and up ahead, the library comes into view, a circular tower that rises out of the landscape, dominating the buildings that surround it. It's my favorite building on campus, but the closer we get, the tighter my stomach twists. The last time I walked this path, my steps led me straight into the arms of a killer. I was robbed, poisoned, mutilated, and nearly murdered.

My knees tremble, but I force myself to keep going, one shaky step at a time. I *have* to do this. That psycho is *not* taking this from me.

Sensing my sudden trepidation, Kirin puts a hand on my shoulder, his energy returning to concerned and protective. "You okay?"

I force myself to nod, but my mouth has gone dry, and I can't seem to find any words.

"Maybe we should come back tomorrow," he says gently. "Give you a little more time to—"

"No," I snap, finally breaking through the nerves. "Kirin, we don't have time. You know the stakes. You just said it yourself—we've got bigger priorities right now."

"But one more day? That's not the end of the world."

"You don't know that. It might be *exactly* the end of the world." I close my eyes and let out a long breath. "I have to do this today, Kirin. The longer I put it off, the harder it's going to be."

He doesn't like it—that much is obvious. His protective energy is kicking into high gear, and I can tell just by looking at him that it's taking some major willpower to keep his mouth shut.

But eventually, Kirin nods. "We'll stay for as little or as long as you want. The minute you want out of there, we leave. No questions. Okay?"

I smile, my fear receding in the wake of his kindness.

We've just reached the front steps when we spot a familiar figure near the entrance.

Dr. Devane nods at us, his face grim.

"Everything okay?" Kirin asks as we approach, even though it's clear everything is *not* okay. "Did Baz get a hold of you?"

"He did," Doc says. "I'm heading over to the suite now, but was hoping to catch you both here first. There's something I need to tell you."

We follow him into the lobby and over to a quiet alcove.

He's shielding his energy, but I can tell by his demeanor that it's bad news.

"There was another attack last night," he says, keeping his voice low. "A mage walking home from water magicks class out at the River of Blood and Sorrow."

"What happened?" I ask, my heart jackhammering. "Is he okay?" My voice trembles, bile rising in my throat. "Was he…" I can't even bring myself to say the words. Instead, I make a slicing motion across my stomach.

Was he carved? Bled? Sacrificed in a twisted ritual to appease the Dark One?

"No." Doc slides his hand around the back of my neck, a shockingly intimate gesture for the normally reserved professor that instantly fills me with warmth. "Nothing like that. He was just a little roughed up, missing a chunk of hair."

"Someone took his hair?" I ask. "Why would they do that?"

"We don't know yet," Doc says. "But I can assure you, no one steals the hair off your head for benevolent magick."

Goosebumps erupt across my arms. Despite the brutality of what Phaines did to me, the idea of someone cutting a chunk of hair from my head feels more sinister. More secretive. Darker.

"I'll update Baz and Ani," Doc says. "In the meantime, I want you both to be *extremely* careful, especially at night."

"You too," I tell him. "You're stubborn and impossible, but not invincible."

A quick smile breaks through his stern face, and then Doc does something that surprises the hell out of me.

He leans down and kisses the top of my head, holding the back of my neck so tenderly it brings tears to my eyes.

"Take no chances," he says. Then, after a quick nod at Kirin, he's gone, his warm touch lingering beneath my hair—a touch I'll carry with me for the rest of the day.

TWENTY-FIVE

STEVIE

Up on the archives level, the entry procedure itself feels the same—hand scanner to get through the first door, then to lock it behind us, followed by the full-body scanner that checks my magickal signature and matches it up with my Academy records. But this time, the body scanner is taking a lot longer to do its thing.

"The system is running checks on your magickal signature like before," Kirin explains. "But it's also checking your vitals for any signs of distress that could indicate coercion or malicious intent."

"What if I'm just anxious?"

"The magick is smart enough to know the difference."

"So you've built an AI empath?"

"That's one way of looking at it."

The machine finally beeps, the lights inside turning green. The same disembodied voice from before invites me to step forward, and seconds later, my phone buzzes with a text—the security code for the final door.

"Go on in," Kirin says from behind me. "But do me a favor and keep your eyes closed. I made some modifications inside and I want to surprise you."

"What sort of modifications?" I narrow my eyes. "Do we have to wear full-on Haz-Mat suits to handle the manuscripts now?"

"No, nothing like that. I think you'll like it, actually." A sweet, shy smile curves his lips, his ears turning red again. "At least, I hope you will. Close your eyes and step inside. I'm right behind you."

I do as he asks, my heart rate kicking up a notch. Seconds later, he's through the machine and standing behind me, his hand coming to rest on the small of my back, gently guiding me forward.

With his mouth close to my ear, Kirin whispers, "Okay. Take a look."

I open my eyes and step into the lab, feeling as if I've just stepped through a portal to another world. Other than the size of the room and the environmentally controlled file cabinets behind their glass walls, everything is completely different.

The walls, once a sterile hospital white, are now a soft, soothing blue, light on top and darker on the bottom, decorated with paintings of various seascapes. The metal tables have been replaced with tables of light blond wood, each one polished to a perfect shine. Weathered white planks line the floor.

"What is this?" I ask, my smile huge. "I feel like I'm in a beach cottage somewhere."

"It's a glamour—we couldn't risk harming the manuscripts with a full remodel, or altering the procedures for handling them. I just thought after what happened here, what you went through… I thought a few changes might help."

"Kirin, you did all this?"

"Cass helped. He's got a knack for mental magicks—glamour is part of that. Plus, he had to smooth things over with Trello first—not a job *I* wanted to sign up for."

I turn to face him, my eyes brimming with tears. "For me?" I whisper.

"The library and the archives have always been a sanctuary for me," he says softly, his pale green eyes shining behind his glasses. "And I wanted that for you, too. Phaines tried to take it from you. I'd like to try to get it back for you, even just a little." He lowers his eyes, his voice dropping to a whisper. "I don't want you to remember this place as you saw it last, Stevie. I want you to remember it new."

"Thank you." I pull him in for a hug, my body instantly relaxing into his familiar embrace. Kirin stiffens, but only for a moment. Then his arms wrap around me, his hand running up and down my back. He rests his cheek on the top of my head, and the full force of his energy hits me— sadness and regret over what we had, now gone; the protectiveness inherent in our brotherhood bond; and there, underscoring all of it, the love he still feels for me.

My heart skips a beat, my stomach turning fizzy. It

would be so easy to fall back into this with him. To erase the slate of our past as easily as he redecorated the archives, painting over the bad memories, hoping to make new ones instead.

But just like the archives redecoration, that would only be a glamour. And I can't risk losing my heart again... Not unless it's real.

"Do you like it?" he asks nervously. "Is it helping? Even a little?"

"It's helping a lot. It's like a whole new world." It's a small lie, one I allow myself despite my general stance against them, because I don't have the heart to tell Kirin that no amount of paint and new furniture could ever make me forget how I last saw this place—my cheek pressed to the floor, the top of Phaines's robes skimming over his boot as he lifted it over my face, the sound of bone crunching as he brought it down...

I close my eyes, forcing out the memory.

Despite what happened between us, the fact that Kirin did this for me at all—that he wanted it to be my sanctuary—that in itself is a balm on my wounded soul.

Pulling out of the hug, I blink away the last of my tears and look up at Kirin with another wide smile, overcome with a sense of rightness and fresh starts, eager to hit the books. "All right, Genius Boy. Let's get to work."

* * *

"Here's what I'm thinking," I say, strumming my fingers on the stack of notebooks Kirin retrieved from the file cabinets. "We've lost Mom's grimoire and the Journey book, so that's out. We may be able to recreate some of the grimoire text using the prophecies in her other notebooks, but that's going to take a lot of time—time we just don't have right now."

"So where do you want to start?"

"I think we should go back through all the translations we've done so far, this time with an eye for clues about the locations of the objects rather than just the objects and legends themselves."

"Good idea. If we can at least narrow it down to general locations, from there we can try to recreate the spells and reveal the specifics."

"I'm especially concerned about finding the Wand of Flame and Fury," I say. "Last night I had another nightmare vision. Sort of." I tell him about Judgment, the undead, the dahlias, and—most importantly—the flaming wand. "Baz and I think it might be *the* wand."

Kirin bristles at the mention of Baz's name, but I plow ahead anyway.

"Do you think it's possible for the Wand to have that much power?" I ask. "To literally raise the dead from ashes?"

"Wands represent the spark of life and creation, so the association makes sense. But necromancy—even in the legends—is intense dark magick. It requires a lot of power, and that's just to reanimate an actual body. Creating life—

re-recreating it, rather—out of ash? I don't know if the Wand has that kind of power on its own. Most of the legends we've read so far suggest the objects are at their most powerful when brought together. That it's their very togetherness that unleashes their innate magick."

"That's what I thought, too, but I can't ignore what I saw. The nightmares… They're visions, I'm certain of it. I'm either seeing what's to come or seeing what the Dark Arcana *want* to come. If it's the latter, that still means it's possible—at least, the Dark Arcana believe it's possible. Either that, or there's *another* crazy-powerful zombie-making wand out there."

"Let's hope there's just the one," he says grimly, rising from his chair to pace the room.

"Here's where I keep getting hung up." I flip open one of the notebooks where I'd recorded my initial thoughts about the legends surrounding the Book of Shadow and Mists. "The Book of Shadow and Mists was actually two books—the Journey Through the Void of Mist and Spirit, and my mother's own grimoire."

"Right."

"But the legends about the Book of Shadow and Mist are thousands of years old. So how is it possible they refer to Mom's grimoire, which is less than thirty years old?"

"I was wondering about that myself," he says, coming to stand behind me. "The Journey book is quite a conundrum too."

Resting a hand on the back of my chair, he leans over

and grabs for my notes on the Journey book, his chest brushing against my arm, making my stomach flutter again.

"What are you thinking?" I ask, hoping he doesn't hear the hitch in my breath. His proximity is messing with my head. My body. My heart. All of it.

Kirin stands up again and flips through my notes. "It's a bound manuscript, but there's no record of it even existing. No information about the author, about any larger works or legends it may have been part of. We only know it's part of Shadow and Mist because you made the discovery, but there's no record of the individual title itself."

A new thought comes to mind. "What if that's because it *doesn't* exist? Not in this realm, anyway."

"What do you mean?"

"What if she brought it back with her from the dream realm?" I turn around to face him, but suddenly he's leaning in close again, so close our noses almost touch.

"Anything's possible," he whispers, breath tickling my lips, but I know he's not talking about my dream realm idea or the book. He's not even listening anymore. Right now, in this moment, there's only Kirin and me, an invisible force pulling us closer, my heart beating so loudly I'd be shocked if he couldn't hear it too.

"Stevie…" My name falls from his lips like a sigh, and he reaches toward my face, looping one of my curls around his finger. A soft smile curves his mouth. "I've always loved your hair."

Heat rises to my cheeks, the gentle touch of his fingers

in my hair bringing me right back to this very room the night he told me he was falling in love with me.

...you're smart, and you make me laugh, and I love the way your mind works, the way you question everything, the way your eyebrow does that thing when you're thinking... I love how you throw yourself into everything you're learning, and how you devour books, and how you always know how to make the perfect tea blend—I've always loved that about you, my queen of leaves. And you're beautiful, Stevie. Every time I look at you, my heart breaks a little more, knowing I'll have to close my eyes at some point and miss your face...

Again I feel that invisible pull, all the old feelings rushing back in, and for a brief moment I want nothing more than to press my mouth to his and pick up right where we left off.

But then I remember how he left me in the stacks, literally with my ass exposed, my pants down around my ankles, my thighs still trembling from his mouth. I remember how he ghosted me for weeks after that. And later, how even after confessing his feelings, he bailed before we had a chance to talk about it. To explore what might be possible. He left me again with no more explanation than this:

Everything I touch, I destroy...

Kirin crashed upon my life like the tide, drowning me in desire and feelings I've never felt before, only to recede, leaving me moored on the beach like an abandoned ship.

My feelings for him haven't changed—I see that now.

I'm still in love with him. I know he feels it, too. But I can't let my heart wash up on the shore. Not again.

I close my eyes, forcing myself to break the connection between us.

"Kirin, I can't," I whisper. "Not after…"

Not after what you did.

I open my eyes to look at him again, and he releases my hair, backing off immediately.

"I… I'm sorry." He stands up, putting some much-needed space between us. "I'm so sorry, Stevie. I wasn't thinking."

"Then?" I snap, letting the anger back in. Welcoming it. "Or now?"

Kirin's face crumples, but I'm done with fielding his guilt.

The anger finally boils over, wiping out the last of the regret, and I rise from my chair to face him head-on. "The thing is, Kirin, last month you told me you couldn't let yourself fall for me because everything you touch, you destroy. You said you didn't want to hurt me. But this past summer, you asked me out in Kettle Black, way before all this started. You said you wanted to hang out and get to know me. Why would you do that if you truly believed it couldn't go anywhere?"

Kirin shoves his hands into his pockets and shrugs, unable to meet my eyes.

Apparently I'm carrying enough anger for both of us, because all he's got is regret.

"Hope, I guess," he says. "A stupid lapse in judgment."

"Well?" I pop my hands on my hips. "Which is it? Hope or stupidity? Because as far as I'm concerned, there's a pretty big gap between those two options."

Kirin looks up at me again, but he doesn't answer. He doesn't *have* an answer. Which is just fine by me, because after everything with Baz, I've got more than enough complications of the penile nature on my hands. Literally *and* figuratively.

I press my fingers to my temples and shake my head. At this rate, the Dark Arcana don't need to kill me. These mages are going to do it for them.

"Let's just focus on the work," I say. "We've got a lot to do."

"Of course, Stevie. I... I understand." He says the words, but his energy tells a different story. He's tormenting himself, hating himself for what he did, wishing things were different between us. He knows he hurt me, and now he's hurting himself.

And he has no idea how deeply I still care for him.

"It's not enough for you to *understand*, Kirin," I say. "I need you to be on the same page with me here. We can't fuck this up. We let things get out of hand that night in the stacks—both of us did. After everything that's happened, I just... It's all been a wake-up call for me. I don't want anyone else to have to go through what I went through with Phaines, or worse. Maybe it sounds crazy, but I *believe* the things I've seen in my visions and dreams. I believe they're coming. And I also believe we have the power to stop them. That means we have to put a hundred percent effort into this work right now. None of us can afford to be distracted—not even for a minute."

"Like you and Baz aren't distracted?" he grumbles, and a fresh wave of jealousy slams into me.

"You don't get a say in what I do with Baz or with anyone else for that matter. You lost that right the night you told me we're not allowed to fall in love."

We square off, both of us glaring at each other as if we're ten seconds from drawing weapons, when all I really want to do is forget everything I just said, run into his arms, and kiss him until he realizes how stupid he's being.

But before I can utter another word, a shrill voice sounds from the other side of the door.

"Yoo-hoo! Is anyone there?"

Janelle Kirkpatrick.

TWENTY-SIX

STEVIE

"Shit," I whisper. "I thought she didn't have access?"

"She doesn't. I made sure the—"

An alarm pierces the air, and magickal cages of red light descend down over the file cabinets.

"Stay here." Kirin bolts for the door and wrenches it open, punching a code into the keypad on the other side.

"Step back, ma'am," he shouts. "You need to get out of the scanner so I can disarm it."

Apparently, she follows his orders, because he punches another code into the pad and the alarm finally stops wailing.

"Goodness, such an ordeal! Are you Kirin Weber?" she asks, her tone dripping with condescension and annoyance. "I'm Janelle Kirkpatrick. The tech guy downstairs said you'd set me up with access to the archives—digital and physical. I wasn't expecting to be treated like a common criminal."

"Just security precautions, Mrs. Kirkpatrick. How did you get through the first door?"

"I scanned my hand and it let me through, but the man downstairs didn't say anything about this scanner monstrosity."

I can't see Janelle from my vantage point, but I can see Kirin's back, ramrod straight, his muscles tense. His protective energy is on high alert, his entire body filling up the doorway, blocking me from view.

Honestly, I'm not even sure how he can stand to be so close to her. That perfume of hers is overpowering, and there's something off about it—like it's gone bad or something. You'd think a woman with money could get herself a better scent.

Petty, I know. But sometimes it's the little joys of nitpicking your enemy that get you through the day.

"I can help you with your login credentials for the research databases," Kirin says, "but the headmistress didn't say anything about adding you to the security system here."

I know that's a lie, but it's a good one. It should buy us a little more time, at least.

"I'm the new librarian and archivist, Mr. Weber," she snipes. "I require complete access to the entire collection, *especially* the archives."

"Fair enough. But until we get that straightened out with Miss Trello, I can't do anything about it."

"Let me in, Mr. Weber."

"Sorry, Mrs. Kirkpatrick. If I let you walk through this

machine again without proper clearance, the magick will see you as a threat and trap you in place. We'll need tech support as well as three security mages to reverse the holding spell. The whole process could take hours."

"I'll wait."

"As the new librarian and archivist, I'm sure you have *much* more important things to do than stand inside a machine all day. We're operating at diminished capacity as it is. The headmistress is relying on you to pick up the slack, Mrs. Kirkpatrick. I'm sure you wouldn't want to disappoint her on your first week at work."

I bite back a smirk. *Go, Kirin.*

"What are you doing in there, anyway?" Janelle asks, and I can just picture her shrewd face, those red lips puckering, her beady eyes narrowing. "Are you alone?"

"I'm working with Starla Milan, one of our first-year students. She's shown an interest in ancient prophecy, and we're quite busy, so—"

"Oh, Starla!" Her energy rolls over Kirin's, barreling right into me. I feel the same annoyance apparent in her tone, but it's mixed with jealousy and vindictiveness, too. Still, I don't sense anything nefarious, which is crazy, considering what we saw on the video feed.

"Such a lovely girl," she continues. "I met her yesterday. I'd love to chat with her."

Kirin's protective energy skyrockets, anger edging in. "I'll be sure to let her know."

"Well, it's no trouble. Why don't I just wait until you're finished up? Outside the machine, of course."

"Starla has another class after this, and your time would probably be better spent speaking with the headmistress about your security access."

Neither of them speaks, and again I picture her lemon-sucking face. She's definitely trying to intimidate him, but Kirin doesn't back down.

That's what you get for trying to spy on me, bitch.

Eventually, she backs down. "I'll be in touch, Mr. Weber. It was nice to meet you. Hopefully, our next meeting will be a little more... productive."

"Good day, Mrs. Kirkpatrick." Kirin shuts the door in her face.

"Thanks for running interference," I say. "Janelle Kirkpatrick is the *last* person I want to talk to today. Or ever."

"I get it. That's the first time I've spoken with her, and I've already had my fill for life. That woman raised Baz?" Kirin shakes his head. "It's almost enough to make me feel bad for the guy."

"Kirin..."

He lets out a deep sigh. "You're right. I shouldn't... I crossed the line today. The comments about Baz, trying to get close to you... I've got no right. I fucked up today, I fucked up then, and no matter how hard I try to make things right, I just keep digging a hole." He reaches for my hands, thumbs brushing over my skin. "I'm sorry. It's just a word, but it's the only one I can say. Over and over, for as long as you need to hear it."

"I don't need to hear it. That's not how forgiveness

works. I need to feel it." I squeeze his hands, offering a small smile. "And I *do* feel it."

It's impossible not to—his deep regret is practically another person in the room.

"I know I screwed up—lost my chance at the best thing I ever..." He shakes his head, letting the rest of the thought fall away. "I know we can't go back to the way things were. Honestly, I'm just grateful you want to be friends at all. I mean... assuming you still want to be friends. I... Do you?"

"I *do*," I say, the last of my anger fizzling out. "More than anything."

"How is it that you're able to forgive me so easily? How can you forgive *any* of us?"

"That's the curse of the empath, I suppose." I release his hands and head back to the table, picking up the notebooks to lock back in their cabinets. "No matter how badly my brain wants me to hold a grudge, to hold on to anger, my heart won't let me. When I reach out for your energy, I can sense your intentions. I know you didn't mean to hurt me. None of you did."

"But I *did* hurt you. Badly. On multiple occasions."

"Don't get me wrong—I feel that pain," I say. "I still feel it, even now. Hurt, betrayal, sadness... I just can't turn it into long-term festering anger like some kind of emotional alchemist. My heart overrides it. That's not to say I forget, or that I'm okay with what happened—I'm not. Forgiveness doesn't mean accepting wrongful treatment or lies. It just means... Well, it just means I forgive you."

"Why do you call it a curse?" Kirin shakes his head, his

brow furrowed. "The capacity for forgiveness… it's a gift, Stevie. A rare one at that."

"It leaves me vulnerable. I'm the queen of second chances, and I've always liked that about myself—I believe everyone deserves another shot. But I also have to constantly guard against letting second chances become tenth chances, letting people take advantage of me. I have to constantly remind myself to confirm my first impressions. Like with Phaines, I didn't reach out for his energy because I allowed my first impressions of him to solidify. In my mind, he was a wise old mentor who wanted nothing more than to help me. If I'd been a little more discerning, I might've seen through it."

"I still think it's a gift," he says. "One with a few strings attached, maybe, but a gift nevertheless. I wish I could do that. Just let things go."

Kirin sighs, and I can't help but wonder if he's thinking about his sister. His family.

"I'm hardwired to forgive people," I say. "But not all people, for all hurts. So many of us just use the word 'sorry' like a spell—as if simply reciting it undoes all the damage. But like any spell, the word is no good if the intentions behind it aren't true."

"For what it's worth—and for lack of a better word—I'm truly sorry, Stevie. And my intention is to make it up to you, whatever it takes. Not so you'll give me another chance." He looks up and meets my eyes, his smile soft and sad. "Just so you'll stop hurting."

"I know." I take his hands, swallowing the knot of

emotion in my throat. Sadness and happiness, regret and hope, all of it tangled up in equal measure. With a tiny smile of my own, I whisper, "I just need a little time."

His smile turns a little brighter. "You continue to surprise me, Queen of Leaves."

We stand together like that for a few beats, looking into each other's eyes, each lost in our own thoughts.

I finally release his hands and gather up my stuff. Glancing at my phone, I say, "I'll check in with Ani later about searching for the Wand. Since he's fire-blessed, I'm thinking that's the object he'll have the strongest connection to."

"Good call. You going to Divination class now?"

"Yep. Maybe today I'll try to divine some good news for once." I laugh, heading for the door. Just before I exit, I turn back with one last smile. "And Kirin? Thank you."

"For what?"

"For making this my sanctuary again."

The smile on his face and the warmth of his energy are enough to carry me through the rest of the day.

That's the thing about forgiveness. When you mean it—when you truly mean it—it fills you both with the best kind of gift there is:

Hope.

ANSEL

It's four in the morning, the sky is the deep, predawn blue of Stevie's eyes, and I can't decide what's more exciting— the prospect of a sunrise hike to my favorite place in the world, or the fact that Stevie accepted the invite to join me.

When she emerges from the Iron and Bone dorms without Baz in tow, my day gets even better.

"Where's your slumber-party buddy?" I ask, doing my best to hide my elation.

Stevie blinks at me slowly, still halfway stuck in dreamland. Her wild curly hair is pulled into a messy bun, her face lined with sheet marks, cheeks pink from the chilly air, and I swear I've never seen anything so beautiful in my life.

"Just me today." She yawns and rolls her sleepy eyes, a sarcastic smile playing at her lips. "Don't look so disappointed, Ani."

"Hey, I get my favorite witch to myself for a *whole* day.

You can't blame a guy for being happy about that. We haven't hung out in forever."

"Forever, as in… a week?"

I press my hand to my heart and make exaggerated doe-eyes at her. "Starla Milan, even a day outside your enchanting presence feels like an eternity to my withering spirit."

"A little too early for confessing your undying love, Sunshine." She laughs, then smacks me in the chest. "But to answer your question, my slumber party buddy is still asleep. I tried to wake him, but he sleeps like the dead. Figured we'd be okay on our own, but if you really miss him that much, go ahead and try to get him up."

"Hard pass. Let's go."

We head down along the pathway back toward Flame and Fury. At this hour, the entire campus is asleep, no sounds but the soft chittering of the last of the night birds and a gentle breeze weaving lazily through the flowers.

"So this sleepover buddy thing," I say. "Is it just that? Or do you still have feelings for him?"

"Maybe? I don't know. I'm still confused. Is confused a feeling? Because I'm drowning in it."

"So Kirin's out of the equation now?"

"I didn't say that."

"But—"

"Hey." She holds up both hands, fluttering her fingers. "You see a ring on this finger?"

I grab her hand, pressing a quick kiss to her palm. "Which one? You've got ten of them."

"Plenty of room for everyone, then." She laughs as we continue down the path, but she doesn't let go of my hand, which is just fine by me.

"I have feelings for *both* of them," she says, "and I'm pretty sure they both know it, though we haven't gotten into any specifics yet."

"Does this mean you no longer think dating more than one guy is shady?"

"I never said dating more than one guy was shady. It's the fact that you guys are all friends that made me feel bad about it."

My heart quickens at the mention of 'you guys,' but I take a deep breath, let it get back to normal. Stevie's not talking about all of us. She's speaking in general.

"But I can't stop my feelings from feeling," she continues.

"True. Feelings gonna feel."

"All I can do is be honest with them, see where this goes."

"Hmm. Sounds like some advice a wise, dashing, incredibly amazing friend once gave you."

"Yeah? I wonder who that could be." She flashes me a smile that kick-starts my heart all over again, then links her arm in mine, resting her head on my shoulder as we continue our walk.

"Despite everything," she says, "I still love Kirin. He's sweet and compassionate, brilliant, thoughtful—well, when he's not being an ass. And Baz makes me feel... I don't know. Wild and uninhibited in the best possible way. He's got a tender side, too—one he hardly ever shows, which makes it all the more rewarding when it comes out. But beyond that? What happens next, what the hell it all means, how we figure this thing out together, I have no idea. Which way?"

She stops and looks up at me, her eyes wide and hopeful.

"Are you asking me to choose for you?" I ask. "Because whoever I pick, the other one will surely murder me in my sleep."

"The path, Ani!" She rolls her eyes again, nodding toward the lands behind Fire and Fury. I didn't realize we'd come so far already. "Which way?"

"Oh! Right. Follow me, my confused little Star."

I lead her along the pathway that will eventually take us up to the top of the Cauldron, the same place we had our picnic awhile back. Only this time, I get to show it to her at sunrise.

She has no idea the surprise she's in for.

"So tell me what the plan is," she says as we make our way up the rocky trail, our breathing become heavier as the landscape slopes upward.

"Well, assuming my theory holds water, if the Arcana objects *are*, in fact, hidden on campus, there's a good chance each one is located somewhere on the land that corresponds with its original element, most likely in a place that has some spiritual significance."

"So you think the wand is around the Cauldron?"

"It's the most spiritual place inside the Flame and Fury lands," I say. "So I thought it made sense to start there."

"Agreed. However, you still haven't explained why I had to wake up at four a.m. for this. Daylight is our friend, Ani. Caffeine is our friend, too, and I didn't even have time to make my tea."

"Fear not, sweet Star. I've taken care of everything." Pulling off my pack, I reach inside for the thermos of tea I brewed for just this occasion. "Nothing fancy like your magick brews, but I think it came out pretty good. Just your basic Irish Black."

She stops to unscrew the lid and take a sip, her eyes closing in pleasure behind a plume of steam. "Oh, Ani. I could kiss you."

"You *could*," I tease, one more flirty comment away from complete heart failure, "but then you'd *really* complicate your love life."

"Ooh, the L-word. So you're saying that one kiss from the fair ginger, and I'll fall hopelessly in love?" She passes the thermos back to me, flashing a cute smile. "Aren't *we* confident?"

Aren't we *dreaming*, is more like it.

Keeping my smile firmly in place, I close the thermos and drop it back in my bag. "In answer to your question, you had to wake up this early because I have a gift for you, and it can only be shared at this specific time."

I start up the path again, the top of the canyon rim coming into view.

"A gift? That's funny. I drew the Ace of Pentacles before I left this morning."

I return her wide smile, excitement building in my stomach. She's going to love this so much—I know it. "Perfect. Come on."

We find our same spot on the rim, and I spread out a blanket and pass her the tea and some breakfast goodies.

"What is it?" she asks, opening the container. "It's still warm."

"Fresh baked blueberry-banana bread."

"Oh my Goddess, Ani! Ace of Pentacles for the win."

"This isn't your gift. I mean, it's *a* gift, and it's for you, but that's not the main event."

I sit down next to her on the blanket, so close our shoulders brush, and the two of us look out across the wide canyon, the red pool at the bottom glittering like a dark jewel. The first orangey-pink hints of sunrise streak the sky.

"This is so beautiful," she says. "If we didn't have all this Arcana craziness to deal with, I think I'd resign from all my classes and just spend every day up here."

I offer a smile and take her hand. I've been up here so many times before, I can read every shade of orange in the sky, sensing exactly when the sun will ascend behind us.

"It's coming," I say softly, gesturing across the canyon, and she turns to look. "Wait for it... wait for it... wait... Now."

"Ani!" Stevie gasps as the first rays of sun hit the back rim, and suddenly the entire canyon before us ignites in a blaze of fire, as if the very rock itself has been lit by some god or goddess, destined to burn for eternity.

I will never, ever tire of this view.

But right now, I'm not looking at the Cauldron of Flame and Fury in all its red-gold glory.

I'm looking at the woman next to me, her mouth caught between surprise and awe and pure joy, tears of wonder streaking her cheeks.

"It's breathtaking," she breathes.

"It is," I say, not taking my eyes off her.

We stay like that for a long while, until the sun is over our shoulders and the canyon dims to its usual red-orange morning glow.

"The Ace of Pentacles," Stevie says. "That was my gift."

"I hope you liked it."

"Liked it?" Dashing away the tears, she leans in and presses a kiss to my cheek, the touch of which I'll feel forever. "No one has ever given me the sunrise before, Ani. I loved it."

"What a coincidence. I've never given anyone the sunrise before."

Her eyes narrow, her brows drawing close, as if she's trying to puzzle something out. But then she smiles again, and all is right in the world.

"Thank you," she says. "Not just for the sunrise. But for everything. For always making me laugh. And for understanding me—trying to, anyway. For not pushing me. For not making me feel weird for falling for more than one guy."

"You're talking to a fire-blessed, Stevie." I stand from the blanket and reach down to help her up. "As far as I'm concerned, the more the merrier."

"I think two is more than enough, though. Right?"

"Why limit yourself?" I haul her up a little too quickly, and she stumbles into me, stopping her fall with her hands on my shoulders.

Goddess, this woman... How the hell did she sweep into our lives so fast, so ferociously?

"Sorry!" Stevie giggles. "I lost my balance. Clearly I need more caffeine—Ani? You okay?"

She's still holding onto me, her face so close, her lips so delicate...

"Stevie, I..." I lose my words, lose myself in the glittering facets of her eyes. There's so much I want to know about her, to learn, and so much more I want to tell her about myself.

Starting with the fact that I'm crushing on her. Maybe more than crushing. The secret's been burning inside me for weeks.

We all agreed not to keep secrets about each other, but how can I possibly tell her I feel this way? That I want to claim one of those fingers of hers? Claim a place in her bed? Claim a place in her heart?

"Hey, you okay?" She cups my face, concern filling her eyes. "Ani?"

"Yeah, I just..." I blink, then pull back. Pull myself together. Give her a nice, bright, sunshiney smile. Because if

I don't, she's going to read it in my energy anyway, and I'm not quite ready for that.

"Just what?"

"Just… nothing. I'm good," I insist. Then, wiggling my brows, "Let's say we head down to the bottom, do a little exploring, and see if we can find this zombie-making wand before the Dark Arcana use it to usher in the end of the world. Sound like a plan?"

She laughs again, a sound that never fails to lift my spirits. "Only *you* could make stopping the apocalypse sound fun."

"It's a gift. Come on."

The trail that leads to the bottom of the Cauldron is steep and dangerous, but Stevie takes point, scrambling down the rocky terrain like a born mountain lion. By the time we reach the bottom, we're both hungry for a little more fuel, so we take a quick break for snacks and water, then spend the rest of the day scrambling up and down the canyon walls, crawling over every crack and crevice in search of anything even remotely resembling the Wand of Flame and Fury.

I'm not sure how many hours we spend down here, but as the sun travels from one side of the bowl to the other, and the two of us become more filthy and tired with every step, I'm pretty sure we've reached a dead end.

"I really thought we'd find something," I say, tossing the last water bottle to Stevie.

"We still might. It's just our first day out. We can't possibly cover every—Ani! She's here!" Stevie bounds across another rocky stretch toward an opening in the canyon wall we've already searched.

I jog to catch up. "Who?"

"The Princess of Wands!"

"Wait—*here* here?"

Stevie points to a spot between us, and I take a step back.

"Don't worry." Stevie laughs. "You're the one she likes best."

"Well, tell her I… I like her best, too." I peer at the space, but all I see is rock. "Is she saying anything?"

"No, just pointing inside the crevice. I think we need to go inside. Yes, she's nodding now."

"We've already checked it out."

"Not *in*, though. Look, it's wider down here." Stevie crouches down and moves aside a few big chunks of loose rock, revealing a larger opening. "We can totally fit."

Before I can stop her, she's securing her headlamp and dropping to her belly, scampering inside the dark crevice like a lizard. I've got no choice but to grab my headlamp and follow her in, hoping she meant what she said about the Princess liking me.

Otherwise, this could be a death trap.

"Let there be light!" She clicks on the headlamp, and I do the same.

We're inside a small chamber just large enough for the two of us to stand up without banging our heads on the ceiling. It's about five feet wide, maybe eight long, with no other obvious crevices or water sources.

"I don't see anything," she says, sweeping her light across the walls. "Do you?"

"I'm not sure. Check this out." I shine my light to show her. The walls are red, just like they are on the outside, but for a black streak stretching from the chamber floor to the ceiling.

"It looks scorched," she says, pressing her hand to the mark. "It feels funny, too. Like… tingly."

"Magick." I press my palms to the wall, immediately feeling the tingle. Seconds later, blue flames ignite in both hands. "Holy shit, the energy is so strong here. It's activating my fire magick without any effort on my part."

"We're getting close."

"But there's nothing here."

We comb through the darkness, running our hands over every inch of rock inside the cavern. All the magick seems to be concentrated along the scorched area, but there's no Wand.

"It's not here," I say.

"I'm not so sure." Stevie leans in close, running her hands over the mark. "Kirin thinks we'll need to recreate the spells from the Book of Shadow and Mists in order to reveal the locations. So maybe it *is* here, but we just can't see it."

"It would explain the spike in fire energy."

"And the Princess," she says. "I feel like she led us to this spot for a reason."

"There's another possibility, though."

Stevie sighs. "That someone beat us to it, and what we're feeling is just leftover energy."

Resigned to the fact that we're not going to find what we're looking for—not today, anyway—she gets back on her belly and leads us out.

Back in the waning daylight, we dust off our hands and take in our surroundings.

"It'll be dark soon," I say. "We should probably head back."

"Hey!" She pinches my cheeks, laughing. "None of that Frowny McBroodyFace stuff. This is a good thing, Ani."

"How so? We spent the whole day searching, with nothing to show for it."

"Not true. Look, whether it's just spelled or long gone, right now, this is the closest we've come to finding *anything*, and I'm choosing to take that as a good sign. Besides, you were right all along."

"About?"

"This. All of it." She spins around on her toes, her giddiness infectious. "It *is* kind of fun, being out here exploring with you. I feel like we're in our own special world."

"Just the two of us."

"Exactly. And I think…" Her eyes narrow, then widen, and she gasps. "Holy flying ballsacks! Look!"

"Okay," I say, turning toward the direction of her gaze. "But if there are *literal* flying ballsacks incoming, this apocalypse just dropped to a whole new level of—"

My words cut off at the sight before me. Swooping down from the sky, a great snowy owl lands on a ten-foot-high rock slab before us, peering down with his all-seeing golden eyes.

"Hello, my friend," Stevie says. "I've missed you."

The owl preens a bit, then lets out a single call that echoes around the bowl.

"He's magnificent," I say, a little star-struck, seeing him up close like this.

"Ani, I think we need to leave." Stevie's tone, happy and sweet just seconds ago, is tinged with alarm. "Generally, he only shows up when something bad happens."

I pull out my phone, but there's no service down here. The last time anyone would've been able to reach us was when we were still up on the rim. That was hours ago.

The owl regards us for another moment, then spreads his wings and takes flight, heading back in the direction of the dorms.

"We need to get home, Ani," Stevie says firmly. "Now."

TWENTY-EIGHT

STEVIE

The moment we reach the rim, a barrage of text messages hit both phones at the same time. Not bothering to check them, I dial Baz.

"Stevie, thank Goddess. We were just about to head out to the Cauldron to look for you guys. Ani still with you?"

"He's right here. What's wrong?"

"Just meet us back at Iron and Bone as soon as you can. Everyone's here."

Alarm spikes in my gut. "What happened?"

"There was another attack."

"Oh my Goddess! Where?"

"Just get here, Stevie. And watch your backs." He disconnects the call, and I grab Ani's hand, both of us hauling ass back to Iron and Bone. By the time we hit the front doors, we're both panting and sweating. But despite the grime, the moment we step into the building, Baz is there, wrapping me up in a crushing hug.

"You fucking scared the shit out of me," he breathes into my hair, his heart banging against his chest, straight into mine. He reaches over and grabs Ani's shoulder, squeezing tight. "Both of you."

"I told you last night we'd be out all day," I say. "And you wouldn't wake up this morning."

"I know, I just… All this shit just went down, and I couldn't reach you guys."

I pull out of his tight embrace. "Tell us what happened."

Baz closes his eyes, pulling me tight once again. Just when I'm about to pass out from the force of it, he lets go, grabbing my hand and opting to crush my fingers instead. "Come on. Everyone's waiting inside."

We follow him into the Iron and Bone common room, the buzz audible even before we reach the entrance. I spot Doc and Kirin immediately, but there are others here, too—Kelly Maddox and Professor Broome. Kirin's sister, Casey, and her fellow agent, James Quintana. Even Isla and Nat are huddled together by the fireplace, the look of worry in their eyes sending a bolt of fear to my heart.

"Stevie!" Isla gasps, and the girls rush forward to greet me, nearly tackling me with a double-hug that's only slightly less painful than Baz's.

Kirin and Doc both give me a once-over, their faces pulled tight with worry.

"Everyone okay?" Doc asks, unable to hide his energy. It washes over me in alternating waves of concern and relief. "No trouble at the Cauldron?"

"We're fine," I say. "What happened? Why is everyone here?"

"I called Isla and Nat when we couldn't reach you," Kirin says. "I wanted to see if they'd heard from you. Isla was with Professor Broome at the time."

"I was having trouble with my dream potion," Isla explains. "We were in the classroom trying to figure it out."

"When I heard what happened," Professor Broome says, "I called Kelly."

Professor Maddox offers a kindly smile. "And I drew the Three of Pentacles crossed by the Nine of Wands this morning," she says with her usual mystical flare, "so when Professor Broome told me what happened, I knew we had to be here."

A muscle in Doc's jaw ticks, and he folds his arms across his chest. I know he was hoping to keep things under wraps, but clearly, that's no longer an option.

"Stevie, have a seat." Doc gestures for the girls and me to take the seats by the fireplace. The three of us crowd into one chair, Isla and Nat basically sitting on my lap.

"Nice to see you again, Miss Milan." Casey takes the other chair, attempting a smile. It glows in the firelight, but no amount of warmth can temper the icy tension in her energy. "Though I wish it were under better circumstances."

"Please tell me no one died," I say, my voice breaking.

"No one died." Casey sighs. "But I'm afraid we've suffered a number of setbacks tonight. Earlier this evening, a third-year witch was attacked en route to her magickal combat class, taken completely by surprise. Shortly thereafter, a graduate mage was attacked outside Blood and Sorrow's Deep Dive Bar and Grill. One hour later, a group of three students reported suspicious activity out by the River. They claim someone wearing a dark, hooded robe attempted to stab them with some sort of ritual blade, but when the perp saw there were three of them, he took off into the woods. Agent Eastman and a few of our security mages are investigating, but we don't have any leads yet."

"Is everyone all right?" I ask. "Were they hurt?"

"Physically, they're fine. None of the bodily injuries were extensive—mostly just scraped knees from falling during the attacks."

"Was it him?" I ask.

Casey knows *exactly* which *him* I'm referring to. "There's nothing in any of the witness statements to make us think it was Phaines."

"But you haven't ruled him out," Kirin says.

"We haven't ruled *anyone* out." This from Agent Quintana, looking supremely uncomfortable at having to speak in front of this little mini-crowd. "Not at this stage."

"You said none of the bodily injuries were extensive," I say, a new flicker of dread working its way through my insides. "What other kinds of injuries are there?"

It's a long beat before anyone speaks again, and when the fire pops behind us, I'm just about ready to crawl out of my skin.

"What other injuries?" I press.

"Well..." Casey glances at Agent Quintana, who nods

stiffly. Meeting my gaze again, she lowers her voice and says, "We didn't want to share this particular detail, so I must ask for your complete discretion. All of you."

The group nods our assent.

"The three students at the River are reporting no anomalies. But both students who were physically attacked tonight—as well as the student from Monday's attack—are missing chunks of hair." She closes her eyes and shakes her head, and I know the bad news is only just beginning. "All three of them are now reporting a total loss of magick."

The collective gasp in the room tells me that this is the first the agents have shared this particular detail.

"How is that possible?" Doc asks. "I've heard of muting spells, but no magick at all?"

Professor Broome and Professor Maddox exchange a worried glance.

"There are certain spells," Professor Broome says. "Dark enchantments. The ingredients are quite rare, some of them even thought to be legends. But if those legends are true, then yes, it is possible to completely strip a witch or mage of their innate magick."

"Is it reversible?" I ask.

Her silence is all the answer I need.

"Well, that's just... horrifying," Nat says. The three of us squeeze closer together.

"Headmistress Trello is working with them now," Casey continues, "trying to lead them through the guided meditation used to connect with magickal affinities—the same one you all participated in when you first entered the Academy.

But so far, none of the affinities have appeared. The students are showing absolutely zero aptitude for magick. It's like they're just… regular humans again."

"I'd like to recommend that all students begin wearing protective amulets," Professor Broome says. "Hematite, black tourmaline, anything like that. Warding and crystal grids for the dorms is a good idea, too."

"Agreed," Professor Maddox says. "And I want you all to continue strengthening your connection to Tarot. Doing so will help strengthen your intuition."

"In the meantime," Casey says, "everyone must continue exercising extreme caution. Limit nighttime travel, don't go anywhere alone, report any suspicious activity immediately. Don't try to convince yourselves you're being paranoid. Better to be overly cautious than dead."

"Or de-witch-ified," Isla says with a shiver.

"So is Trello calling another assembly on Monday?" I ask. "To let everyone know about the attacks?"

"I was wondering about that too," Professor Broome says.

Casey shifts uncomfortably in her chair. "The headmistress feels that we should hold off on announcing any of the attacks until we have more information."

"More victims, you mean," Baz says.

"We're just trying to keep everyone safe, Mr. Redgrave."

"I'm with Baz on this one," I say. "Want to keep us safe? Keep us informed about what's going on."

"That's what we're doing right now," Casey says.

"Keep *everyone* informed, not just this little inner circle."

I glare at her, refusing to back down. "The only reason you're telling us at all is because Kirin's your brother, and the rest of us here are connected by less than two degrees of separation."

"Stevie, that's not… We're doing our best."

"Tell me I'm wrong," I press.

She glares right back at me, but ultimately lowers her eyes. "You're not wrong."

"We don't want to cause a panic," Quintana says—the party line.

"So you think keeping us in the dark is a better bet?" I ask. "With all due respect, Agents, we're not children afraid of the bogeyman here. We're witches and mages attending an elite magickal academy. Show us some trust and faith."

"How do you propose we do that?" he asks.

"Tell *everyone* about the attacks. The hair. The magick. Students need to stick together at all times, to be hyper-vigilant, and to learn how to defend ourselves as well as each other. You want to avoid mass panic, but what's the alternative? You're causing the opposite—mass not-my-problem. Other than the people in this room and the victims themselves, most people aren't taking this seriously because they don't realize how serious it actually is."

The agents exchange a chagrined glance.

"I stand with Stevie on this one," Professor Maddox says from behind my chair, giving my shoulder a reassuring squeeze. "Knowledge is power, and right now, we need to arm everyone with as much knowledge as possible."

"You make good points," Casey finally says. "All of you.

But we are limited by what Anna Trello believes is the best way to keep the Academy safe. She's the higher authority here, so for now, we follow her lead."

"Then we need to talk to her," Professor Broome says. "Fluffy reassuring speeches about coming together as a family sound really pretty at a funeral, but if we want to prevent those funerals in the first place, we need a plan of attack."

"Anna Trello isn't going to be of much use on this one," Doc says. "She's... set in her ways."

"Then we need to figure out a way around her, Dr. Devane," Professor Maddox says, her voice low. "Red tape, rules, regulations... Our job security is not worth a single student's life."

"Or their magick," Professor Broome adds.

The agents consider our words, and I know the moment we've won them over—at least partially; Casey's energy shifts from tense and guarded to resigned.

"If you want information..." She rises from her chair, then crosses the room to whisper something in Agent Quintana's ear.

He nods and clears his throat, then steps forward, not meeting anyone's eyes.

"None of this has been reported in the mainstream press," he says, "but outside the bubble of this academy, eleven more witches and mages have been executed in half as many days. Protests and counter-protests are tearing the country apart. Violent crimes, looting and rioting, destruction... Chaos is running rampant—both magickal and non-magickal. New York City will be under full military control by six a.m. tomorrow morning. The president is considering military requests from Los Angeles and Chicago as well, and it's only a matter of time before the rest of our cities follow suit. People on both sides are terrified, and a scared populace is a dangerous populous."

Ani shakes his head. "So we've got dark magick thugs inside campus, the world going to shit outside campus… Where do we even begin?"

Kirin puts his arm around him. On his other side, Baz and Doc draw closer. Seeing them like that, the brotherhood —*my* brotherhood—gives me more hope than I thought possible just now.

"Agent Eastman is going to recommend to the head-mistress that a curfew be implemented and off-campus travel be forbidden to all but faculty," Quintana says, "and that even faculty travel be limited. Faculty who live off-campus will be asked to relocate to any available housing inside the Academy boundaries as soon as possible."

"Asked or ordered?" Doc asks.

"Asked," Quintana says. "For now, it will be voluntary, but highly encouraged. I can't promise anything beyond that."

"It's for your own safety, Dr. Devane," Casey says, but her attempts to smooth things over fall flat.

There are a few more questions after that, but in the end, the agents have shared all they're willing to share. As more students begin to trickle into the common room after a night of drinking or hanging out with friends, our meeting finally breaks up.

"I'm going to walk the professors back to the Promenade," Kirin says. "I'll check in with you guys later."

"I'll take Isla and Nat back to their dorms," Ani says.

"Nat's going to stay with me at Blood and Sorrow," Isla says. Then, smiling up at me, "Want to join us for a sleepover?"

I glance over at Baz, his eyes blazing with a question, and I nod, my lips quirking into a smile despite the craziness of the night.

"I've got her covered," he says.

"I bet you do," Nat mutters, and I elbow her in the ribs, both of us trying to stifle our smiles.

After I say goodnight to the professors and the girls, Doc approaches me in front of the fireplace, his mouth drawn tight.

"You okay?" I ask him.

"I was about to ask you the same question." He's close now, his voice low and sultry before the crackling flames. "When we couldn't reach you earlier, I thought…"

"I was fine."

"I know. I just automatically feared the worst. It is, as the kids say these days, kind of a *thing* with me."

"Wait." I can't hold back my smile. "Did Dr. Seriouspants Devane just make a… a joke? Like, an actual ha-ha-funny joke?"

He gives me a real grin in return, softening the lines

around his mouth. "Don't get used to it. And don't call me Dr. Seriouspants. I prefer Dr. Serioustrousers."

"Wow, you're in rare form tonight. If you're trying to soften me up, the answer is *no*, I'm not helping you move. You're supposed to ask the friend with the pickup truck, not the one with the broomstick."

"Noted." His grin finally fades, and he puts a hand on my shoulder, warm and reassuring, his dark eyes shining. "We'll get through this, Stevie. Together. I promise."

I cover his hand with mine and nod. "I promise too, Doc. Brothers, remember?"

"Brothers."

"Good. Now get the hell out of here before one of your colleagues sees us talking like this and your infallibly proper reputation is ruined."

Doc laughs and turns to leave, but not before I catch his last retort.

"If anyone ever had the power to ruin me, Miss Milan, it's you."

TWENTY-NINE

STEVIE

After Saturday's stunning outdoor adventure with Ani, spending my Tuesday morning cooped up in the archives feels more like detention than research, despite the relaxing beach cottage glamour. But the attacks this weekend have only served to underscore the urgency of our mission—a mission that keeps expanding at every possible turn.

We must find the Arcana objects.

We must protect said objects.

We must figure out the Dark Magician's plans.

We must devise a counter-plan.

We must inform and protect our fellow students and faculty.

We must sharpen our magickal skills—especially mine, the weakest link in the Brotherhood when it comes to active powers.

Oh, and we must translate Mom's prophecies—the original mission still firmly in place, more important than ever.

There's a word for this.

Futile.

Kirin's downstairs in a meeting with Trello and Kirkpatrick, still working out the so-called kinks in her security clearance—kinks Kirin planted himself. All alone in the archives, surrounded by stacks of my mother's cryptic words and my own attempts at understanding them, I try to stay positive, but despair hangs heavy in the air.

I rest my forehead against the cool wooden table and shut my eyes.

Exhaustion hangs heavy in the air, too.

"Stevie? You okay?"

"Stevie's not home right now. Please leave a message." I lift my head, smile at Kirin as he enters the room. "How was your meeting?"

He glances at the ceiling and purses his lips. "The phrase 'circle-jerk' comes to mind. The good news is I managed to buy us another couple of days."

"How'd you swing that?"

"Easy." He takes his usual seat across from me. "I let it slip that you and I were working on Tarot Language and Symbology and that the Farinkhoff manuscripts should not be disturbed. Naturally, Janelle headed straight for them."

"Farinkhoff manuscripts? Never heard of them."

"Neither have I, but Janelle will be busy looking for books that don't exist for quite some time. Such is the price for being a busybody."

"You're the *best* kind of evil."

Kirin smiles, holding my gaze across the table. Things

have gotten better between us—easier. He hasn't tried to kiss me again, which is… respectable. Disappointing, but respectable. And probably for the best. But sometimes, in the quiet moments between translations and theories, I look at him across our table and can't help but wish he'd just stand up, shove all the books and priceless manuscripts to the floor, throw me down on the table, and—

"What about you?" he asks. "Any luck?"

Blinking away the fantasy, I reach for the notebook I'd been working on, grateful for some other place to force my gaze. Because if I spend one more minute staring into those eyes, I'm pretty sure I'll throw *him* down on the table.

"Listen to this." I flip to the last page and read the latest prophecy of doom:

> *Illusion fills the offered space*
> *Cracked and broken, like its face*
> *Beware the raven's false pretense*
> *It's your doom the heart portends*

> *A spark to cast the flame of life*
> *A blade to cut through mist and strife*
> *A cup to know your heart's desire*
> *A coin to pay to build the pyre*

> *What rises shall fall*
> *What lives shall burn*
> *When magick is free*
> *The darkness returns*

"I've been staring at *that* uplifting passage for two straight hours." I close the notebook and put my head back on the table. "I know this is important, but seriously, Kirin. My eyes are starting to bleed, and if I don't take a break soon, I swear I'll be speaking in rhyme."

"In that case." Kirin stands up, his grin mischievous. "Why don't we get out of here for the rest of the day? Get some fresh air, go out and play?"

"No." I cover my head and groan. "No, please tell me you didn't just—"

"Your eyes are tired, your brain is mush. What better time to get off your tush?"

"Stop! Now my ears are bleeding too!"

"Air magick awaits, and practice you must. 'Cause what if this prophecy thing is a bust?"

"Kill me. Kill me now."

"Spend too much time with your nose in the books, and everyone will... give you... dirty looks?" His grin falls away. "Okay, no idea what happened there. I swear I had it."

"Oh, Kirin. Let's hope your air magick game is stronger than your rhymes."

"I've got some pretty dope-ass rhymes in my collection. I'm just not ready to share them yet."

"Thank the Goddesses for that." Laughing, I stare at the stack of notebooks teetering between us. "This feels... impossible. I mean, I know it isn't. I know we have to keep working on it. But it's..."

"I mean it, Stevie." He comes around to my side and

holds out a hand. "All of this will be here tomorrow. Let's get out of here. Just for today."

"You know what this is, right?" I glance up at him and smile. "This is your Dirty Dancing moment."

"What's a Dirty Dancing moment?"

I press a hand to my chest, aghast. "Kirin Weber! Tell me you've seen Dirty Dancing?"

"I've… heard of it? I think? It's the movie about the baby in the corner, right?"

"Did you grow up in seclusion?" I give him a brief rundown of the plot. "Then there's all this frustration and sexual tension and Baby can't learn the dance moves, and she's having a meltdown about how they've been cooped up inside, then Johnny's all, hey, let's get out of here. So he takes her to this waterhole to practice, and they end up getting all sexy and wet and the whole thing is just epic."

"Clearly, my film education leaves much to be desired. But if you say so, then yes, this is my Dirty Dancing moment." He's still holding out his hand in invitation. "Let's get out of here."

"Just so you know," I warn, taking his hand, "we're *not* getting wet. Not unless you buy me lunch first."

I laugh, but then my words catch up to my ears, and my cheeks burn. "Anyway," I blurt, "love the idea, can't wait, let's go! I could totally use some."

"Wait—lunch? Or getting wet?"

"Air, Kirin. Air!"

Kirin shakes his head, but he's totally smiling. "All right, Queen of Leaves. I know just the place."

THIRTY

STEVIE

Kirin and I ditch the library and head outside, straight for one of the bike racks. The instant my feet hit the pedals, all the stress just melts away.

"You good to go hard?" he asks.

I stifle a laugh, imagining what Baz would do with an opening like that, then nod. "Please. My muscles are absolutely *screaming* for a workout."

"Don't say I didn't warn you." He flashes another mischievous smile, and then he's off, disappearing down the path toward Breath and Blade.

Following his lead, I push hard and fast, gobbling up the distance across the trails, the campus passing by in a blur. It feels so good to get outside and do something physical, it's not long before I'm pedaling like my life depends on it, panting like a dog, laughing the entire way.

The thigh-burn has never felt so good.

Kirin doesn't slow down until we reach the sandstone

Towers of Breath and Blade, and that's only because the trails through the spires are narrow and twisty, too difficult to maneuver in speed-racer mode. He leads me out so far that the climate-controlled warmth of campus fades away, leaving cool, misty air in its place.

When he reaches what I assume is our destination, he rides around to face me, and we both plant our feet, keeping hold of the bikes. Mist immediately surrounds us, a thin gossamer curtain that cools my skin. It reminds me of the mist in my nightmares, only—you know—not creepy.

"What are we doing?" I ask, giddy with anticipation and a runner's high I haven't felt in ages.

"Air Magick 101," he says. "Don't worry—we'll start you off with something easy. But first, a quick lesson in Tarot fundamentals."

"Did Professor Maddox put you up to this?"

"No, but if you do well today, I'll see if I can talk her into some extra credit." Kirin grins. The fresh air seems to have loosened him up, too. "First, air magick is a combination of physics and mental acuity, much like the corresponding suit of swords. But like the swords, it can also be evasive, and can make you work for it."

"How so?"

"Swords energy is one of clarity and illumination, but often that illumination lies hidden just beneath the surface. We need to look beyond the obvious. Explore. Be willing to challenge ourselves. Walk into the mist and make new pathways." He leans forward and blows, swirling the mist before his face, making a momentary space.

"Okay, I'm with you so far."

"Good. Now hop back on the bike and follow me—I want to show you something."

I put my foot on the pedal, ready to push off.

"And Stevie?" Kirin grins with new mischief. "Hold on tight, okay?"

Before I can ask him why, he takes off down the path, swallowed up by the mist.

Not wanting to be left behind, I hop on my bike and zoom after him, the thick air condensing on my face. I've got just enough visibility to see the path a few feet ahead, but nothing more. Kirin has vanished.

"Kirin!" I call.

"Hold on," comes the distant reply. Then, out of nowhere, the pedals on my bike spin faster and faster, all resistance gone.

Suddenly, I'm floating a foot above the pathway. Two feet. Five feet. Ten.

"Kirin!" I shout, gripping the handlebars tight. "Something's happening! *Kirin!*"

"Right here," he says, appearing out of the mist ahead like an apparition, smiling as he zooms back toward me.

"You're doing this?" I ask, laughing. "But… What is it?"

"I told you. Air magick, lesson one."

"I thought you were going to start me off with something small!"

"Yes, *you're* going to start with something small. But I want to show you what's possible first. So for now, just sit back and enjoy the ride."

I do as he instructs, my bike sailing through the air after his, curving and looping around the spires, dipping low, only to race back up again. It's like a rollercoaster, only without friction, without limits.

"Remember, Stevie," he says, coming up behind me. "Everything is energy. Magick is just harnessing that energy and directing it where you want it to go for a desired outcome. Right now, I'm directing air molecules to push us around. To make us fly."

"This feels incredible!" I've flown before—through the energy of my owl familiar—but this is so different. This is me, in my real body, sailing through the sky on a magick bike.

"Close your eyes," Kirin says.

"I can't—I don't want to miss anything!"

"You won't. You'll just be experiencing it differently." He waits for me to obey, then says, "Now, I want you to really focus. Think about the air around you. Really feel it on your skin, in your hair, in your eyelashes. Feel it caressing your body, lifting you. Feel the molecules shifting around you as you move through them."

I focus all of my senses on the air—the coolness of it on my skin, the water droplets in the mist, the dusty desert scent. I hear it rushing past my ears, taste it on my lips, feel it filling my lungs and blowing back out again.

By the time I open my eyes, we're descending, touching down on the ground as soft as feathers landing on snow.

"So," Kirin says, his cheeks red from the cool air, "How did I do? Did my Dirty Dancing moment pass muster?"

"Are you kidding me? Your Dirty Dancing moment is now solidified as a top-five experience of my life. Maybe even top-three. And way better than your rhyme game."

Kirin laughs, then hops off his bike, gesturing for me to follow. We lean the bikes against one of the spires, then walk out to a clearing at the center of several looming towers. The ground here is littered with small, fist-sized rocks. Kirin scoops up two, passing one over to me.

"Remember what I said about feeling the air," he says, placing the stone in his palm and stretching his hand out. "Picture all those air molecules coming together, pushing the stone up from the bottom, lifting it out of your hand. If it helps, you can call on the energy of any swords card that feels particularly relevant. I usually picture the Ace."

He glances down at the rock, and seconds later, it levitates from his hand, then drops back down. "Now you try."

I follow his instruction to the letter, but instead of the Ace, I call on my Princess of Swords, imagining her standing here with her magick sword, commanding the rock to rise, rise, rise. At first nothing happens, but Kirin just stands there patiently, his mere presence encouraging me not to give up.

I close my eyes, focusing on the feel of the rock in my hand, the weight of it, the coolness, the rough texture. I imagine my princess ordering an army of air molecules to rush in and lift it.

And then, suddenly, the rock begins to tremble.

I open my eyes, laughter bubbling out of me.

"Kirin! I'm doing it!" I watch as the rock lifts off my

palm, floating in the air before me. It's a little wobbly, but it's there, levitating. "Oh my Goddess! I'm doing it! I'm doing it!"

Tears spring to my eyes. It's such a little thing, but it's *my* little thing. My magick.

"Yes." He steps closer, his energy beaming with pride. "You are."

The rock finally falls to the ground, and I rush at Kirin, overcome with happiness and warmth and a new sense of possibility that wasn't there just moments ago—not even when he took me flying. He scoops me into his arms and spins me around, laughing at my sudden outburst of affection and glee.

"The more you practice, the more natural it will become." He sets me on the ground, my head spinning, my hands tingling with leftover energy. "Remember, it's already part of you. You're just learning to recognize the subtle feel of different energies, and the feel of your own magick coursing inside you."

I crouch down to grab another rock to try again, but movement on top of one of the shorter spires behind him catches my eye.

"Kirin!" I get to my feet, waving at our new visitor.

Kirin merely grins. "Yes, the owl has been watching you for some time now."

"Do you think he's warning us about another attack?"

"Not this time. It's a function of your magick—it calls to him. Especially when you're working with the air element —owls are associated with knowledge, like the swords, as well as with literal air, like all birds. The more you use your air magick, the more you tune in with it, the stronger your bond with your avian familiar will be."

I pick up another rock—a larger one this time, about twice as big as the last—and go through the process again. Despite the new heft, this time, the rock lifts almost immediately.

From his perch on the spire, the owl seems impressed. At least, that's how I'm choosing to interpret his stately demeanor.

"Look at you, showing off," Kirin teases, giving my shoulder a playful nudge.

"A rock today, a boulder tomorrow."

"Why not?" Kirin's smiling at me again, his warm hand firm on my shoulder. "I'm so proud of you, Stevie. You're picking this up so quickly. It took me a month to do what you've just accomplished in five minutes."

"Really?"

Kirin nods.

"In that case, maybe *I* should teach Air Magick 101."

"Maybe you should."

He's still smiling, locking me in his warm gaze, when out of nowhere my big dumb mouth goes, "Why?"

He cocks his head curiously, but his smile is already faltering, even as I shake my head in a desperate search for the undo button.

We both know what I'm asking, and it's not about teaching Air Magick.

"You want to know why this—us—why it can't

happen," he says softly. "Why I told you I destroy every-thing I touch."

My first thought is to deny it. To drop it. To stop prying and let him off the hook, go back to the part where we're laughing as we make rocks and bicycles fly.

But after everything the two of us shared, if Kirin owes me anything, it's an explanation. So instead, I take a deep breath, steeling myself for the answer, and nod.

Behind him, my owl leaps from his perch, spiraling upward until he's no more than a dot in the mist... And then he's gone.

"I need to tell you more about the Arcana," Kirin says, resigned. "You need to know about our gifts." When he meets my eyes again, all the proud, playful energy dissi-pates, replaced with a heaviness that nearly presses the air from my lungs. "And you need to know about our curses."

STEVIE

We walk deeper into the lands of Breath and Blade, where the terrain turns rockier and the Towers grow even taller and more magnificent. The mist has thickened too, cocooning us in our own hazy, eerie world, the rocky spires twisting upward like dark red fingers grasping for the sun.

"Tarot cards—both minors and majors—contain multitudes," Kirin says. "Light, dark, and every shade in between. Some people see reversed cards as merely the opposite of the upright interpretation, but that's highly limiting. A reversed Ten of Cups, for example, doesn't necessarily mean loneliness or family strife—the opposite of joy and fulfillment. Depending on the question and the other cards in the spread, it could just as easily suggest a need to free yourself from a toxic relationship or a time for seeking inner joy rather than connection with others."

"Or a message that we're blocking some of that upright energy and need to open up to it."

"Precisely. Now, consider it in terms of Arcana witches and mages. If the cards themselves contain multitudes, you can imagine what happens when you take those meanings—that incredibly complex magick—and apply it to a person, with all of our human contradictions and frailties and hopes and emotional experiences. With our unique personalities amplifying the magick, for better or worse."

"Everything seems a lot more intense when you put it that way."

"It is. Take Baz. As The Devil with an earth magick affinity, he's very much rooted to the sensory and material realm. His energy is focused heavily on pleasure, on the physical senses of the body—taste and touch especially. The man can cook too, though he doesn't let that secret out very often. In its positive aspects, The Devil energy brings with it a wealth of sensual pleasures and a deep appreciation for life in its human form—for our experience in these bodies, exploring everything our material realm has to offer. But the darker aspects of his energy can sometimes lead to obsessions, to prioritizing earthly pleasures and experiences at the expense of all else—the emotional bonds associated with water, the pursuit of knowledge associated with air, and the creative and spiritual energy of fire."

"But what would make him give in to the dark side, so to speak?"

"It's not so much giving in as it is a constant balancing act. The potential for darkness is always within him, but the outcome is always going to be influenced by his personality, his choices and actions, his relationships, his magickal practice. Even something as simple as whether he gets enough sleep the night before—all of that can influence the manifestation of his Devil magick."

Talking about pleasure and sleep and Baz sends a flood of heat through my body, and I look away, losing myself in the mist swirling before us.

"So what about Ani?" I ask, eager to move on to less awkward ground. "How does his Sun energy work?"

"As the Sun arcana with a fire affinity, Ani's energy is always going to shine bright—brighter than anyone else in the room. You know how he has that uncanny ability to put people at ease and make everyone laugh?"

I grin. Just thinking about my favorite ginger brings a smile to my face.

"See, that right there?" Kirin points at my face, returning my smile. "That's the Sun energy. Ani will always seek to make people happy. He's adventurous and free-spirited, creative, easy to talk to, and *way* more fun than the rest of us."

I nudge him with my elbow. "Don't sell yourself short, Genius Boy. You've got your fun moments too. I mean, you *did* take me flying on bikes today."

"True. But with Ani... He doesn't just do fun things or have fun moments. He *is* fun. He's light and joy. Laughter. All of it."

"Yeah, I can't imagine he even *has* a dark side."

"It's not dark in the way we think of the Magician now. But as much as Ani has a gift for humor and childlike fun, he can sometimes be naïve, or use that happier side of himself to mask what's hurting him. He also has a hard time taking things seriously. That's the nature of bright-side people in general, because they always want to see the best in every person and situation. But with Ani—the Sun energy—it's just a lot more intense. If he were to give in to his inner darkness, it could very easily lead to vanity and shallowness. Maybe even deception. Add in the fire aspect, and Ani could turn to a lifelong pursuit of passion and pleasure without the underlying joy—similar to the Devil energy in that respect."

"And Doc?" I ask.

"Cass is The Moon arcana and a water-blessed mage. He can tap into emotions, read people and situations, feel and sense things most others can't. Well, *you* probably can, considering your empathic skills. But Cass is very attuned to emotional energies. I know he calls his specialty mental magicks, but really it's emotional magicks. Manipulation happens at the emotional level, not the logical one. Fear, love, desire—it's all emotion."

"Yeah, I can see that."

"Doc, as you call him, challenges us to see what's beneath—to search for deeper truths and meaning, to delve into the depths of our own unconscious realms, to trust our inner voices. But he also has a tendency to lose himself in his own emotions. That's the danger with the Moon energy. It can sweep you away, pull you under, make you lose sight of what's real and what's fantasy. Cass struggles with walking that line sometimes. He's..." Kirin sighs, and I can tell he's weighing how much to reveal. Despite how close I feel to the guys now, I'm still the new kid on the block, and intimacy—physical or emotional—has to be earned.

"It's okay, Kirin." I place my hand on his arm. "You don't need to share Doc's personal demons. That kind of thing doesn't fall under the no-secrets clause."

"I know. It's just… There's still so much for you to learn. I'm trying to give you an overview without totally over-whelming you, and right now, we're still just scratching the surface. A lot of this you'll have to feel your way through, figure it out on your own."

"I'm not on my own, though," I remind him, linking my arm through his. "I've got you guys."

"And we've got you," he says. "Which makes all the darkness more bearable."

We walk a few minutes in silence, the mist swirling around us, tiny droplets of water condensing on my hair. Sensing he's not quite ready to share the details of his own Arcana darkness yet, I decide to bring up my mother instead.

"That day you guys told me about the Brotherhood," I say, "Cass said my mother was part of it. That she was The World."

Kirin nods. "The World is the final card on the Fool's Journey, the last of the Majors. It holds an energy of comple-tion and total fulfillment that I'm sure fueled your mother's passion and dedication to her work. It likely allowed her to see all possibilities, before and after, and to interpret the prophecies with this endless, cyclical nature in mind. But the end of one journey contains the seeds of new beginnings, and I believe that your mother may have succumbed to a darker aspect of this—a feeling that her work was never complete, that she couldn't risk tethering herself to a fixed point in time or space—not even for your father or you. I know some believe she went mad, but it's so much more complex than that. I think she just… She lost herself. Lost all sense of time. Lost her place in the human world, her feeling that she even belonged in it. And even though she ultimately left the Academy and her work behind, a part of her soul likely remained here, still seeking, still endlessly searching."

"Part of that makes me so sad. But it also brings me comfort—you know? Just thinking she's here with me. Does that make sense?"

"She *is* here with you, Stevie. Not just when you see her in your dreams, but every time you open her notebooks. You're touching the same pages she touched, reading over words and passages inspired by her own Tarot mythology and linguistic symbology. Your mother didn't simply translate messages she received from the Tarot. She *interpreted* them—put her own personal stamp on them. You're reading prophecies influenced by her deepest feelings, her beliefs, her hopes and dreams, her wishes, her fears, all of it. Writers—all writers—they leave something of themselves on every page, Stevie. I don't believe it gets any more personal than that."

Warmth rises in my chest as I take in Kirin's words. He's right. I feel Mom with me even now, walking by my side through the strange, otherworldly landscape of Breath and Blade.

There was a time when the very thought of my parents would send me to my knees, unable to shoulder the weight of grief. But every day I spend at the Academy, every day I get closer to my own magick, I feel that weight shift. Lessen. Before I enrolled here, I never imagined that the heaviness of loss would one day fade, even a little. That a smile over a happy memory could turn my tears of loss into tears of gratitude—gratitude that for all the souls in the universe, across all the eons of existence, I was blessed with even a single moment with my parents.

"Thank you," I whisper, and Kirin nods, a new understanding passing between us. Through his work on the prophecies, Kirin brought my mother back to life. Back to *my* life. That will always connect us.

We find a flat, dry patch of rock at the base of a thick spire and take a break, sitting down next to each other to share a bottle of water and some trail mix.

"I understand what you're saying about the light and dark aspects of Arcana energies," I say, popping a handful of peanuts and M&Ms into my mouth. "And sure, maybe there's always a little danger inherent in the darkness. But still… You called it a *curse*, Kirin. None of this sounds like a curse."

"The curse isn't that the light and the dark exist within us—that's just our nature. The curse is that we will always be drawn to both, and anything can happen—at any point —to flip the switch. Humans in general have a hard time staying on the right side of morality—even deciding what the right side *is*. Add magick to the mix—especially magick as powerful as that of Arcana witches and mages—and each of us is a walking nuke. The Dark Arcana are playing out our own worst-case scenarios right now." He turns to face me, his eyes turning serious behind his fogged-up glasses. "Here's the most terrifying part about them. It's not that the Dark Magician wants the objects so he can control magick, or that Dark Judgment may be trying to raise the dead. It's that they represent what each of us has the potential to become. The very things that made them go dark exist in all Arcana witches and mages, Stevie."

"But I don't understand. If we're all such walking nukes, one sleepless night or bad hair day away from a total meltdown, why does it fall to us to protect magick?"

"If you believe the legends, we can thank the original elemental beings."

"Sounds like the elemental beings needed better hiring practices."

"Then they've got a lot in common with Anna Trello." Kirin laughs and removes his glasses, hanging them from his shirt collar and finally giving me a clear view of his eyes. "Anyway, even though it's our sacred duty to protect magick, to stay in the light, sometimes protecting magick means tapping into our darker aspects. But tapping into darkness carries its own consequences."

I blow out a breath. "It's never a straight shot, is it?"

"Not for the Keepers of the Grave, no."

"So what does *my* dark side look like? Do I go supernova or something, blow up the whole world in a blaze of epic glory?"

Kirin laughs at the image, but he's shaking his head. "I've told you we all have light and dark aspects. Across the entire Arcana spectrum, that's mostly true."

"Mostly?"

"There is one exception. Only one." Kirin reaches up and cups my chin, his smile vanishing, his eyes shining with wonder. "The Star is pure goodness, pure love, pure light. You represent hope and healing, wholeness, compassion, forgiveness, inspiration. The fact that you're spirit-blessed, in tune with all magickal elements, only amplifies your inherent Arcana gifts. That night when you first signed the Book of Reckoning—when I said you're the center holding us all together? This is what I meant, Stevie. You make us whole. You give us hope. And when things are at their bleakest—at their darkest—it's your light we'll follow home."

He holds my gaze for an eternity, his eyes shining with emotion, his energy awash with love. Not just romantic love, but something so much more intense—a pure, bright love that transcends all human emotion.

"Kirin," I whisper, my own eyes misting again, but then he lowers his gaze and drops his hand, my skin cooling in the absence of his touch.

"Which brings me back to your original question." He gets to his feet and leans back against the rock spire, his eyes falling closed. "Just as the Star dwells in the realm of light, the Tower lives in darkness. Destruction, chaos, despair—that's my Arcana energy. And if I get too close to you, I'll steal your light away. I'll destroy you, Stevie. No matter how I feel about you, no matter how much it kills me not to touch you again, not to kiss you… If I dimmed your light even a fraction, I couldn't live with myself. I won't take that risk. I can't."

His energy pulses with shame and fear, the darkness swallowing up the light of the pure love I felt just moments ago.

"Kirin." I get to my feet and stand before him, grabbing his hands. "Look at me. Please."

Reluctantly, he does as I ask, his gaze tormented. Haunted.

"I'm not perfect," I say. "I've got just as many flaws and foibles as anyone else. Maybe more. I can make you a list of at least ten recent grade-A fuckups, if you'd like."

"You're talking about your *human* flaws. Of course you have those. But your Arcana magick is… It's *beyond* perfect. There isn't even a word for it."

"If my magick is so damn special, what makes you think your Tower energy would destroy it?"

"It's not the Tower energy itself, but the manifestation of that energy. The way *I* manifest that energy." He releases my hands and crouches down to grab a fist-sized rock. "I feel things intensely, Stevie. *Any* emotion can be blinding for me—love, hate, anger, rage, desire—all of it blurs together, building up inside me until I just…" He squeezes the rock, and in an instant, it pulverizes.

I gasp. "How did you—"

"I thought back to the night at the library. The night I kissed you. The memory brought back the emotions I felt that night—just a fraction of them. And this is the result."

He holds his palm up, and I pinch the red dust between my fingers, remembering that night—Kirin kissing me, dropping to his knees before me, teasing and tasting me until I exploded with pleasure. And then, at the exact moment of ecstasy, a flash of lightning exploded in my mind. The ground trembled, right along with my body. Books leaped from the shelves, glass shattered, and a raging fire consumed everything in its path...

"But it was just a vision, Kirin. *My* vision. None of that stuff actually happened. Even the books that fell off the shelves... That was just my regular ol' human expression of big-O excitement."

I crack a smile, but Kirin isn't convinced.

"What you saw *was* a vision," he says, "but not how you think. It wasn't imagined. It was a glimpse into the future—the very near future. An actual peek at what *would've* happened that night had I not immediately suppressed my energy. And that was just the emotional resonance of me giving *you* pleasure. Imagine if I'd let you do the same for me?"

I take a step back, trying to process this. "So you're saying you can't... You've never had sex before?"

"No, it's not... It's just..." He shoves a hand through his hair. "I'm not explaining this right. It's not the physical sensations that send me over the edge. It's the *emotion* behind them. What I feel for you... It was magnified in that moment—magnified by a thousand, because that's how emotion works for me. The more intense the emotion normally, the more intense the effect magickally. And for me, that can literally spell disaster."

"But the Tower is so much more than just chaos and destruction. It's about clarity—those shocking moments of insight that make you question everything you've ever held true. It's about knocking down all the old shit so we can heal and rebuild. People are afraid of the card because in most interpretations, it looks scary as hell. But there are so many positives about that energy. Don't you see that?"

"You're right." Kirin slumps back against the rock, shaking his head. "But something about how I carry that energy... It's different. Yes, the Tower Arcana is the one who ushers in those moments of clarity, but the rest of it... It's me. Just me. Whatever crossed wires or broken shit exists inside me, the end result is that I destroy—"

"Everything you touch?" I ask, throwing his old words back at him, because yes, *now* I'm getting pissed. "I don't buy it, Kirin. Not for a second. You're not broken. I don't know what happened to make you believe that, but you're not."

"I never should've brought you into this. Not... not emotionally."

"We're Arcana brothers now. You wouldn't have been able to keep this secret."

"Maybe not. But I never should've let myself believe we could be anything more than that—more than brothers."

"You're *assuming* we can't. You still haven't convinced

me." I cross my arms over my chest. "Frankly, I think you're being a big, scared, melodramatic jerk."

"Stevie, I—"

"No. You're acting out of fear, using your Arcana energy as an excuse, and I'm sorry, Kirin, but that's absolute bullshit. And here's another newsflash, in case it isn't obvious enough: I still love you. That hasn't gone away, no matter how much I've tried to force it."

"You're the Star," he says softly. His lips curve into a gentle smile, but it holds as much anguish as his eyes. "You want to fix me, just like you want to fix Baz and Cass. Even Ani. It's the same reason you know exactly what kind of tea to make, and why your body heals so quickly. You're a healer. Fixing what's broken or missing inside someone— that's the essence of who you are."

"Why?" I snap. "Because that's what some dusty old book says the Star card means? I'm destined to flit around patching up holes and giving people emotional Band-Aids and chicken soup?"

"No. Because the healing energy inherent in the Star amplifies your compassionate, giving nature. Your magick, your affinities, your Arcana gifts, and you—it's all wrapped up together in one amazing, strong, beautiful package."

"You don't get it, Kirin. I don't want to *fix* any of you— not like that. But I can't help it if I understand implicitly what you need. That's part of my gift, and I wouldn't trade it away—no matter how hard or frustrating it is."

"How is that frustrating? I'd kill for a chance to know what the people I care about need most."

"Yeah? Try knowing exactly how to help someone you love, then watching them refuse your help or try to convince you they don't need it in the first place. Watch them walk away from you with some ridiculous excuse about trying to protect you, all because they're too afraid to face their own shit."

Kirin glares at me, but there's nothing he can say to that.

"And you know what else, Genius Boy?" I close the space between us again, my whole body buzzing with anger. "Super-special Arcana Star power or not, if there's some part of me that can help my friends feel less alone? That can show you that you all deserve kindness and friendship? That can give you understanding and love? Then hell yes, I'm signing up for that."

"You don't understand!" Kirin grabs my shoulders, his eyes blazing. "Love, passion, worry, fear of loss—all the feelings that come with relationships—it's all too much for me. Especially where you're concerned, Stevie. I can't *let* you help me feel those things or show me what I deserve. That's what I'm trying to tell you. I can't—"

"No, Kirin. That's what you're trying to tell *yourself*. And it's a good story, too. I'm sure whatever happened to you—whatever it was that caused you to create that story in the first place—I'm sure it was rough. But however badly it sucked at the time, that moment has passed. What you're left with now is just this story about how you can't get too close to anyone because you'll lose control. I know because I've done it. All the lies we tell ourselves? They're just something our brains invent to try to protect us from all the things our hearts don't want to believe. To protect us from experiencing the crushing pain that comes from being human, no magick required."

In an instant, the fire leaves his eyes, and he lowers his hands and leans back against the rock again, his shoulders slumping. A wave of pain crests between us, his energy so strong and forceful he's practically drowning in it.

My own anger fizzles out, my heart breaking for him.

"Kirin." I reach for his hands again, softening my voice. "When you told me about the other Arcana, you mentioned everyone's gifts right along with their challenges. Yet when it comes to your Tower energy, you're so ashamed of the destructive aspects that you've completely neglected all your light. All the good things about you, about the Tower, about how you uniquely manifest that energy. You said it yourself—we all contain multitudes, just like the Tarot."

This gets a small smile. "You're turning my logic around on me. Not fair. Smart, but not fair."

"The day I was arrested at Kettle Black, you were there. My life changed in a shocking, single moment. I thought it was over."

"It *was* over. That part of your life is gone. Even if we defeat the Dark Arcana and restore the peace outside our boundaries, you will never get that life back."

"No, but that wasn't your fault. And when I look back on that moment now, two things come to mind. One, I wouldn't change how it happened. Not now, knowing what I am and what I'm meant to do here. Knowing that I'm destined to be part of the Brotherhood that protects magick and our fellow witches and mages. If Doc or anyone else from the Academy had come to me under any other circumstances, I don't think I would've enrolled. I would've stayed in my current life, totally stuck. No magick, no purpose, no sense of belonging. And worse—no Arcana mages driving me crazy at every turn." I reach up with one hand and cup the side of his face, my thumb stroking his thin layer of stubble. "I wouldn't have gotten the chance to know you like this, Kirin. To know any of you."

"And two?" he asks. "What's number two?"

"I'm so glad you were there when it happened. Not just because you took care of Jessa, but because you were my rock. The Tower—it's not just about what crumbles. It's about what's left standing when the dust settles. What's worth saving and fighting for. The thing you hold on to when everything else is utterly lost." I bring my other hand to his face, our bodies so close I can feel the warmth of his skin radiating through his shirt, straight into my chest. Into my heart. "Kirin, you say that I'm the light you'll follow home. Well, you were my light, too. Not just that day at the café, but my first day on campus. My first day in the library, working with Mom's prophecies. You're *still* my light."

His eyes glaze with new emotion. "Stevie…"

"I'm not afraid of you, Kirin Weber. You could bring all these spires down around us right now, and I still wouldn't be afraid. So please stop being afraid of yourself."

I stand up on my tiptoes and press a long, lingering kiss to his cheek, then rest my head against his chest. His hands slide around my back, holding me close, and we stay like that for the span of a hundred heartbeats, a thousand, a million, cocooned in mist and silence and the bonds of friendship between two souls trying to find their way back to something more.

But then, just behind our rock, a shadow takes form in the mist, the tattered blue fabric of her dress fluttering in a soft breeze, the glint of a metal sword shining through the fog.

"Kirin," I whisper. "We've got company."

"Is the owl back?"

"It's the Princess of Swords." I pluck the glasses from his shirt collar and slide them back onto his face. "And we need to follow her."

THIRTY-TWO

STEVIE

My Princess is as fast as the wind, as elusive as the mist.

"Hurry! This way!" I grab Kirin's hand and we jog after her, racing deeper into the misty cage of towering rock formations. With every footfall, the fog thickens around us, obscuring most of the landscape. Each time I fear we've lost her, I catch a glimpse of blue fabric, or a lock of dark hair, or the black wing of the raven perched on her shoulder, and onward we charge.

We're so far off the path, I'd never be able to find my way back to campus alone. Just when I'm about to call off the chase and turn back, the Princess stops in her tracks, turning to face us with a sly smile. All around her, the mist vanishes, revealing a strange new sight.

"What is this place?" I ask, turning to take it all in. It seems we've wandered into a grove of standing stones, made from seven red sandstone slabs topped with massive stone spheres as smooth as a drop of water. They form a perfect circle, like seven upside-down exclamation points standing guard.

"It's definitely man made," Kirin says. "Some sort of ancient gateway or maybe a place of worship."

"You've never been here?"

"I've never seen anything like this in my life."

"Kirin," I whisper, afraid that anything louder will shatter the silence, the reverence of this magickal place. "I think the sword may be here."

Before me, my Princess bows her head. And then she's gone.

"What makes you say that?" he asks.

"Ani's theory is that the Arcana objects are buried on Academy grounds, each one hidden in the most spiritual location of its corresponding elemental landscape." I press my hand to one of the massive rock slabs, magick tingling across my palm. "If this isn't the most spiritual place inside the Towers of Breath and Blade, I can't imagine what is."

"You have a point." Kirin steps up beside me, reaching out to touch the rock. "But I'm not sensing anything. Are you?"

"A little. This is the same thing that happened last weekend at the Cauldron. The Princess of Wands led Ani and me to that scorched cave."

"But you guys said the wand wasn't there."

"No, but *something* was. Some leftover energy connected to the wand in some way. I'm sure of it." I move from stone to stone, running my hands up and down the rocks, searching for some sort of indicator. "But at the Cauldron, it was Ani who felt the energy the most, not me. Wait... Look!"

I spot an opening at the base of one of the standing stones, a dark hole about two feet in diameter, hidden behind a large boulder. Crouching down, I hold up my palm and call on my witchfire. Silver flame dances to life in my hand, illuminating the space below.

"There are stairs. Let's go." Taking the lead, I gingerly make my way down the rough stone staircase to a large chamber beneath the stone circle. "Kirin, this is incredible!"

I lift my palms and call up more witchfire, casting the chamber in pale silver light. It's much larger than the space Ani and I found—about the size of the Iron and Bone common room. The ceiling is about twenty feet off the ground.

"It's down here somewhere," I say, my voice echoing. "I can feel it. It's like it's calling to me or something."

"I feel it now too." Kirin holds up his hands, silver-blue magick crackling in the air around us like tiny sparks. "It's definitely swords energy."

"I know. I can practically feel the sword in my hands— almost like I'm holding the real thing."

"Really?" Kirin cocks his head, still staring at the magick sparking on his hands. "I wonder..."

"Wonder what?"

"Stevie, the sword that's appearing in your nightmares —the same one that appeared in your first meditation when you met your Princesses... What if it's the Sword of Breath and Blade?"

"But I thought it was just a magick sword from the Princess. Like a protective gift or something."

Kirin shakes his head. "I've never heard of a magick sword that adjusts in size and weight to perfectly suit its handler. Do you realize the kind of magick that would require? Look, this magick here..." He waves his hands, causing the sparks to flare and cascade around him. "It's beyond powerful. And the Princess led you here for a reason, just like the Princess of Wands led you and Ani to the caves."

"Because Ani's a fire mage. Wands are his affinity."

"And swords are mine, but you're blessed with all four. Perhaps your air magick is your strongest affinity. Maybe it's even stronger than mine." Kirin's brow furrows, thoughts spinning behind his eyes. "Let's try something."

Kirin removes a Tarot card from his pack and places it on the ground before us, right in the center of the chamber. "The Seven of Swords sometimes suggests hiding or obscuring, as well as seeking or revealing that which is hidden or obscured. If we can tap into that magick together, maybe it can help us narrow down the search area."

"Brilliant idea." I stand before him. "What do you need me to do?"

"I'll say the spell. When I take your hands, I want you to close your eyes and focus all your energy on finding the sword—the one from your nightmares. Picture it, just as you've seen it in your visions. Imagine yourself holding it again—feel the texture and shape as your fingers wrap around the grip, test the weight of it as you hold it in your hand. Hear the sound it makes as it cuts through the air. Feel its power coursing through your veins."

"Got it."

I close my eyes, and Kirin takes my hands, his touch warm and comforting, a familiar anchor in an otherwise baffling mystery. I do as he asks, focusing my memory and will on the sword from my visions, pouring all of my desire into finding it.

Kirin recites his spell three times:

> *Magick of air, magick of mind*
> *You know what we seek, so help us to find*
> *Protection we offer, guidance we ask*
> *Let that which is hidden now be unmasked*

As the final verse fades into silence, a soft, otherworldly breeze stirs my hair, and the ground rumbles.

"Stevie, look!"

I open my eyes and glance down to see a stone pedestal rising from the ground between us, pulsing with silver-blue light. The top is smooth and unbroken but for a deep groove carved down the middle, nearly bisecting it. Suddenly my right hand begins to tingle, and though I can't see it, I feel the exact shape and weight of the sword handle as if I'm clutching it tight.

The stone channel glows inside, brighter than the rest. I see now that it's the perfect size and shape for a sword. As I run my hand along the groove, my witchfire ignites on its own, brighter and stronger than I've ever seen it before.

"Holy balls," I breathe.

"Was it like this at the Cauldron?"

"For Ani, I think. I could feel the presence of the magick, but it affected him a lot more strongly. This is... new for me." I pull my hand back, and the witchfire and pedestal magick both fade, leaving us in darkness.

I call up my witchfire again, a pale imitation of the magick I felt only seconds ago.

Kirin peers into the groove. "There's nothing there."

"Not anymore. But I think the sword *was* here. I can feel its energy—almost like a memory."

"Like it was moved?"

"Maybe? The connection is still so strong, though. If this is what Ani felt at the Cauldron, then we're *definitely* on to something. I don't know what it means yet, but I do know we're getting closer. I can feel it."

"We need those spells, Stevie. If they're the key to revealing the location of the objects, that's our best bet for finding them before the Dark Arcana."

"But we don't have the books, and Phaines has essentially vanished into the mist."

"Then there's only one thing to do." Kirin glances up at me, his eyes wild with excitement. "We need to make our *own* Book of Shadow and Mists."

THIRTY-THREE

STEVIE

Thanks to my Dirty Dancing day with Kirin, complete with flying bicycles, levitating rocks, an owl sighting, a brutal fight, a sweet embrace, a Princess chase, and an epic Lara Croft-style discovery, I don't make it back to campus in time for my Tarot Divination and Spellcraft class. Rather than dwell on it, I decide to let Kirin fill the guys in on our discovery while I meet the girls for happy hour and a little retail therapy at Promenade.

Yes, we've got spells to recreate and ancient magickal objects to discover and attackers to thwart and dark armies to fight, but sometimes even a badass warrior witch needs a night off with some good friends, a few martinis, and a new pair of shoes.

Okay, *three* new pairs, but still.

"Out of an abundance of caution," Nat says, flipping through the martini menu on the heated patio at Sea and

Sky Bar after our successful shoe store raid, "I think I need to get the peach martini as well as the chocolate."

"Good call," Isla says. "Out of an abundance of caution, of course. These days, you can never be too sure when a given drink might be your last."

I laugh and roll my eyes. "Have you two ever heard the saying, beating a dead horse? Until it's dead? Like, really really really dead from all the beating you gave it before it died? And now it's completely dead?"

"Hmm." Isla taps her lips. "Out of an abundance of—"

"No. I hereby declare a moratorium on that phrase for at least one semester."

"Stevie," Nat says, passing me the menu, "pick a drink. You need to calm down before you cause unnecessary panic."

"Is self-defense against two severely annoying witches an acceptable plea for murder of said witches by cocktail straw?" I flash a psychotic grin. "Asking for a friend."

"Speaking of friends," Isla says. "Where's Jessa? She should be here for this. By video chat, at least."

"I know." I smile, thinking of my best friend. So much has happened in the last couple of weeks, but Jessa's never far from my thoughts, no matter how crazy things get on campus. "She's off-grid for the next few weeks. She's in the middle of moving back to Mexico."

"As soon as she's settled in," Isla says, "we need to figure out a way to turn her into a witch so she can enroll at the Academy."

Nat nods. "Way better than video chats anyway."

"I'm totally on board with that plan," I say. "Once we figure out who's trying to steal our magick and possibly kill us, of course."

"Of course," Nat says. "Out of an—"

"Moratorium on the phrase, or moratorium on your face," I shoot her another faux-murderous glare. "However, I totally agree about the last drink stuff, and am therefore on team one-of-everything. I'll start with the appletini."

We put in our drink order, then I excuse myself from the table. "I need to run a quick errand across the way. I'll be back in just a sec."

"Wait, where are you going?" Isla asks.

"It's a secret," I tease. "Be right back."

"Pharmacy?" She wriggles her brows. "Out of condoms already? I told you, you should've gotten the jumbo pack."

"Or just talk to Professor Broome about the birth control potion," Nat says.

"There's a birth control potion?" I stop in my tracks. "How did I not know this?"

Nat shrugs. "Maybe because you grew up in a mundane house and never got the magick sex talk?"

"Birth control potion, huh? What will they think of next?" Grinning, I make a mental note to check in with Professor Broome. But for now, I'm on another sort of mission. "Don't drink my drink!"

I scoot outside, leaving the girls to their wild speculations about my sex life. They're not wrong—I *am* almost out of condoms. But the pharmacy is not the store on my list today.

* * *

"Stevie!" Kelly's face lights up as I step into Time Out of Mind. "I'm so glad you stopped by. Just a social visit, or can I help you find something?"

"Partly social, partly shopping." I point to the glass jewelry case at the end of the room. "I'm actually looking for some protective jewelry—hematite, specifically. It's for Isla and Nat."

"I'm so glad you're taking this seriously." She shakes her head, her mouth pulling into a frown. "Kate—Professor Broome—we still can't believe our esteemed headmistress hasn't taken more action on this. The attacks this weekend were absolutely appalling, and those poor students still haven't regained their magick. Pardon me for saying so, but on this point, Anna's got her head shoved way up her ass, and I told her just that."

"I take it your talk with her didn't go as planned?"

"It's like Agent Appleton said. Anna believes keeping the information under wraps is the best way to keep everyone safe." Her energy pulses with anger and frustration, but then she takes a deep breath and lets it go. Turning back to me with a smile, she says, "Come with me. I've got just the thing."

She leads me to the case and opens it up, taking out a few different trays of necklaces, bracelets, and rings.

"Professor Broome handcrafted most of this jewelry," she says, "so you know it's the good stuff."

Since Isla always wears her teardrop pendant, I decide

on bracelets for each of them. For Isla, I find one with inter-locking silver links shaped like ocean waves, each one dotted with an embedded hematite stone. I pick out a rose-gold charm bracelet for Nat, dripping with tiny hematite spheres.

"The gifts aren't the only reason you stopped by," Kelly says, wrapping each bracelet in a black gift box with a cream-colored bow. "The cards told me I'd see you here today."

"Really?"

Kelly nods. "They also told me it was time to give you this."

She reaches beneath the counter and pulls out an old journal with a soft brown leather cover tied with a long red cord that wraps around several times. A silver moon and star dangle from the ends of the cord, winking in the light.

"What is it?" I whisper.

"Open it and see for yourself."

I do as she asks, unwinding the cord. The moment I turn the front cover, my hands begin to tingle, the touch of magick warming my skin. Each page is hand-written, drawn with ancient runes and symbols I don't even recognize. I run my fingers across the page, hoping my magick will illuminate more words like it did with my mother's notebooks, but nothing happens.

"Is it a journal?" I ask. "A grimoire?"

"Perhaps," she says. "I've never been able to translate it. It's my hope that you'll be able to unravel its mysteries. It was meant for you, Stevie."

"Kelly, it's beautiful, and I appreciate the vote of confidence. But I'm a first-year witch with almost no magickal background. I haven't even begun to study runes or magickal symbols yet—I'm still trying to get a handle on the Tarot."

"I'm aware." Kelly smiles. "I'm not sure studying our runes and symbols will help. This book is… different."

"Is it from the library?"

"Not any library in this realm."

"Where did you get it?"

"It was your mother's." She reaches across the counter and covers my hands with hers, her eyes sparkling. "She dreamed it."

THIRTY-FOUR

STEVIE

I head back to Sea and Sky in a daze, the gift bag draped over my arm, the dream-book still clutched in my hand, still giving off its warm magickal vibe.

"What is *that*?" Isla asks, glancing at the book as I rejoin them at our table. "It looks about a thousand years old."

"I think it might be," I say.

"Is that what you went to get?" Nat asks.

I shake my head, my thoughts still hazy.

"Then where did it come from?" she asks.

There's a bright green appletini sitting on the table before me, and I reach for the glass and take a long sip, focusing on the sweet-tart flavor, the pleasant warmth of the alcohol sliding down my throat. When I set down the glass, I glance up at Nat with a dazed smile. "It came from a dream."

Nat laughs.

Isla laughs.

I just stare at the book.

"I don't think she's kidding," Nat whispers to Isla.

"Maybe she was drinking without us," Isla says.

"She's not kidding," I say, "and she's not drunk." I glance back up at the girls and take a deep breath, knowing I'm about to change everything between us. To *risk* everything. But I've held this in long enough. Nat and Isla are my closest friends here, and they've been there for me at every turn. I trust them. I owe them the truth—as much as I'm able to share—in honor of our friendship and for their own safety.

All of our lives may depend on it.

"Remember when I told you guys my enrollment at the Academy was a crazy story?" I ask, flagging down the waiter for another round of drinks. "I think it's about time I told it."

Out of respect for the guys and my sacred oath, I don't tell Nat and Isla about the Brotherhood, or the fact that I'm one of the fabled Arcana Majors destined to protect magick. But after confirming we're alone on the patio, I let everything else pour out of me—my parents' mysterious history at the Academy, followed by their hasty exit. How I was raised in a mundane household where magick was a four-letter word. The attack on my friend Luke that led to my arrest and imprisonment, and Dr. Devane's role in helping me escape. My mother's prophecies and their possible connection to the magickal attacks happening beyond our borders, and my work with Kirin to translate them.

I also tell them about my visions, my nightmares, the Dark Arcana legends, and our quest to find the sacred objects.

They listen attentively, heads bent close together, eyes full of concern and astonishment. But no matter how crazy my story sounds, their energy continues to wash over me in warm, supportive waves, never once faltering.

"So you and Kirin are trying to find the link between your mom's predictions and what's going on with the witch and mage attacks outside?" Isla asks.

I nod. "As well as the attacks here on campus."

"And you believe this is all connected to the legends of the Dark Magician," she says.

"Him specifically, yes, but also the Dark Arcana in general. We believe there are at least four of them working together, maybe more. Professor Phaines was one of them—the Hierophant."

"Oh my Goddess," Nat breathes.

"He didn't just assault me. He tried to do a ritual sacrifice on me. He thought he could channel my magick through my blood and use it to read the spells."

"Does APOA know about all this?" Isla asks. "Is that why they're trying to keep everything under wraps?"

"Kirin said his sister asked about the Arcana objects," I say, "but as far as I know, she hasn't said anything beyond that. I'm pretty sure APOA is more focused on the magickal attacks on campus and their connection to the attacks happening outside. But they're pretty secretive themselves, so who even knows?"

"So you and Kirin are what—planning to take on this psycho Magician by yourselves?" Nat asks.

"Baz, Ani, and Dr. Devane are also involved," I say. "I told you how Dr. Devane got me out of prison. He brought me here at Anna Trello's behest. Kirin is the researcher, and he's been working on my mother's prophecies all along. Baz and Ani are just… part of the package."

Isla sighs. "No wonder they're all so protective of you."

"It sounds crazy," I say. "It *is* crazy. But all this Dark Arcana stuff… It's bringing us closer."

Close as brothers… among other things.

"So what does Trello think about all this?" Isla asks.

"No idea, honestly." I shrug. "It's funny—she's the one who sent for me. She knew my mother, and as far as I know, she's the primary reason my parents were booted out of the Academy. Now she believes Mom's prophecies were right —that we need to translate them if we stand a chance against whatever's going on outside. Supposedly, I'm the only one who *can* translate them. I'm basically her star pupil in that respect. But the entire time I've been here, I've hardly seen her. Hardly had any communication with her at all since the first day."

"She's shady AF," Nat says, and Isla agrees. "And why is she trying to keep all this a secret, anyway? If she knows about the Dark Arcana legends, shouldn't she be rallying us all together? Figuring out how to train us to defend ourselves? Defend each other?"

"I think she's either hoping we're wrong, or that we can take out the Dark Arcana without involving anyone else." I down the rest of my drink. "On that point, I can't blame her. I don't want to drag anyone else into this, either. We don't even know what we're up against. Not really."

Isla grabs my hand, her eyes shiny with tears. "There are five of you, Stevie. Just five. Whether this ends up being just a bunch of crooked mages like you initially thought, or the actual Dark Arcana rising up to reclaim magick and enslave us for all eternity, five is not enough."

I open my mouth to argue, but she's absolutely right. Five people against an army—possibly one that can't be killed. Five people against a world gone mad, against human authorities executing witches and mages on live television, ensuring the population stays terrified and angry. No matter who's behind all of this, no matter if it's connected or not, we don't stand a chance on our own.

"You need more people," Nat says.

"I know," I say. "Goddess, I know. I just... We can't let anyone find out about the Arcana objects, and I'm scared of dragging anyone else into this."

"Who says anything about dragging?" Isla glares at me as if my protectiveness is an utter affront to every last one of her sensibilities. "Stevie, did you honestly think you could drop all this on us and think we *wouldn't* have your back?"

"Newbie witches," Nat says, a smile tugging at her lips despite the heaviness of our conversation. "So hard to train these days."

"You guys, I love you. Seriously. But I can't ask you to—"

"Do you hear something?" Isla asks Nat, her eyes glittering with mischief. "Like the annoying buzz of a witch trying to talk us out of getting involved?"

Nat downs her chocolate martini, then looks at us with a wide smile. "The only thing *I* hear is the sound of three witches getting ready to beat some serious Dark Arcana ass."

I crack up at that, even as the tears well in my eyes.

I'm afraid for them. I'm afraid for all of us. But I'm also glad they're on my side. And they're right—I need them. We need each other—all of us do. All these secrets and lies, hiding information, the abundance of caution Trello is so stuck on—that's what's going to be our downfall.

The only way we're going to survive this thing—whatever *this thing* turns out to be—is if we stick together.

"All right, Charmed Ones," I tease. "Since you insist on throwing yourselves into the path of danger anyway..." I remove their gift boxes from the Time Out of Mind bag and hand them over.

"Ah, so *this* was the mysterious errand," Isla says with a smile. She opens her box and pulls out the bracelet, her eyes going wide. "Stevie, this is gorgeous! Goddess, it's perfect!"

"Wow, it's so beautiful!" Nat says, opening hers. "Is this hematite?"

I nod. "Professor Broome wants everyone to start wearing protective amulets, and I noticed you guys don't have any."

"Thank you so much, Stevie," Isla says. "I love it."

"Me too," Nat says.

The girls help each other fasten their new bracelets, then pull me in for a group hug, the three of us simultaneously laughing and crying in the way only true girlfriends can.

But our Hallmark moment is interrupted by a sound that sends icy shivers down my spine.

"Well, isn't this cozy?" a cool voice says, and I glance up to see Carly's pals Emory and Blue slink out of the shadows from the alley next to our patio.

They were eavesdropping. There's no doubt about it.

"Did you enjoy drinks and gossip, girls? Because let me tell you, we certainly did." Beaming at us with fake, menacing smiles, the girls turn on their heels and walk past the patio, heading into the French restaurant next door.

"Holy shit," Isla says. "Do you think they heard us?"

Dread drops in my stomach like a boulder. "Every fucking word."

I whip out my phone and send an S.O.S. text to Doc. *Epic fuckup—you can yell at me later. I need your help NOW.*

He responds immediately. *Where are you? What happened?*

Blue & Emory overhead me telling Nat & Isla about highly sensitive info, I reply, hoping it's enough to make the point.

Are they with you now?

They just went into Café Marchande.

On my way, he replies.

Should I meet you?

No. You should go home, Stevie. Immediately. And try VERY HARD not to put anyone else's life in danger on your way back.

My heart sinks, guilt heating up my insides. *I'm really sorry, Doc. :-(I know I screwed up bigtime.*

No response.

I wait another minute, but the phone is silent.

There's nothing more I can say, and Nat and Isla know it. Wrung out and exhausted, I pay the bill and head back to the dorms with my witch sisters, none of us daring to speak another word.

If Doc can't fix this, I may have just signed a death warrant for every person on campus.

THIRTY-FIVE

STEVIE

The next morning, I invent a new brew for the special occasion of encountering the wrath of Dr. Devane. I'm calling it Get On Your Big Girl Broomstick and Deal With Him—the perfect blend of energizing pu-erh, yerba mate for focus and endurance, and melted chocolate—you know, just in case this is the very last thing I get to drink.

I also brew a special to-go pot for Doc—a soothing blend of lavender, mint, vanilla, and chamomile I've christened Calm the Fuck Down.

It's going to be a long and grueling day.

So, with an hour to spare before Mental Magicks, I take a deep breath, square my shoulders, and walk into his classroom, ready to do battle with the one man who's challenged me more than anyone else at Arcana Academy.

He's seated at his desk in a white dress shirt with the sleeves rolled up, his pale blue tie held firmly in place by the silver academy pin. His suit jacket is draped over the back of his chair, and for a brief moment, he doesn't see me.

He looks calm. Peaceful, despite the stress of everything going on.

But his energy, unguarded for the moment, is tired.

Now or never, girl.

"Dr. Devane?" I begin, holding up his tea mug like a peace offering. "I made you some—"

"Oh, Miss Milan! What a lovely surprise." He turns to me and grins, his teeth glinting like the fangs of a wolf, his tone dramatic and exaggerated. "Come in and shut the door, please."

I do as he asks, then turn to face him, once again holding up the mug. "Tea?"

"No, thank you." He gestures for me to take a chair at the front of the classroom, all his calm, peaceful energy sailing away. "You look well. How are you feeling this morning?"

"I'm fine," I grind out, dropping into the chair. "Doc, can we kill the theatrics? I came here to say—"

"Did you sleep well?" he asks.

"Fine," I repeat. "I need to—"

"Well, I'm so glad *one* of us is rested." He rises from the chair behind his desk, pacing the room before me. "Care to know how I spent my evening?"

I fold my arms across my chest and glare. So it's going to be one of *those* conversations. Okay, then. Best to let him get it all out of his system now.

Because I didn't just come here to apologize. I came for a

fight. And what I have to say next? It's going to *really* piss him off.

"No?" he presses. "Come on, Miss Milan. I thought sharing was your new favorite pastime."

"Go ahead," I say. "Get it off your chest. I know I deserve it." After all, when I texted for help last night, I did give him permission to yell at me later.

"Allow me to enlighten you," he says. "Rather than unpacking my belongings into the terribly small apartment to which I was highly encouraged to relocate—the one located above a store that sells nothing but incense that smells like hot garbage and old socks, mind you—I had the distinct pleasure of tracking down two first-year witches, inserting myself into their dinner plans under false academic pretenses, and using highly unethical forms of mental manipulation to make them believe they'd overheard you and your friends talking about a movie you'd seen rather than whatever highly sensitive information you deemed safe enough to share with your friends in a public space, after we spent the better part of an evening not ten days past stressing the importance of secrecy above all else. If that weren't maddening enough, I also had to pick up the check." Doc shoves his hands through his hair, fuming. "Do you understand how expensive Café Marchande is, Miss Milan? Do you understand what Goddess-awful dinner companions Blue Haydensport and Emory Sanchez are? Do you understand how much trouble you're in right now?"

Doc's still pacing like a wild animal, his energy so wound up he can't even shield it from me. Certain he's said all he can on the matter, I give him a moment to pull himself together before attempting a response.

"May I speak?" I ask.

"Oh, by all means. Please do speak, Miss Milan. At least this time, we're alone."

Ignoring the dig, I say, "Firstly, I came here to apologize—that's a given. I take full responsibility for what I did. It was reckless, stupid, and if you hadn't been there to clean up the mess, things could be a hell of a lot worse for all of us right now. I know that, and I'm sorry, Doc. Truly sorry."

"What, precisely, are you sorry for?"

"That I shared dangerous information—information that could compromise our mission and the safety of all involved—in a public place." I lower my eyes, cringing inside, already knowing how this next part will go over. But I can't back down now. Not after everything I shared with Isla and Nat. Not after everything I've come to believe. "But—"

"There's a *but*?" He explodes again, his face turning the color of the Cauldron at sunrise. "You have the audacity to come in here with a *but*?"

"Actually, yes. I do." Drawing on the strength of my friends, of my mother, of every witch who ever stood up for what she believed in, I rise from my chair and face him, ready to do serious battle. "I'm sorry I was careless in public. *But*... I'm not sorry I opened up to Isla and Nat. They're my closest friends here, their lives are in danger, and they have a right to know what's going on."

I cross my arms over my chest and hold his gaze,

waiting for him to explode. To lash out in the worst way possible. To yell and scream, to tear up my Brotherhood membership card and deem me unworthy to walk the halls of this Academy.

But though his eyes blaze, the rage and frustration inside him recede, and Doc finally exhales, raising his hands in a cease-fire.

"Okay, Stevie," he says, his tone much gentler now. "Obviously, you came here with an agenda of some sort. So why don't you just tell me what's on your mind?"

"I want you to know that I didn't share anything about the Brotherhood. I took an oath to keep that secret, and I wouldn't betray you guys like that. We *are* brothers, after all."

A look of pride crosses his face, but he quickly schools his features.

"But I did tell them… well… basically everything else. They know about my parents and my work on the prophecies, my visions and nightmares, our fears about the Dark Arcana legends, our search for the arcane objects, and the possibility that all of this magickal danger is connected to the attacks happening outside."

Doc nods and sits on the edge of his desk, gesturing for me to pass him the tea.

"Like I said, I told them all that stuff because I feel they have a right to know." I hand over the mug. "But they also want to help us. We're preparing for a possible war, Doc. Five of us won't cut it. We need an army of our own."

"Two first-year witches? That's hardly an army, Stevie."

"It's a start."

Doc doesn't respond, but he does sip the tea, his energy immediately relaxing.

Calm the Fuck Down for the win!

"I'd also like to bring in Professor Maddox and Professor Broome," I say. "They're allies, Doc. Both believe that Trello is doing us all a huge disservice by keeping things under wraps. And both were close with my mother. Professor Broome even made this necklace for her." I touch the Eye of Horus at my throat. "You saw them that night at Iron and Bone after the attacks. They're on our side. They can help us."

"They can expose us," he says, shaking his head. "Stevie, I hear what you're saying—I've thought about it myself. I know our numbers are small, but bringing others into this... It's too risky. They could get hurt, or worse—turn on us, either intentionally or simply by letting some crucial bit of intelligence slip to the wrong people. We can't take that chance."

"Then we're taking an even *bigger* chance thinking we have what it takes to battle the Dark Arcana." I step closer, feeling my own anger simmer. Why can he not see the obvious here? "Not to name-and-shame, Doc, but one of us is still green—i.e., *me*—and another is practically over the hill." I glare at him. "Yes, that would be *you*. Frankly, we could use all the help we can get."

"Snark about my age all you want, Stevie. We simply *can't* involve anyone else. This is our responsibility. The *Brotherhood's* responsibility. No one else's."

"Our responsibility is to protect magick, not to die trying." I step closer, closing the last of the space between us. He's still holding the tea mug, both hands wrapped around it, and now I reach up and cover his hands with mine, gentling my tone. "We can't do this alone. It's gotten too big, even for Arcana Mages. We need to start trusting other people, Doc, or magick is going to fall into the hands of the Dark Arcana and we're all going to die."

Doc looks into my eyes, his energy a war zone of conflicting emotions. He knows I'm right, but he's also terrified. Not just about the battles to come, but for me. Of all the threads weaving through his energy, that's the heaviest, the brightest, the one I focus on now, trying to understand it.

He's terrified he's going to lose me. And if that happens, he won't be able to live with himself.

The realization knocks something loose inside my chest, and I gasp, my heart skipping a beat.

Doc closes his eyes and shakes his head, pressing his lips together like he's trying to keep the words locked up.

"Doc," I say softly, squeezing his hands. "If it were Baz or Ani coming to you with this, or Kirin, would you shut it down so easily?"

He looks up at me again, his gray eyes full of pain and torment, a thousand ghosts floating up between us.

What is it that haunts you? I want to ask. *What is this ancient pain?*

Doc opens his mouth to speak, then closes it, shaking his head. Instead, he pulls away from me and rises from the desk, going back around to sit on the other side, putting the barrier between us once again.

"You're right," he finally says. "I wouldn't be so quick to shoot down one of the others."

"Why not?" I press. "And don't bother trying to lie to me. I'll know right away—your energy gets all squirmy."

"First of all, I do not get *squirmy*. And secondly, Miss Milan..." He reaches for the tea again and takes a sip, ducking my gaze. When he finishes, he still won't meet my eyes, but at least he has an answer for me. "Something about you has... affected me."

"Affected you how?"

"I've always felt protective toward my students—first-year students, especially. Despite the fact that you're all adults, you're still young and inexperienced adults, and you've come here to learn magick in all its forms. Students place their trust in me—trust I don't always feel worthy of, but do my best to honor, teaching and guiding them to the best of my abilities."

"I know you do," I say. "You're an excellent professor. And I'm not just saying that so you'll bump up my grade. I mean it, Doc."

He flashes an all-too-brief smile. "Yes, well. For whatever reason, when it comes to you, my protective instincts kick into overdrive."

I shake my head, annoyance creeping back in. "You told me this already. You feel super protective of me, it goes beyond the Brotherhood bond, you can't explain it, blah blah blah."

"Well, it seems you've already got your answer, then."

"So when you say I affect you, it's just this overprotective thing you've got going on?"

He nods, avoiding my gaze again.

"You're squirming," I say. "Energetically speaking, of course."

He opens his mouth to deny it, but we both know there's no point.

My heart's kicking into overdrive, and I've got a feeling Doc's is doing the same crazy dance. I know I'm cruising onto dangerous ground, and some tiny voice inside me tells me I should probably let this particular sleeping dog lie, but I can't. I need to know the truth. Because whatever connection I feel to Doc—whatever connection I feel to all of them —it goes well beyond our Brotherhood bond.

And maybe I just need some reassurance that I'm not the only one who feels it.

"I need to ask you something," I say, "and I need you to be totally honest with me, no matter how inappropriate or downright awkward you find the question. Deal?"

"With a lead-up like *that*, how could I refuse?" A smile tugs at his lips, and I relax, remembering some of the nicer moments we've shared together. The tacos at Lala's place. The way he stocked my tea pantry and loaded me up with the best climbing gear available. His ministrations after my rattlesnake vision. Every time he's ever worried about me, or shown even a modicum of kindness.

"Sometimes," I say, my voice no more than a whisper, "when you look at me, when you touch me... I feel this...

like a connection, but more than that. I don't even have the words for it, really. But I feel it with the other guys, too. The only difference is…" I swallow the knot in my throat and close my eyes. "You're the only one who tries to fight it."

"I… I don't know what you mean."

"Are you attracted to me, Dr. Devane?" I open my eyes to find him staring back at me, his own eyes wide, his neck turning red behind his tie.

"This conversation is *definitely* not appropriate for…" He loosens his tie, his eyes roaming the room, everywhere but on mine. "It's simply not appropriate."

"I think we're well past what's appropriate. I'm ready for what's true. Besides, you promised you'd be totally honest." A sigh escapes my lips. It's not exactly fair, pushing him into this line of questioning without explanation. Without giving up a little of my own carefully guarded control. "Doc, whenever I'm around you—any of you—I feel a connection that goes beyond anything I've ever felt before. It's like a pull, but deeper. I… I feel things. Not just for Kirin and Baz, either. Ani is suddenly getting under my skin in ways that a friend should definitely not. And even you, as grumpy as you are, there's something…" I close my eyes, trying to focus my scattered thoughts. Trying to steady my pounding heart. "I need to understand if that's part of the Brotherhood bond, or something else."

"Something else?" he asks.

"Do all Arcana witches and mages feel… feelings? For each other, I mean?"

He considers me for a long, uncomfortable beat, and for

a minute I worry he's going to send me away, shutting down this conversation for good.

But eventually he lets out a long breath and shakes his head.

"All Arcana," he says, "unless they're actively shielding like Phaines was doing, feel some sort of connection to each other. A recognition, perhaps, or a sense of familiarity and trust. *That's* the bond. But what you're talking about..." He lowers his eyes, his brow furrowing. "No, Stevie. That's something else entirely. If all Arcana felt this level of connection, I suspect the four of us would've experienced these feelings toward one another in your absence, regardless of gender identity or sexual orientation." He glances up at me again, and when our eyes meet, he offers a soft smile. "So no. I don't think this is connected to the Brotherhood bond at all."

I take a deep, steadying breath, unsure how to process this. Part of me was still hoping I could blame magick or destiny or any other outside force, but I can't. Which means I'm just getting *all* in my feels over four impossibly sexy, super overprotective, infuriating-in-every-possible way mages, with no one to blame but me. The woman who once said mages were bad news and love was reserved for other people.

Just like magick.

I try again, one more time, just to be absolutely clear. "So what you're saying... It means..."

Doc rises from his chair and comes back around to join

me in front of his desk, stopping right in front of me, closer than close.

"It means that whatever you're feeling," he says softly, "whatever *any* of us is feeling, it's not magick." He takes my hand, his touch warm and gentle, and presses it to his chest, holding it in place. I feel his heartbeat, wild and strong and powerful, its frantic rhythm a mirror to my own. Gone are the ghosts from his eyes, replaced now with heat and passion, with possibility, with wonder.

"It's something infinitely more powerful," he whispers, leaning in close, "and infinitely more terrifying."

His warm breath carries with it the sound of the ocean, the roar of the waves against the shore, the distant howl of a wolf beneath the moonlight, and he lowers his mouth to mine, our lips nearly brushing…

A hard rap on the door startles us both, and I turn away, heat shooting through every one of my limbs.

Doc clears his throat, resuming his position behind the desk.

"Come in," he calls out.

Agent Eastman enters, stern and severe as ever—a much-needed bucket of ice water dumped right down my pants.

"Dr. Devane, I was hoping you could spare a minute or two before your next class."

Doc glances at his watch, his forearm muscles rippling in a way I never quite noticed before and probably shouldn't be noticing now, but holy hell my heart is still dancing inside my chest, my blood still singing with the unexpended energy of that almost-but-not-quite kiss.

"I've got about ten minutes," Doc says. "How can I help you, Agent?"

Eastman glares at me, probably remembering how annoying I was the day he checked out my security system. "It's a *private* campus security matter, if you don't mind."

Doc clears his throat. "Agent, I—"

"It's fine," I say, saving Doc the awkwardness of shooing me out after what just happened. Or didn't happen. "I'll be back in a few minutes for class."

Doc holds my gaze another beat, a whole bunch of unsaid things passing between us, then finally nods.

The moment I reach the hallway, my phone buzzes with a text.

Thank you for the tea, Miss Milan.

Then, seconds later, another one.

And for keeping my days full of surprises.

THIRTY-SIX

STEVIE

With the faculty and staff under intense scrutiny from APOA, the next week is pretty grueling on the classroom front. All the professors are upping their game, pushing us to learn more, do better, and quote-unquote make good choices, which basically translates to more homework and much harder tests.

In the face of everything at stake, it's hard for me to prioritize things like ten-page essays comparing and contrasting the symbolism of clouds and birds in the swords suit, but I have to remember that until I reach an agreement with Doc and the other guys about getting more people on Team Keepers of the Grave, the search for the Arcana objects is our responsibility and no one else's. I can't expect the faculty to put classes on hold or give me and the guys special treatment just because we're trying to save the world from the invasion of the Dark Arcana.

I mean, I'll probably ask for extra credit when all is said

and done, but still. Right now, we have to keep living our regular lives, just like everyone else.

Doc and I have not revisited our conversation—not about letting a few more students and professors into the circle of trust, not about the Brotherhood bond, and *definitely* not about the near-kiss that still sends my stomach somersaulting every time I think about it. It's just as well, though. We've all been so busy juggling schoolwork and the mission to find the objects, there's not a lot of time for personal detours. Not now.

After much nagging and tantrum-throwing, Janelle Kirkpatrick finally got her security access, so after locking all of our sensitive work in a password-protected file cabinet, Kirin and I have been spending most of our time in the stacks. It's not easy dodging her creepy, lurky, highly over-perfumed ass, but so far we've managed to do just that, combing through dusty books and manuscripts in search of legends and lore that might help us recreate the Book of Mist and Shadow.

But my luck runs out today when I wander off on my own to fetch a book for Kirin from the section on Arcane Occult Languages. Just before I reach the row I need, hushed, angry voices from between the shelves stop me cold.

"Don't you want to help your mother?" The first one hisses.

"I do," comes the second, clearly terrified even at a whisper. "I'm trying my best."

"Try harder, *daughter*, or your precious house of cards will crumble. Do you want to end up like Amelia?"

Amelia? If she's talking about Amelia Weatherby… She was one of the Claires—a friend of Carly's who left the Academy last month when her aunt Danika Lewis was executed on live TV for the crime of witchcraft.

I duck into the row beside them and peer through the shelves, catching sight of Janelle and Carly. Carly's crying, her eyes red and puffy, her shoulders slumped. Janelle, as poised and polished as ever, looms over her, glaring at Carly as if she were no more than a nuisance, a piece of gum stuck on the bottom of her Jimmy Choos.

"You disgust me," Janelle says. Then, out of nowhere, she slaps Carly hard across the face, the crack echoing down the row. "I never should've trusted you. You're no better than—"

"Carly, hey." I pop up at the end of the row, plastering on a smile. "We've been waiting for you over in the Tarot Interpretation section."

Carly turns to face me, her energy a mixture of confusion, embarrassment, and relief.

"I know it sucks you got stuck helping me," I say, "but I really need it. Maddox will fail me if I don't nail the next paper."

Carly forces a smile, tucking her hair behind her ears before she turns back to look at her mother. "I'll talk to you later, *Mother*. I need to take care of this."

Janelle says nothing—just smiles her fake plastic smile,

that awful red lipstick blaring out like a traffic light, her perfume nearly making me gag.

I walk with Carly toward the Tarot Interpretation section, as fast and far away from her mother as we can get.

"Thanks for the save," Carly says. "Guess we're even now, Twink."

And with that, she turns toward the exit and disappears down the stairs.

* * *

"I've been thinking," Kirin says.

"And this is news because…?"

He smiles, nudging me with his knee. "Hear me out."

We're sitting side by side on the floor in the Dream Interpretation section on a Friday night, trying to locate information that might help us translate the dream grimoire Kelly Maddox gave me, hoping against the odds it'll help us recreate the spells we need to locate the Arcana objects. We've been doing some form of this dance all week—sitting between the stacks, pulling random books off the shelves, skimming and flipping, taking notes, desperate for a lead— any lead—that can bring us one step closer.

So far, we haven't made all that much progress.

But at least the company is good.

"I get what you're saying about the wand," Kirin continues. "But if your dreams are any indicator, I still believe the sword was meant for you. Therefore, I think we should focus on finding the sword first."

"But if Dark Judgment gets his hands on the wand—"

"He may already have it, Stevie. In your dreams, he uses it to raise the dead, and you're wielding the sword."

"*Sometimes*. I'm *sometimes* wielding the sword. Other times, I'm wielding a bouquet of dead flowers or a holly branch or a rabbit."

"*Sometimes* with the sword is plenty enough to go on right now." Kirin slides a book back into place on the shelf above his head, then looks at me, his eyes pleading. "We need to find the objects. All of them. But if there's even the slightest chance you can use that sword, we need to make that the priority. Then at least you won't be totally defenseless."

I want to argue, but there's logic to his reasoning.

"Tell you what," he says, pushing his glasses up his nose. "Give me one more week. If we don't make any progress by next Friday, we'll regroup and focus on the wand instead."

"Throw in a few more lattes, and you've got yourself a deal." I hold out my hand, and Kirin grabs it for a shake, giving it an extra squeeze before letting go.

"So, believe it or not, I've been thinking too." I lean across him and grab one of the books I'd been working with earlier, flipping to the section I last read on Dreams and Divination.

But this time, when I turn the page, The Moon card falls out.

I laugh, picking it up for a closer look.

"Yes, Mom," I tease. "I know. I'm getting to that part."

Kirin, used to my randomly appearing Tarot messages by now, shakes his head and smiles. "I take it this has something to do with dreams?"

"Remember the other day when I was talking about Mom's grimoire, wondering how it could be part of the Book of Shadow and Mists when that legend is thousands of years old?"

Kirin nods.

"Totally obvious in retrospect," I say, "but the only way that makes sense is if it's not Mom's grimoire itself that holds the key. It's the spells and prophecies *contained* in that grimoire—spells and prophecies she divined from another source. One we might be able to connect with directly, bypassing the need for all the translations, thereby recreating the spells."

"What are you saying?" he asks, excitement bubbling out of him.

I hold up the Moon card between us. "I think she may have brought the Journey book back from the dream realm, then divined the full prophecies through the Tarot. So all we need to do is find another Journey book—or something equivalent—and divine our own meanings. Maybe that's how this whole thing works."

Message received, the card vanishes from my grasp.

Kirin looks at me intently, his eyes sparkling in the way I've come to associate with new discoveries and exciting academic challenges. "Stevie, you might be onto something here."

"Might be?" I smack his knee and laugh. "This is

genius-level insight right here, my friend. You are in the presence of greatness."

"I never doubted it for a second," he teases, his eyes still holding mine. Suddenly I'm hyperaware of everything—our knees touching, the soft murmurs of students on the other side of the library, the comforting smell of parchment and lemon oil.

Looking at Kirin, I feel the pull of those mesmerizing green eyes, the memories of our last kiss in the stacks conspiring to make me lean in closer, to reach for him, to want him with every maddening beat of my heart.

Kirin lowers his mouth to mine, and our lips touch, soft and tender as a warm breeze, shattering the very last wall left lingering between us.

I thread my hands into his hair and deepen our kiss, fireworks exploding on my tongue.

"Stevie…" Kirin breathes, and I moan against his lips, desperate for the hot press of them one more time…

A flash of movement at the end of the aisle sends us scattering, and I grab the nearest book off the shelf and pretend to flip through it, glancing up to find Ani staring down at us, his caramel eyes alight with some new mischief.

"Wow," he says, barely holding back his grin. "You really *can* learn new things at the library!"

"I found it!" I blurt out, holding up the book as if Ani didn't just catch us making out.

Ani swipes it from my hands and peers at the title. "Never Too Old to Party with the Priestess: How to Plan an

Arcana-Themed Birthday for Your Magickal Inner Child." He shakes his head. "Stevie, we talked about this."

"First of all, you are totally making that up. And second of all, we're busy, so if you're not here to help us research, then farewell, my ginger-haired friend. Adieu!"

"I'm definitely not here for more homework," he says, "but something tells me neither are you."

I roll my eyes, but Ani never fails to make me laugh. "Why are you here?"

"I'm here," he announces, handing over a white binder stuffed with papers, their edges stained with splotches of mysterious origins, "to collect payback."

"What dark magick is *this* questionably sticky grimoire?"

"*This* questionably sticky grimoire is your destiny," he says in a breathy impersonation of Professor Maddox. Then, with a quick shrug, "At least for tonight."

"Is this hot sauce?" I bring the binder to my nose and sniff one of the unidentifiable stains. Hot sauce confirmed. Eww.

"Don't think of it as hot sauce. Think of it as payback."

I flip through the pages. "Song lists?"

Ani wriggles his eyebrows.

"Tonight?" I snap the binder shut and hand it back to him. "You're kidding, right?"

"*You're* kidding if you think I'm letting you hit up Hot Shots dressed like a yoga-teaching librarian. A hot yoga-teaching librarian, but still. Come with me, woman." He reaches for my hand and hauls me up from the floor, then wrinkles his nose. "You smell like old books and desperation."

"My new signature scent." Laughing, I glance down at Kirin, who's got his head bent over another book, his hair sticking up where I ran my hands through it. He's so intensely focused, I'm not even sure he remembers kissing me.

"Kirin," I say, "you coming?"

No response.

"Kirin?" I nudge his shoulder with my knee, and he finally glances up. "You ready to call it a day? Do something a little less—"

"Nerdy?" Ani asks.

"I was going to say academic."

"Either way," Ani says, "it's way past time to fulfill our rockstar fantasies and drink copious amounts of alcohol to mask our deep inner shame. You coming?"

Kirin looks at me, his eyes blazing behind his glasses, but I can't get a read on him.

Please say yes. Please, please say yes. Just this once...

"No, you guys go ahead," he says, and my heart sinks.

"Are you sure?" I ask.

"I need to finish up here, then I've got a ton of work to catch up on at my computer."

"So I'll stick around and help," I say.

He hesitates only a moment, then shakes his head. "No. I want you to go out and have at least one night of fun. Might be your last chance for a while."

"You sure?"

"Positive."

"Well, if you change your mind, you know where to find us."

"I do. And Stevie?" He beams up at me, a half-smile tugging his lips. "Sing something witchy for me."

Without hesitating, I kneel down in front of him and press another kiss to his surprised lips, not caring that Ani's still watching. "Count on it."

THIRTY-SEVEN

ANSEL

"No, this absolutely won't do." I run my eyes over Stevie's current ensemble—her third attempt of the evening. "I mean, you look amazing in everything, of course. But tonight I need something a little *more*. Something... I don't know. Extra. *Super* extra."

"Listen, Tim Gunn. I'm wearing six-inch heels, a red leather mini, and a sheer white camisole. That's not extra enough?"

"No. No it is not."

"This shirt is so see-through, if I had pierced nipples, every passerby would be able to identify the exact shape and metal composition of my studs!"

"That was... oddly specific. And also kind of exciting."

She stomps her foot. Definition of adorable. "This is ridiculous, Ani. It's just Hot Shots!"

"Think of your legions of adoring future-fans."

"Think of my overly exposed nipples!"

"Um… okay?" I close my eyes and grin, and Stevie smacks my arm.

"This is a terrible idea. I should be at the library helping Kirin figure out the spells."

"No can do, Stevie Boo-Boo. Hit the books any harder, and your pretty little head is going to explode. And I say that in the least condescending way possible. Make-out sessions aside, you and that adorable genius of yours are on burnout highway."

"That's…" She blows out a breath and shrugs. "Accurate. I do kind of need this tonight. Even if we just go for a few songs."

"That's the spirit. Besides, you *can't* bail." I pull out my phone and scroll through the student directory for Nat and Isla's numbers, then send them an invite. I send one to Baz, too, complete with a bunch of fruit and vegetable emojis to confound him—he still doesn't understand what the eggplant means. "Now the whole gang's expecting you."

"Ani. You don't have a gang."

"*We* have a gang. And they're all coming. Well, aside from Kirin, who's currently in a three-way with his computer and his bookshelf, and Cass, who's much too proper to spend a night drinking in public with his students." I sense her wavering again, and I swoop in for a hug. "Come on, Stevie. You need a break. We all do. One night of fun, then it's back to saving the world tomorrow. Okay?"

"You know I can never say no to you, Ani."

"Perfect." I release her and shoo her toward the

bedroom. "Now go find something sexy and fierce to wear. I want sparkles. I want spangles. I want vampire sex kitten."

She narrows her eyes at me. "I'm not sure whether I should be highly offended, slightly terrified, or completely turned on right now."

I'm saved from having to respond by her ringing phone.

Her face lights up when she sees who's calling, and I immediately know it's Baz.

"Hey!" she says, holding the phone to her ear. "Yeah, I'm here with Ani. He's helping me get dressed." Stevie laughs and rolls her eyes. "Because any time *you* help me get dressed, I end up naked and late."

Baz's voice rumbles through the phone, and she smiles again.

"We'll revisit that idea later." She glances at me, then away, her cheeks blushing. "No, don't worry. We're almost done. We'll just meet you downstairs."

She hangs up and looks down at her outfit. "Okay, I know what I'm going to wear. And this time you can't say no."

"Is it sparkly?"

"Yes, it's sparkly! Goddess, Ani! You're obsessed!"

"I like sparkles, what can I say?" I grin, then grab the songbook off the countertop. "Tell you what. I'll go down and meet Baz, you go get sparkled and spangled. I'm trusting you, Stevie. Don't disappoint me. We've got songs to crush and hearts to break."

"You know something?" She smiles, lighting up the

whole room, then grabs me in another tight hug, pressing a big fat smooch to my cheek. "Even when you're driving me nuts, you're still the best."

I close my eyes and hold her tight, inhaling the sweet scent of her hair, and for just a minute, I almost believe she's really mine. That *I'm* the one who put that sexy blush on her cheeks, that smile on her face.

That Stevie, unlike everyone else I've ever loved, won't light a match, burn down that bridge, and walk out of my life for good.

* * *

"Too bad we can't get Cass to come out." Baz leans against the hearth in the common room, flipping through the songbook. "I'd kill to see him on stage."

I crack up at that. "Oh, sure. I can just picture him letting loose with a crazy rendition of Frank Sinatra's *Witchcraft.*"

"Sinatra? That's not entirely fair. He's not *that* old. Maybe The Eagles, *Witchy Woman*?"

"Nah, too easy-listening. Wait, I've got it! Santana, *Black Magic Woman.*"

"Fuck, that's totally a Cass song." Baz snaps the book shut. "Maybe one day we'll have to drug him, kidnap him, and throw his ass up on stage."

I laugh and flutter my eyelashes. "A girl can dream."

Truth is, I'd love it if Cass would hang out with us. But he's a professor, we're his students, and he's not going to cross that line, ever. Just like we'll never get Kirin's ass out of the library for a night out. Kirin doesn't like the bar scene —always worried something's going to set him off.

I get it. Still, it doesn't make it any easier. Outside the Brotherhood meetings, it's rare that the four of us get to be in the same room together. It'd be nice if we could do it for fun reasons rather than just for crisis management and post-tragedy clean-up.

I'm about to ask Baz what his thoughts are on the matter when Stevie enters the common room, and all my thoughts evaporate.

She's wearing thigh-high black boots and a long-sleeved silver dress that stops a few inches above the knee, the fabric hugging every curve, catching the light as she moves. Her hair is twisted into a loose mass of curls on top of her head, a few pulled down around her face, showing off a pair of silver hoop earrings.

But it's her smile that really does me in.

She's stunning. That's the only word for it. And if I had to actually concentrate to make my heart beat and my lungs fill with air, I'd be dead by now.

"Right, Ani?" Baz's voice cuts into the haze, and I tear my eyes away from Stevie and look at him, blinking rapidly.

"Sorry, what?"

Baz shakes his head and laughs. "Oh, you've got it *bad*, man."

"I've got… what?"

He cuts his eyes to Stevie, who stopped near the

entrance to chat with a few guys playing D&D, then back to me. *That's* what."

"It's not… Stevie and I are just… I mean…"

Baz holds up his hand, his eyes fiery. But not angry fiery, I note with relief. More like… amused fiery.

"Truth is," he says, "we *all* feel something for her. Even Cass, much as that bastard will never admit it."

I shake my head, denial at the ready. "It's just the bond, Baz."

"Yeah?" Baz laughs. "Then why don't you stare at *me* with that sappy, goopy-eyed look?"

I laugh and turn down my nose at him. "You're not my type."

"But she is," he says. It's not a question.

I lower my eyes. There's no use denying it anymore— not to my brothers. My best fucking friends. "Yeah," I whisper. "I think maybe she is."

"Why?"

"What do you mean, why? Maybe because I spend my whole fucking day trying to come up with ways to make her laugh? Because the days I get to go adventuring with her are the best of my life? Because one smile from Stevie can get me through all the fucked-up family shit? Because being around her makes me believe all this bullshit is worth fighting for? Because—"

He holds up his hand again, cutting me off. "You made your point."

I glare at him, waiting for the smartass comeback, the "keep dreaming, buddy" that's bound to come.

But Baz only nods, wrapping his hand around the back of my neck and giving it an affectionate squeeze.

"Wait… That's it?" I ask, incredulous. "I lay my soul upon this hearth before us, and you just… nod and squeeze?"

He considers me a moment, then cocks a devilish grin. "Nothing left to say, brother. You took the words right out of my mouth. Kirin's too, I suspect. And yeah, like I said, Cass is probably writing the same love song."

I glance back at Stevie, who's dutifully inspecting the miniature monsters her friends have positioned on their game map, and blow out a breath. "So where does that leave us?"

"Depends on her, I guess," he says. "What she wants. How she feels."

"And you're telling me you're cool with it?"

"With sharing her?" Baz shrugs. "Not exactly my first choice, but come on. As far as competition goes, I could do a lot worse than the Brotherhood, and so could you."

I stare at him open-mouthed, trying to process this.

"Look," he says, "don't act so surprised. Everyone knows Stevie and I have been spending a lot of time together. And everyone also knows she's been in love with Kirin since… I don't know. Back when he was hanging out at her tea café, I guess. She and I have talked about that. And yeah, as much as I'd love to keep her all to myself? I would never, ever want her to choose. I'd never ask her to do something that would break her heart, not even for a minute."

I nod, taking in his words, a surge of gratitude rising up inside me.

"Don't look at me like that," Baz says. "I'm not the one you want to kiss, remember?"

We both glance back over at Stevie, still smiling, the whole D&D gang utterly captivated by her. She catches us watching her and waves, her smile brightening.

"Thank you," I say, then shake my head. "For understanding about all this. But seriously, Baz. Stevie and I... She doesn't feel that way about me. As far as she's concerned, I'm firmly in the big-brother zone."

"I wouldn't be so sure about that, Gingersnap. I mean, you're not *my* type by any stretch, but you've got a certain appeal." He narrows his eyes, pretending to consider me. "I could see it."

I crack up. "Yeah, well. You know what they say. Once you go red, you—"

"Don't finish that sentence, or you'll end up dead?" Baz grins.

"Who's ending up dead?" Stevie joins us at the hearth, standing between us and looping an arm over each of our shoulders. "Are you two brutes threatening the first-years again?"

"Hell no," Baz says. "Only the D&D guys."

"Sorry, kids," he calls over to them. "She's got her hands full."

"Baz!" Stevie gives him a playful smack on the chest. "You guys are terrible. Both of you. Now take me to Hot

Shots before I change my mind and this bomb-ass outfit goes to waste."

"As you wish, Little Bird."

The three of us head over to Hot Shots, walking down the red stone path arm-in-arm, Stevie in the middle, each of us taking turns thinking up the best karaoke revenge songs we can spring on each other.

Farther up the path, three women head our way.

"Ah, fuck," Baz grumbles, and I can tell from his tone *exactly* who's about to ruin the moment.

That tone is reserved for one person and one person only.

"Hey, Carly," I say, eager to keep things cordial as she and her friends approach. The last thing I need is Carly's Baz infatuation—and its ensuing bickering—destroying my Friday night vibe. "You guys heading to karaoke?"

"We *were*," Carly huffs, flipping her dark hair. "But Hot Shots is a total bust tonight."

"Dead crowd?" I ask.

"No crowd. No anything. The place got flooded—it's closed."

"You're kidding?" Stevie asks.

Carly glares at her, then rolls her eyes. "Yes, Twink, I make a habit of spreading rumors about bars being closed just for kicks. Hilarious, right?"

Stevie smiles. "Well, great talking with you, as always. I think we'll go check it out anyway."

"Suit yourselves," Carly says with a shrug. "But seriously. Waste of time. They've already shut it down."

We continue on our way, leaving the Claires in the rearview. Still, it takes me a minute to shake off the bad mojo. Carly has a way of sucking all the light out of the room on the best of days, and tonight she seems particularly off. I can't quite put my finger on it, but something in her demeanor was just… odd. Nervous, almost.

"Ani, you okay?" Stevie asks, ruffling my hair. If she sensed anything off about Carly's energy, she isn't mentioning it.

"Yeah." I blink away the image of the Claires, focusing instead on Stevie's big blue eyes. "More than okay."

"Good." She beams at me, then takes my hand, giving it an affectionate squeeze. "Okay, boys. I've decided on my first song."

"Don't leave us in suspense," Baz says.

"Edge of Seventeen, by the singer with the best name ever."

"Who?" Baz teases.

"Hello? Stevie Nicks!"

"Badass," I say, just as Hot Shots comes into view.

And then, right when I start to think the night might turn out okay after all, the fucking bar explodes before our eyes.

THIRTY-EIGHT

KIRIN

She saunters into my office and crosses the room, flashing that gorgeous smile that lights me up from the inside. I take a breath to speak, but she presses her finger to my lips.

"Don't talk," she whispers, straddling me in the chair. "Don't breathe a word."

Suddenly she's naked, her hot flesh radiating through my jeans, making me ache. Instinctively, I cup her ass, pulling her closer and pressing my mouth to her breast.

She moans my name, writhing in my lap as my cock grows harder, every inch desperate for her touch.

But the longer she stays with me, the darker my thoughts turn. My body craves her, needs her, but my heart can't take it. It hammers wildly in my chest, my nerves buzzing, every muscle screaming in agony as the fear rises inside, bile churning in my gut, my vision turning red with lust and rage and the pain of a thousand lifetimes...

Behind us, the bookshelves tremble and collapse, and my desk follows next. Ignoring the chaos, she laughs and fumbles with my zipper, finally freeing my cock from my jeans.

"Take it," she whispers, positioning the tip at her hot, wet entrance. "Take all of it."

"I can't."

"Shh," she says again, then lowers herself onto my rock-hard cock, taking me in deep, claiming my mouth and sucking the very last breath from my lungs.

The windows explode and the floor buckles and the walls crack and crumble down, but still, she doesn't stop.

I come with a shuddering gasp, and when I finally open my eyes, the rest of the world is burning to ash, and she's still laughing. Laughing and laughing until there's nothing left of the world we knew but memory and ash.

"Kirin," she finally says. "Wake up…."

* * *

"Kirin, wake *up!*"

I bolt upright with a gasp, blinking away the last remnants of my dream. In its place, three figures take shape in my office.

Baz, glaring at me with his arms crossed over his chest.

Ani, smirking.

And Stevie, dressed like she just stepped off the set of a music video, so stunningly beautiful I wonder if I'm still dreaming.

"Did we disturb you, Sleeping Beauty?" Baz asks.

I glance down at my desk, willing my heart rate to return to normal. "What time is it? What's going on?"

"You just slept through an explosion, that's what's going on."

"What?" I'm out of my chair in a flash. "What the hell happened?"

"Someone blew up Hot Shots," Ani says.

"Holy shit! Did anyone get hurt?"

"See, that's the crazy part," Baz says. "Apparently, not fifteen minutes before the explosion, the manager cleared out the whole place. Said a pipe burst and it was flooded. And the explosion itself was totally contained—it didn't touch anything other than the bar."

"So the Flame and Fury dorms weren't damaged?" I ask, trying to make sense of it.

Baz shakes his head. "Totally unscathed. The manager got out of the bar in time, too."

"Convenient," I say. "I assume he's suspect number one."

"Eastman and Quintana are grilling him now," he says. "They've implemented a curfew."

"And I see you're all following orders, as usual," I say. "Where's Casey?"

"We didn't see her," Stevie says. "But guys, seriously. I don't think the manager did it. Think about it—who has the most to gain from blowing up a bar with no one in it? In a controlled explosion, where no one got hurt?"

"No idea," Ani says.

"He didn't do it," Stevie says. "This has magick attack

written all over it. Either someone got to him, or the whole thing was a setup."

"To what end, though?" Baz asks. "No one got hurt."

"To scare the shit out of us and use it as leverage to take away more freedoms," she says, and the rest of the pieces fall into place.

"You think APOA is behind it?" I ask.

"Think about it," she says. "Agent Quintana said Eastman was pushing for a curfew as well as cutting off travel. They want us all locked up and scared."

"But why?" I ask. "Just so they can complete their investigation?"

"That doesn't add up," Ani says. "They're investigating magickal attacks on students. Why would they stage another one, just so they could keep investigating what they're already investigating?"

"But if it's not APOA, that leaves who?" Baz asks. "The other attacks were actual *attacks*. People got hurt, or got their magick stripped. This was just theatrics. Scare tactics."

"Something isn't adding up," Stevie says. "In my gut, I feel like APOA was involved in this. But there's only one reason I can think of for them wanting to keep all of us out of their hair with a curfew and more restrictions."

She glances up at me, and I read her thoughts in her eyes.

"They're looking for the Arcana objects." I shove a hand through my hair, remembering Casey's interest in the matter. As much as I hate to think my sister's involved in something like this, I can't rule it out.

"So what the hell do we do now?" Baz asks.

Stevie drops into a chair. "We just sit here for a few minutes and think."

"What were you doing, anyway?" Baz asks me, his eyes trailing down my body, stopping at my crotch.

It's only then that I realize I'm still rocking a halfway raging hard-on.

"Must've been some dream," he says.

My eyes instinctively dart to Stevie, and Baz laughs.

"I see," he says. "So you were having freaky dream-realm sex with my girl? I'm not sure how I should feel about that."

Stevie rolls her eyes. "Slow your roll, Mr. Possessive. We've got bigger problems right now."

Baz nods toward my annoyingly persistent hard-on. "Bigger than *that*?"

I shake my head, unable to let this go unaddressed. "From a purely technical standpoint, no. I was not *having* dream-realm sex with her. I was dreaming *about* having sex with her. *Actual* dream-realm sex would require both of us to travel to the dream realm together, at which time, if we mutually decided to engage in… Well, that's how it would work. Just wanted to clear up any misconceptions there."

Baz glares at Stevie, but his eyes hold a hint of humor. "Do you have anything to say about this?"

She winks at me. "What happens in the dream realm stays in the dream realm, right?"

"Again, from a technical standpoint," I say, "the realms don't work like that, either. When something happens in the dream realm, it leaves impressions that can have ripple effects into other realms. So, for example, if two people who know each other in real life decide to have sex in the dream realm, the effects of that could ripple into their *actual* real life. Physical as well as emotional—anything from pregnancy to rumpled sheets to real feelings of love and desire, or—as is sometimes the case—regret."

I glance up to find all three of them staring at me open-mouthed.

"You have too much free time on your hands," Baz says.

Ani laughs.

But Stevie has tears in her eyes.

Before I can ask her what's wrong, she's on her feet, leaning across my desk to pull me in for an awkward hug.

"Kirin, I could kiss you." She grabs my shoulders, a grin stretching across her face. "In fact, screw it. I'm totally gonna kiss you."

She plants one right on my mouth, soft and sweet and deep, all-too-quickly turning into a laugh.

"Right here, baby," Baz says, pointing at his mouth. "If you're handing them out."

She releases me and turns toward Baz, capturing his mouth in an equally deep kiss.

"Not to beg," Ani says, holding up a finger, "but—"

I have no idea whether he's kidding or not, but Stevie cuts him off, grabbing his shirt collar and hauling him in close, pressing her lips to his.

Ani's eyes widen, his hands sliding around her back, a soft moan slipping from his mouth.

By the time she breaks away, all of us are dazed and baffled. And more than a little turned on.

"I know where they are!" she exclaims, her smile stretching wide.

"What?" I ask.

"The Arcana objects!" she says. "Well, the Sword and Wand, for starters. What time is it?"

"Almost midnight," I say. "Why? What's happening, Stevie?"

"Do you remember how to get to those standing stones?" she asks.

"I think so. Why? What's going on?"

"Call Doc," she instructs. "Ani, you call Isla and Nat. I'll call Professor Maddox and Professor Broome. Tell everyone to meet us behind Breath and Blade in twenty minutes. Hurry—we don't have much time, and we need all the help we can get."

She grabs her phone, and the rest of us follow suit, everyone talking at once.

Judging by the slightly slurred, rugged tone of his voice, it's clear Cass is half-drunk and half-asleep when he answers my call. Still, I press on, Stevie's sense of urgency infecting us all and sobering him up fast.

"Get dressed," I tell him. "Meet us out behind Breath and Blade as soon as you can. It's an emergency."

Leaving no chance for argument, I hang up.

"Sorry for the late call," Stevie says, presumably to one of the Professors. "I can't explain now, but I need you and Kelly to meet us on the path behind Breath and Blade. Bring some blankets and whatever dream potions we need to encourage shared dreaming and dream retrieval." She takes a breath, her smile still shining bright. "Yes, exactly. It's only a theory, but it's solid. I'll explain everything later. See you soon."

"Isla and Nat are good to go," Ani says, hanging up his phone.

"We need to go," Stevie says, grabbing my hand. "Come on."

My head is still spinning, thoughts crashing together too fast to make any sense inside my addled brain.

"Right now?" I ask. "At midnight?"

"Now is the *perfect* time." She flashes me another grin, her whole body vibrating with adrenaline and excitement. "It's dream time."

It hits me then, the realization exploding inside me.

"The objects… They're in the dream realm," I say. "Holy shit."

Stevie nods. "That's why we can feel the magick at the Towers and the Cauldron, but not the objects themselves. There's a ripple effect—the magickal connection resonating across realms."

"So they *are* on campus," Ani says, just as astounded as the rest of us. "Just not *this* version of campus, exactly."

"Brilliant," Baz says. "Fucking brilliant."

"Let's go." I grab the sweatshirt from the back of my chair and head for the door. If Stevie's theory is correct, we may have just found the key to deciphering the cryptic map we've been chasing since we first uncovered the Dark Arcana legends.

But when I haul open the door, I find a woman blocking our exit, her grin sly and malicious. Behind her, another woman lurks, red lips pulled into an unnatural smile.

"Casey? Janelle?" My mind is reeling, my eyes darting back and forth between them. I angle myself in front of Stevie, blocking her from view. "What are you two doing here?"

Casey glares at me with cold, empty eyes, and my blood turns to ice.

Despite all our years of estrangement, despite all the arguments that came before it, despite everything that's happened on the long and winding road of our relationship, one thing I can say with absolute certainty is this:

The woman staring back at me now is not my sister at all.

"Haven't you heard, little brother?" She flashes another wicked grin, then lifts her gun, pointing it directly at my chest. "There's a curfew now. And I'm here to enforce it."

THIRTY-NINE

CASS

Trust. A concept that's simultaneously as solid as bedrock and as fragile as a glass bubble.

I fear it. I loathe it. I long for it.

Despite my years at Arcana Academy, despite the camaraderie of the faculty and staff, the only people I've truly come to trust are my Brothers. Kirin, Baz, Ani, and now Stevie. Our Star. Everyone else is either an enemy or a liability. That's how I've operated. It's how I've kept us safe.

Yet some part of me knows Stevie was right when she came to me last week. We *can't* do this alone—not anymore. There's too much at stake, too many enemies, too many threats. Not even the strength of our bond is enough to see us through this war. Not if we want to end up on the winning side.

And so it is, we've come to this night, nearly a dozen witches and mages gathered beneath a starry sky and the awe-inspiring standing stones at the center of the Breath and Blade lands.

I wanted to trust. I *still* want to trust.

But trust would be a hell of a lot easier if I wasn't on my knees with a gun pointed at my head.

"Stop wasting time," Casey Appleton barks, pressing the muzzle to the base of my skull.

Professor Broome glares at her, her gaze equal parts pleading and angry. "The ritual can't be rushed, Agent. Not if you want it to succeed."

Casey sighs, but the pressure against my skull lessens a fraction. I don't dare breathe. Don't dare move. My eyes find Stevie's in the darkness, and she smiles, a beacon of hope on an otherwise hopeless night.

She's skyclad, lying on a pile of blankets beneath a threadbare sheet, Baz and Kirin lying on either side of her. The men are also nude; Professor Broome believes dream sharing works best when the participants have as much skin-to-skin contact as possible. Positioned at equal intervals around them, Ani, Nat, and Isla hold space, casting a protective circle, their concern for their friends outweighing their concern for their own lives.

If not for the threat of death, this might have been a brilliant plan.

But behind me, the gun speaks volumes, and Janelle Kirkpatrick continues to pace, desperation and greed driving her onward.

"Hold out your palms, please," Professor Maddox says calmly, and the three prone Arcana brothers obey. With a ritual athame, she makes a quick, clean slice across their palms, then orders them to join hands.

"Your flesh and blood now form an unbroken connection. Close your eyes and feel the power of that bond. The intimacy of it. Use this to call each other into the dream, to find each other if you lose your way, and to bring each other back. It's the only thing tethering you to this world."

She speaks the truth. She removed their protective jewelry before the ritual began, as grounding stones like hematite would interfere with their ability to dreamshare and return safely. So now they're entering a realm full of danger, totally unprotected.

My only hope is that they'll find less danger there than we've got right here. That somehow, despite the bleak odds, they'll find a way to escape this—even if it means leaving the rest of us behind.

"Dr. Devane?" Professor Broome calls. "It is time."

I wait for Casey to grant me permission, then I crawl over to the blankets, kneeling at their feet. Casey moves to follow, but Professor Broome holds up a hand.

"Since you and Mrs. Kirkpatrick have clearly established yourselves as threats, if either of you enter the protective circle, the ritual will be ruined."

"Bullshit," Casey snaps.

"Would you like to take the risk?" Broome asks, her voice as calm and unbending as steel. "Now, when you're so close to achieving your ends?"

Casey hesitates, then takes a few steps backward, granting us a small bubble of privacy.

Raising her gun, she takes aim at Ani and says, "If I sense so much as a *tingle* of magick, a *whiff* of an attack plan, he's gone."

"No one will attack," I say. "You have my word."

She barks out a dry laugh. "Let's hope your promises to me are stronger than your promises to them."

I wince at the jab, feeling it cut straight through me. A tear slides down my cheek, but that's the only one I will allow tonight.

Kirin meets my eyes, his own shining with regret. He gave up trying to talk sense into his sister an hour ago, his voice hoarse from the effort. There was nothing he could say. Whatever came over Casey, whatever poisonous thoughts infected her mind, she's singularly focused now. She wants the sword, and she believes Stevie knows how to retrieve it. Nothing will sway her from that course.

"I will guide you into the dream realm with a meditation," I say, looking each of them in the eye, forcing myself to remain calm. Steady. To hold the hope that's quickly fading from their eyes, despite the weight of the darkness threatening to pull me under too. "Listen to the sound of my voice and follow it to your destination, holding tight to each other always."

My voice breaks on the last part, but I clear my throat and smile, touching their feet, hoping it's not the last time I get to touch them. See them. Know them.

Know her.

If I let it, my heart could shatter right now for all the things that never got to be.

But I can't let it. I *refuse* to let it.

They need me to stay strong.

With our three Arcana brothers still clasping hands, Professor Broome retrieves a glass bottle from her bag, filled with a mixture of water, herbs, and crystals. She unstoppers the bottle and gives it a gentle swirl, the herbal scent floating into the night air.

"The potion will help you find what you're searching for, communicate with any necessary guides and spirits, and find your way back with the object intact." She holds it first to Kirin's lips, then to Baz's. Each man takes a deep drink.

When she presses it to Stevie's lips, Stevie's nose wrinkles, followed by another gentle smile that threatens to undo me completely.

"That smells terrible," she says softly.

Professor Broome strokes her hair. "It's the Fairy's Breath. You're the only one who can smell it."

Stevie nods and takes a sip, finishing her dose. But just as Professor Broome sets the bottle aside, a soft gasp escapes Stevie's lips, her eyes widening, her mouth parting in shock.

"Fairy's Breath," she whispers. "That's it!"

I narrow my eyes, searching her face, keeping my voice low enough to avoid detection from our captors. "Stevie? What is it?"

"The smell. I've been smelling it for weeks, and it's been driving me crazy because I couldn't remember what it was.

Janelle *reeks* of it—always has. And tonight, for the first time in all the times I've seen her, Casey does too."

"What are you saying?" I whisper.

Professor Broome's eyes widen, some new realization dawning on her face. "Fairy's Breath is used to enhance spirit communications and channeling, but it can also be used for possession."

"As in demonic?" I whisper.

"As in *any* entity—good or evil, spiritual or earth-based, magickal or otherwise—that seeks to possess a human body and use it to achieve its own ends."

"That's not Casey *or* Janelle," Stevie whispers. "Someone has possessed them."

Kirin's eyes alight with new hope. Relief.

Beside her, Baz lets out a breath I'm certain he's been holding all night.

"Dark Arcana," I whisper. "It must be."

"What's taking so long?" Janelle snaps.

"Mrs. Kirkpatrick," Professor Broome replies, her tone as steely as ever. "Each time you interrupt the ritual, we must begin again. Please stop with your incessant questions. You will have your treasure soon enough, but only if you let us work in peace."

"But—"

"Furthermore," she continues, "the whole point of this ritual is to guide them into a dream state, for which they must be asleep. Even the slightest interruption or sound could wake them, and we'll be forced to start at the beginning. Understand?"

This does the trick, and Janelle and Casey both back off again, though they're still watching us closely.

"What next?" Professor Maddox whispers.

I close my eyes, thinking as quickly as I can. "For now, we need to go through with the ritual. We can't let on that we know. If they come back with the sword, there might be a way… I don't know. I need more time."

"I've got other herbs and potions," Professor Broome says. "We may be able to devise a spell to force out the entities or bind them to something else."

"Keep thinking," I say. "In the meantime, we'll move forward with the ritual as planned."

"We'll find the sword, Doc," Stevie whispers. "It's here, just beneath the stone circle. I promise we'll come back with it."

Despite the dire circumstances, a smile spreads across my face. "I have no doubts, Miss Milan, that if the sword exists—if it's in the dream realm as you believe—you of all people will find a way to bring it back."

She returns my smile, her eyes shining with new hope.

"Come back to us," I whisper, laying my hands on them one last time. "All of you."

They nod and shift closer together, hands clasped tight, the bonds of Brotherhood and love and friendship wrapping around us all, a bright light that can never be dimmed.

Swallowing the tightness in my throat, I smile and say, "Shall we begin?"

Stevie, Kirin, and Baz nod, their eyelids finally drifting closed.

Professor Maddox places three Tarot cards on Stevie's chest—The Moon, to encourage lucid dreams; The High Priestess, for inner wisdom; and the Ace of Swords, for the swift recovery of the Sword of Breath and Blade.

Then I recite the meditation.

Kneeling together in silent solidarity, clinging to blind hope, the Professors and I watch them drift off to sleep, their breathing deep and even, their young faces smooth and untroubled.

I let out a soft sigh of relief.

"What do we do now?" Professor Maddox whispers.

The uncertainty presses on my heart, threatening once again to shatter it. But I promised Stevie I'd be strong, that I'd keep our allies united in hope. And no matter what Casey believes, my promises to the ones I love—to my brothers—they *are* strong. Unbreakable, in fact. So, despite the desperate pain in my chest, I draw on Baz's rock-solid strength, on Kirin's keen intellect, on Ani's optimism, and on Stevie's healing light, her hope, and her love.

I turn to Professor Maddox and offer an encouraging smile.

"The only thing we *can* do," I whisper. "We trust."

This story continues in book 3, Spells of Flame and Fury!

Will Stevie and her red-hot mages survive the epic journey to the dream realm, and if they do, what awaits them on the other side? Find out what happens next in **Spells of Flame and Fury!**

* * *

Are you a member of our private Facebook group, <u>Sarah Piper's Sassy Witches?</u> Pop in for sneak peeks, cover reveals, exclusive giveaways, book chats, and plenty of complete randomness! We've got a great community of readers and fans (and fellow Tarot lovers too!), and we'd love to see you there!

XOXO
Sarah

Paranormal romance fans, do you know I've got another sexy series ready to heat up your bookshelf? The Witch's Rebels is a complete supernatural reverse harem series featuring five smoldering-hot guys and the kickass witch they'd kill to protect. Read on for a taste of book one, Shadow Kissed!

SHADOW KISSED EXCERPT

Survival instinct was a powerful thing.

What horrors could we endure, could we accept, could we embrace in the name of staying alive?

Hunger. Brutality. Desperation.

Being alone.

I'd been alone for so long I'd almost forgotten what it was like to love, to trust, to look into the eyes of another person and feel a spark of something other than fear.

Then *they* came into my life.

Each one as damaged and flawed as I was, yet somehow finding a way through the cracks in my walls, slowly breaking down the bricks I'd so carefully built around my heart.

Despite their differences, they'd come together as my protectors and friends for reasons I still didn't fully understand. And after everything we'd been through, I had no doubts about who they were to me now. To each other.

Family.

I didn't know what the future held; I'd given up trying to predict it years ago. But I didn't need my Tarot cards or my mother's old crystal ball to know this:

For me, there was no future without them. Without my rebels.

"Gray?" His whisper floated to my ears.

After several heartbeats, I took a deep breath and opened my eyes.

I heard nothing, saw nothing, felt nothing but the demon imprisoned before me, pale and shattered, fading from this realm.

"Whatever you're thinking," he said, his head lolling forward, "don't."

Looking at him chained to the chair, bruises covering his face, blood pouring from the gashes in his chest, I strengthened my resolve.

His voice was faint, his body broken, his essence dimming. But the fire in his eyes blazed as bright as it had the day we'd met.

"Whatever horrible things you've heard about me, Cupcake, they're all true..."

"Please," he whispered, almost begging now. "I'm not worth..."

His words trailed off into a cough, blood spraying his lips.

I shook my head. He was wrong. He was *more* than worth it. Between the two of us, maybe only one would make it out of this room alive. If that were true, it had to be him; I couldn't live in a world where he didn't exist. Where any of them didn't exist.

This was my fate. My purpose. My gift.

There was no going back.

I held up my hands, indigo flames licking across my palms, surging bright in the darkness.

The demon shuddered as I reached for him, and I closed my eyes, sealing away the memory of his ocean-blue gaze, knowing it could very well be the last time I saw it.

* * *

2 Weeks Earlier...

Don't act like prey, and you won't become it. Don't act like prey...

Whispering my usual mantra, I locked up the van and pushed my rusty hand truck down St. Vincent Avenue, scanning the shadows for trouble.

It'd rained earlier, and mist still clung to the streets, rising into the dark autumn night like smoke. It made everything that much harder to see.

Fortunately it was my last delivery of the night, and I'd brought along my favorite traveling companions—a sharp stake in my waistband and a big-ass hunting knife in my boot. Still, danger had a way of sneaking up on a girl in Blackmoon Bay's warehouse district, which was why most people avoided it.

If I hadn't needed the money—and a boss who paid in cash and didn't ask questions about my past—I would've avoided it, too.

Alas...

Snuggling deeper into my leather jacket, I banked left at

the next alley and rolled to a stop in front of the unmarked service entrance to Black Ruby. My hand truck wobbled under the weight of its cargo—five refrigerated cases of O-positive and three AB-negative, fresh from a medical supplier in Vancouver.

Yeah, Waldrich's Imports dealt in some weird shit, but human cops didn't bother with the warehouse district, and the Fae Council that governed supernaturals didn't get involved with the Bay's black market. The only time they cared was when a supernatural killed a human, and some-times—depending on the human—not even then.

Thumbing through my packing slips, I hoped the vampires weren't too thirsty tonight. Half their order had gotten snagged by customs across the bay in Seattle.

I also hoped someone other than Darius Beaumont would sign for this. I could hold my own with most vamps, but Black Ruby's owner definitely struck me as the shoot-the-messenger type.

No matter how sexy he is…

Wrapping one hand discretely around my stake, I reached up to hit the buzzer, but a faint cry from the far end of the alley stopped me.

"Don't! Please!"

"Settle down, sweetheart," a man said, the menace in his voice a sick contrast to the terrified tremble in hers.

My heart rate spiked.

Abandoning my delivery, I scooted along the building's brick exterior, edging closer to the struggle. I spotted the girl first—she couldn't have been more than fifteen, sixteen at most, with lanky brown hair and the pale, haunted features of a blood slave.

But it wasn't a vampire that'd lured her out for a snack.

The greasy dude who'd cornered her was a hundred percent human—just another pervert in dirty jeans and a sweat-stained henley who clearly thought runaway kids were an easy mark.

"It'll all be over soon," he told her.

Yeah, sooner than you think…

Anger coiled in my belly, fizzing the edges of my vision. I couldn't decide who deserved more of my ire—the asshole threatening her now, or the parents who'd abandoned her in the first place.

Far as I was concerned, they were the same breed of evil.

"Well now. Must be my lucky night." The man barked out a wheezing laugh, and too late, I realized I'd been spotted. "Two for the price of one. Come on over here, Blondie. Don't be shy."

Shit. I'd hesitated too long, let my emotions get the best of me when I should've been working that knife out of my boot.

Fear leaked into my limbs, and for a brief instant, I felt my brain and body duking it out. *Fight or flight, fight or flight…*

No. I couldn't leave her. Not like that.

"Let her go," I said, brandishing my stake.

He yanked the kid against his chest, one meaty hand fisting her blue unicorn hoodie, the other curling around her throat. Fresh urine soaked her jeans.

"Drop your little stick and come over here," the man said, "or I'll break her neck."

My mind raced for an alternative, but there was no time. I couldn't risk going for the knife. Couldn't sneak up on him. And around here, screaming for help could attract a worse kind of attention.

Plan B it is.

"All right, big guy. You win." I dropped the stake and smiled, sidling toward him with all the confidence I could muster, which wasn't much, considering how hard I was shaking. "What are you doing with a scrawny little kid, anyway?"

He looked at the kid, then back at me, his lecherous gaze burning my skin. The stench of cigarettes and cheap booze lingered on his breath, like old fish and sour milk.

"I've got everything you need right here," I purred, choking back bile as I unzipped my jacket. "Unless you're not man enough to handle it?"

His gaze roamed my curves, eyes dark with lust.

"You're about to find out," he warned. "Ain't ya?"

He shoved the kid away, and in one swift move, he grabbed me and spun me around, pinning me face-first against the bricks.

He was a hell of a lot faster than I'd given him credit for.

"So you're an all talk, no action kind of bitch?" He wrenched my arms behind me, the intense pain making my eyes water. His sour breath was hot on the back of my neck, his hold impossibly strong, my knife impossibly out of reach. "That ends now."

A few blocks off, an ambulance screamed into the night, but it wasn't coming for us. The kid and I were on our own.

"Mmm. You got some ass on you, girl." He shoved a hand into the back pocket of my jeans and grabbed a handful of my flesh. "I like that in a woman."

Of course *you do.*

After all these years making illegal, late-night deliveries to the seediest supernatural haunts in town, this wasn't my first rodeo. The one-liners, the threats, the grabby hands… Human or monster, guys like this never managed to deviate from the standard dickhole playbook.

But this was the first guy who'd actually pinned me to a wall.

At least he'd ditched the kid. I tried to get her attention now, to urge her to take off, but she'd tucked herself behind a Dumpster, paralyzed with fear.

The man pressed his greasy lips to my ear. "No more bullshit, witch."

You don't know the half of it, asshole.

He didn't—that much was obvious. Just another dude with a tiny dick who tossed around the word "witch" like an insult.

My vision flickered again, rage boiling up inside, clawing at my insides like a caged animal searching for weak points.

It wanted out.

I took a deep breath, dialed it back down to a simmer.

God, I would've loved to light him up—spell his ass straight to oblivion. But I hadn't kept my mojo on lockdown for damn near a decade just to risk exposure for *this* prick.

So magic was out. I couldn't reach my knife. And my top-notch negotiating skills had obviously failed.

Fuck diplomacy.

I let my head slump forward in apparent defeat.

Then slammed it backward, right into his chin.

He grunted and staggered back, but before I could spin around or reach for my knife, he was on me again, fisting my hair and shoving my face against the wall.

"Nice try, little cunt. Now you eat brick."

"Don't!" the girl squeaked. "Just… just let us go."

"Aw, that's cute." He let out a satisfied moan like he'd just discovered the last piece of cake in the fridge. "You'll get your turn, baby."

Okay, she'd saved me from a serious case of brick-rash —not to mention a possible skull fracture—but now she was back on his radar. And I still couldn't get to the knife.

Time for plan B. Or was this C?

Fuck it.

"Hey. I've got some money," I said. "Let us go, and it's yours."

"Yeah?" He perked up at that. "How much we talkin'?"

"Like I said—some."

Lie. At the moment, I was loaded. Most of the $3,000 I'd already collected tonight was in the van, wrapped in a McDonald's bag and shoved under the seat. I also had $200 in a baggie inside my boot and another $800 in my bra, because I believed in diversifying my assets.

My commission depended on me getting the cash and van back to the docks without incident. I couldn't afford incidents. Rent was due tomorrow, and Sophie had already covered me last month.

But I couldn't—wouldn't—risk him hurting the kid.

"It's in my boot," I said. "Left one."

"We'll see about that, Blondie." He yanked me away from the wall and shoved me to the ground, wet pavement biting into the heels of my hands.

With a boot to my back, he pushed me flat on my stomach, then crouched down and grabbed my wrists, pinning them behind me with one of his meaty hands. With his free hand, he bent my leg back and yanked off my boot.

Bastard.

"I hope you feel good about your life choices," I grumbled.

Another wheezing laugh rattled through his chest, and he coughed. "Choice ain't got nothin' to do with it."

Whatever. I waited until he saw the baggie with the cash, let him get distracted and stupid over his small victory.

The instant he released my wrists and went for the money, I pushed up on all fours and slammed my other boot heel straight into his teeth.

The crunch of bone was pure music, but his howl of agony could've called the wolves.

I had just enough time to flip over and scamper to my feet before he rose up and charged, pile-driving me backward into the wall. The wind rushed out of my lungs on impact, but I couldn't give up. I had to keep fighting. Had to make sure he wouldn't hurt the girl.

I clawed at his face and shoved a knee into his groin, but *damn it*—I couldn't get enough leverage. His hands clamped around my throat, rage and fire in his eyes, blood pouring from his nose and mouth as he spit out broken teeth.

He cocked back an arm, but just before his fist connected, I went limp, dropping to the ground like a pile of rags.

The momentum of his swing threw him off balance, and I quickly ducked beneath his arms and darted behind him, crouching down and reaching for the sweet, solid handle of my knife.

"You can't win," he taunted as he turned to face me. Neither his injuries nor the newly acquired lisp diminished his confidence. "I'm bigger, stronger, and I ain't got no qualms about hurting little cunts like you."

Despite the tremble in my legs, I stood up straight, blade flashing in the moonlight.

"Whoa. Whoa!" Eyes wide, he raised his hands in surrender, slowly backing off. "Hand over the knife, sweetheart."

"Not happening."

"You're gonna hurt yourself, waving around a big weapon like that."

"Also not happening."

"Look. You need to calm the fuck down before—" A

coughing fit cut him short, and he leaned against the wall, one hand on his chest as he gasped for air.

I held the knife out in front of me, rock steady, finally getting my footing. Chancing a quick glance at the girl, I jerked my head toward the other end of the alley, willing her to bolt.

Her sudden, panicked gasp and a blur of movement beside me were all the warning I had before the dude slammed into me again, tackling me to the ground. My knife clattered away.

Straddling my chest, he cocked back an arm and offered a bloody, near-toothless smile. "Time to say goodnight, witch."

"Leave her alone!" No more than another flash in my peripheral vision, the kid leaped out from behind the Dumpster, flinging herself at our attacker.

She scratched and punched for all she was worth, eyes blazing and wild. I'd never seen anyone so fierce.

But he simply batted her away like she was nothing. A fly. A gnat. A piece of lint.

She hit the ground hard.

I gasped, heart hammering in my chest, shock radiating through my limbs. She *wasn't* a fly or a gnat. She was a fucking child in a unicorn hoodie, lost and scared and totally alone, and he'd thrown her down.

Just like that.

Still pinned in place, I couldn't even see where she'd landed.

But I would never forget that sound. Her head hitting

the pavement. The eerie silence that followed. Seconds later, another ambulance howled into the darkness, nowhere close enough to help.

"What did you do?" I screamed, no longer caring who or what might've heard me. "She's just a kid!"

I clawed at the man's chest, but I was pretty sure he'd already forgotten about me.

"No. No way. Fuck this bullshit." He jumped up to his feet, staggered back a few steps, then took off without another word.

Still trying to catch my breath, I crawled over next to the girl, adrenaline chasing away my pain. Blood pooled beneath her head, spreading out like a dark halo. Her breathing was shallow.

"Hey. I'm right here," I whispered. "It's okay, baby."

She was thin as a rail, her wet jeans and threadbare hoodie hanging off her shivering frame.

"Jesus, you're freezing." I shucked off my jacket and covered her body, careful not to move her. "He's gone now. He can't hurt you anymore."

I swept the matted hair from her forehead. Her skin was clammy, her eyes glassy and unfocused, but she was still conscious. Still there, blinking up at me and the dark, cloudy sky above.

"What's your name, sweet pea?" I asked.

Blink. Blink.

"Hon, can you tell me your name?"

She sucked in a breath. Fresh tears leaked from her eyes. That had to be a good sign, right?

"Um. Yeah," she whispered. "It's... Breanne?"

"Breanne?"

"Sometimes Bean."

"Bean. That's a great nickname." I tucked a lock of hair behind her ear, my fingers coming away sticky with blood. "Hang in there, Bean. I'm going for help."

"No! Don't leave me here. I—" She reached for me, arms trembling, skin white as the moon. "Grape jelly. Grape—"

Grape jelly grape, she'd said. And then her eyes went wide, and I watched the spark in her go out.

Just like that.

"Bean!" I pressed my fingers beneath her jaw, then checked her wrist, desperate to find a pulse.

But it was too late.

Here in the middle of vamp central, the sweet kid in the unicorn hoodie—the one who'd ultimately saved *my* life— was dead.

* * *

Ready for more? Dive into the sexy supernatural world of The Witch's Rebels! Order your copy of Shadow Kissed now!

ABOUT SARAH PIPER

Sarah Piper is a witchy, Tarot-card-slinging paranormal romance and urban fantasy author. Through her signature brew of dark magic, heart-pounding suspense, and steamy romance, Sarah promises a sexy, supernatural escape into a world where the magic is real, the monsters are sinfully hot, and the witches always get their magically-ever-afters.

Readers have dubbed her work "super sexy," "imaginative and original," "off-the-walls good," and "delightfully wicked in the best ways," a quote Sarah hopes will appear on her tombstone.

Originally from New York, Sarah now makes her home in northern Colorado with her husband (though that changes frequently) (the location, not the husband), where she spends her days sleeping like a vampire and her nights writing books, casting spells, gazing at the moon, playing with her ever-expanding collection of Tarot cards, binge-watching Supernatural (Team Dean!), and obsessing over the best way to brew a cup of tea.

You can find her online at SarahPiperBooks.com, on TikTok at @sarahpiperbooks, and in her Facebook readers group at Sarah Piper's Sassy Witches! If you're sassy, or if you need a little *more* sass in your life, or if you need more Dean Winchester gifs in your life (who doesn't?), come hang out!

www.ingramcontent.com/pod-product-compliance
Lightning Source LLC
Chambersburg PA
CBHW060948190726

48286CB00005B/1478